Luck of the Witch

Crypt Witch Cozy Paranormal Mystery - book 1

K.E. O'Connor

K.E. O'Connor Books

LUCK OF THE WITCH

Copyright © 2021 by K.E. O'Connor

ISBN: 978-1-9163573-9-6

Written by: K.E. O'Connor

Chapter 1

As I slid through the familiar tingle of the magic barrier surrounding Willow Tree Falls, I had one mission on my mind. Find the biggest brownie I could and head home for a night curled up on the couch with Wiggles.

I tried to brush green dust from my black pants. It was unpleasantly sticky, and I only succeeded in smearing it down my thigh. That was the trouble with rogue demons. They had no concern about messing up your clothes when you dragged them back to prison.

I'd spent the best part of a week tracking this particular demon. Abigar had been sly and uncooperative. He had not come quietly. In fact, he'd whined and pleaded for a second chance. He'd even offered me a stash of gold if I'd let him go.

I twisted my long dark hair over one shoulder and adjusted the heavy bag containing Abigar on my hip.

There was no way I could let a demon who was that much trouble loose on the rest of the world.

My stomach gurgled, and my mission to find the brownie intensified.

A group of young witches raced out of Star Fairfax's dance studio, almost slamming into me in their haste to escape the sweaty tutus and bouncy floors that were the torture of dance lessons.

Two of the girls pulled up sharply and stared at me before covering their mouths and running away, laughing as they did so.

"That's Tempest Crypt, the witch I told you about," the small redheaded girl with an inability to whisper spoke from behind her hand. "She eats demons for breakfast."

The other girl turned her wide dark eyes toward me before grabbing her friend's hand and running off.

"You'd better run," I muttered. "I don't make a habit of eating demons or little girls, but I might make an exception in your case."

I slowed as I passed Heaven's Door, my sister, Aurora's magic store. The place was bustling as usual. It was the most popular store in Willow Tree Falls. Everyone loved Aurora. She was Little Miss Perfect and never put a foot wrong. If she wasn't my sister, I'd hate her.

As if sensing my presence, Aurora's gaze lifted to the window, and she smiled. She beckoned me into the store.

I shook my head and carried on walking. I was too exhausted, and when I was tired, I wasn't safe to be around, especially not when it came to Aurora.

I inhaled deeply and smiled. My favorite smell drifted out of Sprinkles bakery. Patti must have just taken a fresh batch of goodies out of her oven.

I increased my pace and pushed open the door to the bakery.

Patti Kayes stood behind the counter, loading the shelves with chocolate chip cookies. She did something magical to whatever she baked. It always tasted heavenly and left you wanting more. I was a sucker for her brownies. The bigger the better, and the more chocolate, the happier I was.

I approached the counter, my eyes glued to the sweet treats behind the glass.

Patti tapped the top of the counter with a long finger to get my attention.

I looked up and met her green eyes. "I don't see any brownies. My mission is brownie retrieval."

Patti chuckled as she placed the cookies down. Her wild red curls were hidden neatly under a white floppy baker's cap. "They're coming. I had a feeling you'd be back today, so I made an extra batch."

"You're keeping tabs on me?"

"Nothing so sinister. I had some of Angel Force in earlier today on a coffee run. They were worried because you hadn't been in touch and were asking around to see if anyone knew anything and if you might be in trouble."

I shook my head. I'd done this job as a favor for Angel Force. They were kind of like the police in non-magical communities, just not so efficient. The angels monitored illicit demon activity from Willow Tree Falls, keeping an eye on the rest of the world and making sure no demons became too troublesome. "Those puffed up angel farts don't know what they're talking about. We don't all have time to go gossiping when on a job. They know I won't let them down."

Patti eyed the lumpy bag I had attached to my belt. "He's in there?"

"Where else?"

"Your family will be happy to have him back inside."

"This one was a giant pain in the butt. But he didn't escape from the prison. He escaped Angel Force when they were transporting him."

"That's demons for you. Always up to no good." Patti grinned at me. "How many brownies do you need?"

"As many as you've got."

She laughed. "I cooked a batch of fifty."

"Oh, well, I'll take a dozen."

"Good plan. That's breakfast, lunch, and dinner sorted for a few days."

I snorted a laugh. "If I'm lucky."

"Give me two minutes. I'll box them up for you. Fresh out of the oven, so they're still warm and gooey."

I lounged against the counter as I waited for my brownies, my gaze going around the pretty pastel pink and blue cafe. It was late afternoon, so the only customers were retired people or young moms. Several of the clientele didn't meet my gaze. I didn't mind. I had a bitchy side that could emerge at inappropriate times. He was called Frank. Frank was a demon, and he came out when I least wanted him to.

"A dozen brownies ready to go." Patti placed a box on the counter.

I handed over some money, resisting the urge to rip off the lid and stuff my face full of brownies. "Have I missed anything while I've been gone?"

"Only all the nonsense in the build-up to the mayoral election." Patti handed me my change. "I can't imagine anyone wanting that job. All they get is hassled day and night about inconsiderate neighbors, overgrown hedges, or boundary disputes. Who wants to deal with that?"

"All the ego maniacs who put themselves forward," I said. "I saw the bunting up across the street. Is that to do with the election?"

"It's supposed to make people more excited about them," Patti said. "I'm not even sure I'll bother to vote. Maybe I will if there's an *any other option*. I don't know about Axel, Mannie, or Deacon being the new mayor. None of them seem quite right for the job."

"If you don't vote, you risk getting some idiot filling the role." Willow Tree Falls' incompetent but harmless current mayor, Grenville Kirby, was retiring after twenty years on the job. He was stepping down for a life of blissful peace and a passion for playing golf extremely badly.

"Any idea who you'll vote for?" Patti asked.

"Whoever is least likely to cause Cloven Hoof any problems." That was my business. I specialized in providing exotic drinks with a little pinch of magic. I also did a healthy sideline in natural pick me ups that came with a side order of magic bliss. It was the perfect way for people to unwind after a stressful day.

"I heard talk about Cloven Hoof at one of the candidate's meetings," Patti said.

I sighed. Not everybody loved Cloven Hoof. "Who's gunning for me this time?"

"I'm not sure but check what they were talking about. You don't want to find yourself thumped with a new business tax or restrictions on use."

"I'd like to see them try." I grabbed the brownies. "Thanks for the heads-up." My happy brownie induced mood was dented by the possibility of somebody interfering with Cloven Hoof, and it led me to the door of the Ancient Imp. I needed a drink and an update on who was talking about my business. No one knew the local gossip better than the Ancient Imp's owner, Petra Duke. People always talked more freely when they'd had a few drinks. Petra was always happy to listen.

She was behind the bar when I entered, wiping a clean cloth over the already clean surface. Her long black hair had a sweep of silver running down either side. Her eyes were lined with black kohl, and her mouth was painted red. She nodded at me as I stopped by the bar.

"The usual?"

"Make it a double." I leaned on the bar, enjoying the woody, earthy scent the building always had. It had a lot to do with Petra's earth witch roots.

"Are those demons causing you trouble again?" Petra placed a tall glass full of sparkling lemon water in front of me. I rarely drank alcohol. It didn't do Frank any good.

"This one had his moments, but I squashed him."

"Cora was in here with your Auntie Queenie last night. She said all the demon cracks are sealed. They've had a quiet few days since you've been gone."

"I've heard that before," I said. "There will be someone below causing mischief before too long."

"You should be grateful. If it weren't for their mischief, you'd be out of a job."

"Cloven Hoof keeps me busy enough. Speaking of which, do you know which mayoral candidate is looking to cause me trouble if they get into post?"

Petra laughed. "I wondered when you'd hear about that."

"It's true?"

"A couple of residents who live close to Cloven Hoof have mentioned your late license, and they want to see it restricted."

"I open late to meet customer demand. I don't like working past midnight. If there was no demand, I wouldn't do it. Half of the people who come in after hours live in the houses near Cloven Hoof."

"I'm not the one with the problem." Petra raised a hand. "It won't happen. It's all hot air to get people interested and get them out voting next week."

"Whose hot air are we talking about?"

Petra narrowed her eyes, a wicked smile on her face. "Mannie Winter."

"That self-righteous dwarf comes in at least once a week. Why does he want to shut me down at night?"

"He wants to be seen as the next mayor of Willow Tree Falls. He has to be seen working to meet his followers' requests."

"I've got a request for him. I'll tell him what it is when I've jammed my foot up his butt."

Petra chuckled and looked over my head as the door to the Ancient Imp opened.

I groaned as I recognized the smell of sweaty, sulfur coated bodies. Willow Tree Falls did a roaring tourist trade, thanks to its allegedly magical hot spas and healing stone circle. Non-magicals came from hundreds of miles to sample these elixirs of a long life and good health. They either spent their time meditating within the stone circle or splashing around naked in the naturally warm thermal spas that sat on the edge of the forest.

They were tourist gimmicks. Non-magicals couldn't access the real properties of the stones or the spa water. But it meant Willow Tree Falls was thriving, and local businesses did well out of the tourists who visited throughout the year.

"I feel ten years younger." A plump non-magical with damp blonde hair sat in the seat next to me.

"Me too," her companion said. He was equally damp looking and sulfur smelling.

Petra turned her attention to them and took their drinks order.

"We should come back every year," the woman said, "and bring Denise and Bobby. It will do wonders for his aching hip."

I took a sip of my lemon water. The non-magicals bugged me. They were so sure of themselves yet had no clue what was going on beneath their noses. If it weren't for my family, their world would be in chaos. They had no clue what was beneath their feet. If they did, there'd be no way they'd hang out in Willow Tree Falls.

The woman glanced at me and smiled. "Are you here for the thermal spas?"

"Nope, I live here," I said.

"You're so lucky. You must use them all the time. Your skin's glowing, and your hair has a lovely sheen."

"Thanks, I use a great foundation."

The woman tilted her head. "Tell me your secret. What is it?"

I glanced at Petra and winked. "Actually, it is the spas. Did you cover yourself in the mud when you were there?"

The woman's eyes widened. "I didn't know we were supposed to. We swam about a bit and assumed whatever is in the water would be absorbed through our skin."

I shook my head, forcing myself to look serious. "You'll only get some of the benefits if you do that. For an immersive treatment, you need to dive under the water, grab a handful of mud from the bottom and cover your bodies in it. That way, you'll get the maximum benefits and have glowing skin."

"We should go back," the woman said as she tugged on her friend's hand. "I don't want to miss this opportunity while we're here."

Her friend looked longingly at the pint of beer that had just arrived. "We can go back tomorrow."

"You should go tonight," I said. "It's good to be covered in the mud under a full moon."

"Tempest, maybe you shouldn't," Petra cautioned.

I couldn't help myself. Non-magical tourists were so annoying. "Lots of mud, a full moon, and then you lie on the banks of the spa and let it dry for at least an hour."

"That sounds amazing. Thanks for the tip. We'll do that."

"My pleasure." I drained my lemon water. And when they did, they'd be met with our not so friendly toothless werewolf, Brian. He liked to hang out at the spa in full shaggy werewolf form and scare tourists. He could do them no harm with his gums and blunt claws but still enjoyed chasing them out of his territory, especially when they were naked.

I grabbed my box of brownies, nodded a goodbye to Petra, and headed out of the Ancient Imp. I spotted more tourists heading toward the pub and was glad I'd left when I did.

"Coooeeee! Tempest, have you got a second?" The piercing tones of Puddles Lavern drilled into my head.

"Not now. I'm busy." I kept walking, my head down.

"I hate to trouble you, but I need to check when your rent is coming in."

I gritted my teeth as I slowed. I was a week late in paying. Puddles ran Gnome Place Like Home, the village's realtor and letting agency. I leased Cloven Hoof's building from her, including the apartment above it.

"The money's on its way. As you can see, I'm back from an out-of-town gig. Angel Force will have paid me by now. I'll drop off a check tomorrow."

"That's good to hear. We can't have you getting behind on payments. I've got several people interested in taking over the running of that building if you're struggling." Puddle's lips were painted a glossy pale pink to match her candy floss hair. She was a short, curvy hedge witch, who thought clashing candy floss colors were the latest trend.

"I've been busy. You'll get your money."

"Of course, I trust you." Her gaze landed on the box of brownies. "Have you been to Sprinkles? I'm starving."

"I have." She was not getting her hands on my brownies.

"What did you get?"

"Brownies."

Puddles mouth formed a little O of delight. "They're my favorite."

"Mine too." My fingers tightened around the box.

She glanced up at me and frowned. "I should get back to work."

"Good idea." As I turned in the direction of Cloven Hoof, I saw a blur of movement heading toward me.

Puddles backed up several steps. "You should tell him to slow down."

"You have met Wiggles?" I said. He was my best friend, a stocky tan mutt, who had the ability to track me down whenever I arrived back from a job. I never knew how he managed to get out of Cloven Hoof. He was a ninja escape artist with a keen sense of smell, especially when brownies were involved.

Puddles scuttled backwards to the safety of the door of her office.

I held up a hand. Wiggles didn't appear to be slowing down. "Wiggles, stop!" It was too late. He launched himself into the air and straight into my arms.

Wiggles landed on top of me, and we crashed to the ground, the box of brownies squashing between us.

"Stop. Heel. Sit." I shouldn't have wasted my breath. Nothing I said would deter Wiggles from his enthusiastic licking of my face.

I laughed as I gave in and ran my fingers through his wiry fur. "I've missed you too, you fur ball." My gaze went to the squashed brownies, and I groaned. I shimmied, and the box plopped to the ground, the brownies flopping out. They looked like sad little puddles of melting perfection.

Wiggles jumped off me and went to investigate his carnage.

I looked up to see Puddles smirk before heading back into her office.

Wiggles made a grab for a brownie, but I stamped on it. "Chocolate is not good for you."

He made a grab for another, and we did a dance as I kept standing on brownies and grinding them into the dirt to stop him from getting his teeth into them.

Wiggles sniffed the bag containing the demon and growled.

"Yes, I'm still carrying, so be careful. We don't want to let this guy loose." I scooped up the destroyed brownies and was about to put them back in the box when I spotted one pristine brownie sitting in there.

I dumped the rest of the brownies in the nearest trash can and reverently carried the single brownie back to Cloven Hoof, Wiggles trotting along beside me.

Once through the black, shiny double doors, I walked into the bar. It was quiet, only a few customers occupying the booths and a couple sitting at the bar. It never got busy here until the end of the working day. It got really frantic at weekends.

Merrie Noble, bar manager extraordinaire, stood behind the bar polishing glasses. "Welcome home. Did you have a successful trip?"

I patted the bag. "Job done. How's everything been here?"

"No problems. We had a few tourists trying to get in the other day. I gently persuaded them that this wasn't the place for them and they'd be happier trying the Ancient Imp."

We were always careful not to let non-magicals into Cloven Hoof. Magic had a strange effect on them. The magic barrier around the building did a good job, but occasionally, they broke through.

"There are a lot of them out there. We need to keep an eye out for them."

"The non-magical detector is operational," Merrie said as she flipped her long blonde braid over one shoulder. "They won't be getting in anytime soon."

Wiggles rested his paw on my knee as I sat at the bar and opened the lid of the brownie box.

Merrie poked her head in hopefully. "You've eaten nearly all of them."

"I had a Wiggles related incident. He came to say hello. Most of them ended up in the dirt."

Merrie chuckled. "I wondered if you were back when he barged down the stairs and out the door before I could stop him."

I grinned as I eased off my boots. I already felt more relaxed being home. I'd run Cloven Hoof for three years, transforming it from a dodgy biker bar into a reputable joint that served high-end products.

"I'll be in my booth if anybody needs me." I grabbed my brownie and walked away from the bar.

I'd just settled in my favorite seat and taken the first bite of brownie when I stiffened. Somebody was watching me.

Chapter 2

I kept my attention on Wiggles. He lounged by my feet, his tongue hanging out and his tail draped over my feet. That was a clear sign that whoever watched me wasn't a serious threat.

"You shouldn't be here," I said as I turned and saw my sister.

Aurora emerged from the shadows. She approached me cautiously. "I wanted to see how you got on out of town."

"I got the demon." I kept my gaze averted, my heart kicking up a gear. She shouldn't be here. She knew what she was doing was stupid by being this close to me after I'd been working.

"I need to talk to you."

"Another time."

"This can't wait. It's important. I need your advice about a date."

I shifted in my seat. My sister had the weirdest notions when it came to what was important. She was obsessed with finding the perfect guy.

"Whoever it is, get rid of him. If you're having doubts, then he's not worth it."

"He's a mayoral candidate."

"Even more reason to turn him down."

"He's a good-looking guy, though. It's Deacon Feathers."

My eyebrows rose. Deacon was one hot half-angel half-human. He was like an Adonis with a squint. He was muscled, blond and had piercing blue eyes. One eye was always half-shut as if he was thinking about some complicated puzzle, or maybe he was just constipated. I could never tell.

"Anyone running for mayor will have an ego too big for you to handle."

Aurora sighed. "He's a nice guy. We've been on a few dates already."

It looked like I wasn't getting rid of my sister any time soon. I checked in with Frank. He seemed content and wasn't kicking up a fuss because his desired object was almost within touching distance. "What's the problem?"

"There's somebody else."

"You're two-timing Deacon?" My sister would never do such a thing, would she?

"No, nothing like that. It's nothing serious with Deacon. I think he might like me though. He's dropped hints about making us official soon."

"Do you think he's looking for a trophy wife to support his campaign?"

"Tempest! It's not like that. He is sweet and funny. I like him."

"Do you like the other guy more?"

"That's the problem. I think so. He's different. Older than me."

"You're dating a sugar warlock?"

Aurora drew closer to the table. I held my hand up and shook my head. "Bad idea. I'm exhausted."

Her smile faded. "I trust you not to hurt me."

"Then you're an idiot." I took a large bite of brownie. Sugar always helped keep Frank occupied.

Aurora's gaze lowered. "I don't know what to do. I've agreed to go on another date with Deacon tonight, but I don't think it's right. Maybe I should give him another chance. He is fun, but…"

"He doesn't set your panties alight like the old dude does?"

Aurora laughed. "It's not all about sex. I never thought I was into older guys. This one is special."

"Then you've solved your own problem. Date him and ditch Deacon."

"I don't want anybody to get hurt."

"They definitely will if you don't make up your mind. You can't leave two guys hanging." Aurora was always the good girl. The one with the perfect white magic spell ready to help anybody at a moment's notice.

I kicked out a stool, the sugar from the brownie giving me a hit of energy. "Sit down, you're making the place look untidy."

Aurora grinned at me as she took her seat. "What would you do in my position?"

"Date neither of them. They sound like more trouble than they're worth. An old rich dude or an up-and-coming egomaniac. Hard pass on both."

"Neither of them is like that. They're both sweeties, just in different ways." Aurora shrugged, and her hand drifted to my half-eaten brownie. She pulled off a piece and popped it into her mouth. "I could go on one more date with both of them. That would make up my mind."

"Or make you more confused. Perhaps neither of them is right for you, which is why you're finding it so hard to make a decision."

Aurora licked chocolate off her fingers. "You could be right. I'm doomed to a life alone, never finding love or happiness."

"You've just described my life."

"Tempest! That's not true. You decided not to date."

"They're not exactly queueing up outside the door to get me to change my mind."

"Your work keeps you busy." Aurora waved a hand in the air. "Then there's the whole… demon thing."

I flinched in my seat as Aurora alluded to my unwelcome passenger. Every time I let my guard down, Frank took advantage, especially when Aurora was around. "You should go."

"This is nice. We should do it more often."

"Not today. Get out of here." Frank stirred inside of me, finally alert to Aurora's presence. I felt his hot, sticky energy slide up my windpipe, like a gross bout of acid indigestion. An unpleasant side effect of containing such a strong demon inside me was the burps.

Aurora carried on, seemingly oblivious to my trouble. "Mom wants to see you for lunch tomorrow. We're all getting together. Can you make it?"

"Sure, I'll be there." I gritted my teeth as I fought with Frank to stop him from getting a foothold. If he did, Aurora would be at risk.

"Are you having problems with the one we never talk about?" Aurora's gaze turned cautious, and she stood slowly from her seat.

"My only problem is you. Get out of here. Now."

Aurora backed away. "Sorry, I didn't mean to cause you any trouble. I missed you; that's all. I miss not having my big sister around to talk to when I have a problem."

"You should be used to it by now." I squeezed my eyes shut and pressed my fingers against the bridge of my nose. A gross tasting sulfur belch shot from my lips as Frank made his presence felt.

Aurora turned and hurried away. "See you tomorrow?"

I nodded as I watched her leave, my throat burning and my eyes hot. "Frank, you son of a demon. You are not having my sister." The hot burn sank back into my stomach, and a faint chuckle filled my head.

That was too close. I had to keep Aurora out of my life as much as possible. It was better for her if she wasn't around me. Better for my whole family. I didn't trust Frank not to try to take a pop at one of them out of spite.

I could never stay in Willow Tree Falls for long. There was always too much temptation for Frank.

Tomorrow, I'd go to Angel Force, get a new job, and get out of here for another week or two. Willow Tree Falls and my family were better off without me.

Chapter 3

No matter how hard I tried to ignore it, the persistent thumping sound wouldn't go away.

I rolled over and groaned, covering my head with a pillow.

Wiggles wriggled in under my arm, nudged the pillow away, and licked my cheek.

"You have my authority to go eat whoever is making that awful noise."

Wiggles laid next to me and continued to nudge the pillow off me.

With a resigned groan, I pulled myself out of bed and stomped downstairs, through the empty bar and to the front door of Cloven Hoof.

Lula Greenwood stood in front of me. She had elected herself the unofficial village's gossip and was ideally placed to fulfill that role as the owner of Sweet Pixie Beauty, the only hairdresser and beautician in Willow Tree Falls.

"Has somebody died?"

Lula's almond-shaped eyes widened. "Not that I know of."

"Is the village burning down?"

"Erm, no." She glanced over her shoulder.

"Has the demon prison collapsed?"

"The demons are fine, I think."

"Then you have no reason to be banging on my door. Go away."

"Wait! I had to come and tell you as soon as I heard." Lula bounced on her toes.

"I'm not interested."

"Aurora's been arrested."

I scowled at her. "My sister would never be arrested. You've made a mistake."

"I promise you, I haven't. I saw her being taken away not half an hour ago."

"Taken away by?" I rubbed my eyes, wondering if this was a horrible dream.

"Dazielle. She never leaves the office unless it's serious."

I grimaced. Dazielle ran Angel Force. She led a group of twelve angels who spent most of their time polishing their halos and preening their feathers. "Are you sure it was Aurora?"

"Positive. They marched right into Heaven's Door and brought her out. It looked like she was crying when they took her."

What had my sister got herself into? I should leave this alone. One night of sleep was not going to make me safe to be around. "Does our mom know?"

"I came here first. I was going to drop by Cora's place next and let her know what's happening."

"Do that. This must be a mistake by the angels. It won't be the first. Any idea what they've taken her in for?"

"It's terrible what people are saying," Lula said as she ran a hand down her long, silky hair. "I hope it's not true."

"Tell me." Aurora's worst crime was being too sweet or stroking a puppy for too long.

"Some people are saying she's been arrested for murder."

I choked out a laugh. "Then this is all a huge mistake. My sister can't squash an ant. She wouldn't kill anybody." I needed to stay out of this. This mess could be sorted by Mom.

"Aurora must need a friend right about now," Lula said. "I went and asked if I could speak to her and got turned away. Apparently, they're still processing her. I knew she'd need a friendly ear, though."

"I bet you did." Lula would be hot on any gossip trail, just waiting to spread it around as quickly as she could. I let out a sigh. I needed to see what had happened. I couldn't abandon my sister if she'd made a mess of things.

"I can wait here for you while you get ready." Lula eyed my sleep shorts and faded gray tank top. "We can go to the station together."

"No need. I know the way." I closed the door in her eager-looking face. I needed strong coffee with a magic hit if I was getting into this mess.

I hurried upstairs and pulled on clean black pants and a fitted black shirt. I grabbed the ripe smelling bag full of captured demon and clipped him to my belt. He would enjoy a trip to see the angels just as much as I would.

I headed down to the bar. We had a state-of-the-art coffee machine that I'd never quite figured out how to use. I managed to make an expresso and dumped in a heaped teaspoon of stardust. It would give me the right natural boost of energy to get me through this and hopefully keep Frank satisfied.

As soon as my family found out what had happened to Aurora, they'd invade Angel Force's headquarters. My family was a handful. A big, powerful magical handful, who couldn't afford to get distracted by this.

"Stay here, Wiggles," I said as I pulled open the door. "Keep this place safe until I get back."

He whined as he watched me leave. He hated me going anywhere without him, but Angel Force was no place for Wiggles. They'd spend all their time petting him and feeding him treats like he was their toy to play with.

I raced along the street and had made it ten steps past Puddles' office when she shot out the door. "I heard about Aurora. I hope everything is okay."

"It's all a mistake. She'll be out in no time." I kept walking.

"Oh, that's good to hear. Have you got my check?"

I grimaced. In my haste to get to Aurora, I'd forgotten about the overdue rent. "Later. I'll get it to you later."

"I do need that money," Puddles called as I raced away.

"You'll get it. End of the day, I promise." Puddles was a pain, but I always paid my bills.

"Give my best to Aurora."

I ignored her and continued to hurry along the main street of Willow Tree Falls until I reached Angel Force. I barged through the double doors and had to blink several times. Everything was white. It was such a cliché. It wasn't as if residents didn't know the place was run by angels. They had the name emblazoned over the door in glowing lights to hammer home that they were pure, angelic beings that wafted around with those ridiculous wings doing good deeds.

I stomped to the desk where Sablo stood, her perfect blonde hair in a coil on top of her head. She stood her ground as I stopped in front of her and craned my neck. Angels were tall.

"I'm here to get my sister out."

Sablo pursed her perfectly full lips. "Aurora is about to be questioned."

"What's she being questioned about?"

The doors behind me burst open. My mom, Cora, was the first through the door. She was followed by her sister, my aunt Queenie, Uncle Kenny, and just behind them was Granny Dottie and Grandpa Lucius.

I shook my head. Did the whole family have to turn up? I'm surprised they didn't drag my cousins along as well. We could have had a picnic.

Mom grabbed me in a hug. "What's going on? We just heard what happened. How is our baby?"

"Aurora is twenty-three. She's not a kid, and I've no idea how she is. I just got here." I extracted myself from Mom's embrace. "I was about to spring her out."

"Nobody is springing anybody out," Sablo said sharply.

"Somebody mentioned a murder." Mom turned her dark, intense eyes on Sablo. "I can't believe that. Not my little girl. You're barking down the wrong hole if you think she's involved."

"Up the wrong tree, Mom, not down the wrong hole." Mom always messed up her metaphors.

"You know what I mean. This is a big mistake."

"Aurora is being questioned in relation to a death," Sablo said.

The whole family erupted into cries of protest.

Sablo held up a hand and waited until they'd quietened down. "We are questioning her to get more information and discover what she knows about it."

"We must all be there," Mom said.

"That's not possible," Sablo said. "But Aurora has asked for one of you to be present." Her gaze went to me.

I stepped back and shook my head. "That's not a good idea." Angels made Frank twitchy. Therefore, I was also twitchy. When I was twitchy, Aurora was in danger.

"She says you know the process. Apparently, you've been arrested before."

I shrugged. "That was a long time ago. Aurora would be better with someone else. Auntie Queenie, you should go in."

Auntie Queenie chewed on the large pastry she had in her hand. "I get so nervous under pressure. I might blurt out my secrets and be the one to end up behind bars."

I shook my head. Auntie Queenie did have something of a murky past. "Grandpa Lucius?"

He patted my arm. "You go in. Your sister needs you. She's asked for your help."

They were crazy letting me anywhere near her. They knew what risk I posed to Aurora. I couldn't abandon her, though. She was terrible under pressure. "Fine, I'll go in for the questions."

"I'll take you there now," Sablo said.

After reassuring Mom I wasn't going to let Aurora get stuck behind bars, I followed Sablo through a doorway and along a white corridor. She knocked at a door and opened it to reveal a small interview room with a table and chairs.

Dazielle sat on one side of the table and my sister the other.

Dazielle's teal-colored eyes narrowed a fraction when she saw me. "Come in, Tempest. Aurora has asked for your presence in this interview."

I nodded and hurried to sit next to Aurora. "How are you doing? What are you doing in here?"

"It's been a horrible misunderstanding." My sister's normally perfect cheeks were blotchy and her eyes red. I'd always taken comfort that she was an ugly crier until today. "They think I killed Deacon Feathers."

My eyebrows shot up. "Why would they think that?"

"We're about to find that out," Dazielle said. She nodded to Sablo, who closed the door behind her.

"My sister would never kill anybody," I said. "You know her."

"I'll admit I was as surprised as you. But her intimate relationship with Mr. Feathers is well-known."

"So, you jump to a conclusion and assume she killed him because of that?" I glanced at Aurora. "You didn't kill him, did you?"

"Of course not." Aurora dabbed the end of her nose.

Dazielle tapped a finger on the top of the table. "When was the last time you saw Deacon Feathers?"

"Two days ago," Aurora said as she grabbed my hand and held on tight.

"What did you do when you met?"

"We had a coffee at Unicorn's Trough. Brogan can back me up if you need a witness. He served us."

"What did you talk about?"

"Nothing special. I guess you could say we were on a date. We were getting to know each other."

"Is your relationship with Mr. Feathers intimate?"

"That's none of your business," I said.

"It is. Jealousy and unrequited love are good motives for murder."

"We weren't intimate," Aurora said. "That was our third date. We'd held hands a couple of times, and he'd kissed me on the cheek but nothing more."

"Did he want more? Did he try to push you into something you weren't comfortable with and you snapped?"

"My sister never snaps," I said.

"Somebody did because Deacon's dead," Dazielle said.

Aurora stifled a sob. "I didn't do it. I didn't see him yesterday."

I glanced at her. She'd just lied. Aurora had told me she was supposed to meet Deacon last night.

"What were you doing last night if you weren't with Mr. Feathers?" Dazielle asked.

"I was stocktaking at Heaven's Door. I do it every Thursday night."

That was another lie. Aurora hated stocktaking. She did it about once a month and only when customers started mentioning certain stock was low.

"We found a note in Deacon's calendar to say he was meeting you for dinner at seven thirty. Are you saying that date never happened?"

Aurora nodded. "We had a change of plans. We were going to meet, but then I couldn't. I realized I was long overdue getting my records up-to-date and new stock ordered."

"I thought you said you did a stock take every week. Things can't get that far behind in seven days."

Aurora blushed. "It might have been two weeks since I did my last stock take. Business has to come first. Deacon understood when I let him know."

"So, you did see him yesterday?" Dazielle asked.

I kicked Aurora under the table. She was making too many mistakes. Even I was suspicious of her.

"Oh, yes, my mistake. Only for a few minutes. It was after I'd seen Tempest. I dropped by Cloven Hoof to talk to her. Then I went straight to Deacon's and told him I couldn't make our date."

Dazielle looked at me. "Is that true?"

I nodded. "Aurora came by after I got back from my job." The bag with the demon in still sat on my hip.

"What did you talk about?"

"Family stuff. Nothing you'd be interested in."

Aurora nodded. "After that, I spent the evening at Heaven's Door. I did my stock take and then went to bed. It was a dull evening."

"Not so dull if you snuck out and killed Deacon," Dazielle said.

"I'd never hurt him. He was so lovely."

"How did he die and when?" I asked Dazielle.

"We're still determining the cause of death," Dazielle said. "He died around midnight. One thing we do know is that your sister was one of the last people to see Deacon alive."

"Where did he die?"

"He was found in his bed at home."

"I'm innocent." Aurora sniffed loudly and wiped her nose.

Something was off here. I was angry with the angels for arresting my sister, but her story didn't stack up. She was hiding something. I wasn't going to dig it out of her under the watchful gaze of Dazielle.

"If you don't have concrete proof that Aurora is involved, she's not staying here any longer," I said.

"She can leave," Dazielle said. "I decided it best if we question her here to speed things up. Deacon Feathers was an important member of the community. He was a potential mayor. We are under pressure to get this solved quickly."

"So, you dragged in the first victim you could lay your feathery paws on to try to force a confession?" I shook my head. "That's not going to happen. Aurora gets out of here, right now."

Dazielle's top lip curled. "Aurora you may leave. But stay in Willow Tree Falls. Don't go anywhere. I will have more questions for you."

"She's not going to skip town," I said. "She's done nothing wrong."

"Of course I won't," Aurora said. "I want to help in any way I can. I promise you I had nothing to do with Deacon's death. I liked him. I considered him a friend."

"A friend with benefits?" Dazielle asked.

"Don't say any more." I stood and pulled Aurora to her feet. "Let's get you out of here."

Dazielle jumped up and opened the door.

I unclipped the demon bag from my belt and passed it to her. "You'll be needing this."

Dazielle scowled and held the bag out at arm's length as a foul sulfur smell drifted from it. Demons always got angry when they were too close to an angel. "You should have taken him to processing as soon as you got back. Can't you take him to the crypt now?"

"You wanted one escaped demon collected and brought to you. That's what you paid me for, and that's what I've done. You can process Abigar and transport him yourself."

Dazielle glared at me. "Very well. And if you're interested, I've got another job coming up next week."

Although we didn't consider each other friends, she knew how good I was at chasing down demons. I glanced at Aurora, who hovered in the hallway, clearly anxious to leave. "I might be. Let me have the details another time." An out-of-town job was what I needed. It would give me distance from my sister. My work here was done. Aurora was out of the cells, which meant I could leave too.

Dazielle nodded. "I'll be in touch."

I hurried Aurora back to the desk where Sablo stood. Aurora had to fingerprint a couple of documents before she was allowed to leave, but we were finally free.

"My sweet girl, whatever have they done to you?" Mom fussed around Aurora, running her hands over her hair as if checking for injuries.

"They just questioned her. It's nothing," I said.

"Somebody killed Deacon," Aurora whispered, big, unshed tears glistening in her eyes.

"You had nothing to do with it," I said. "Did you?"

"No, as I said in the interview, I was at the store." Aurora glanced at me before looking away. She knew I was on to her.

If she wasn't going to tell me the truth, there was nothing I could do. Aurora was out of harm's way, and I needed to get out of Willow Tree Falls before I caused her any problems. Problems of the demon kind.

"We'll figure out the truth," Mom said. "Your sister will figure this all out."

"I can't." I slowed from my sneaky retreat to the doors. "I'm busy with Cloven Hoof. And the angel farts have another job for me."

Sablo cleared her throat and glared at me.

I shrugged. I never hid my contempt of them. That really would be rude.

Granny Dottie tutted. "You need to look after your sister."

"That's what I'm trying to do," I growled and tapped a finger against my chest.

"You can't abandon her when she needs you most," Granny Dottie continued, seeming happy to forget about the demon residing inside me who wanted to kill Aurora.

"She's got all of you," I said. "She's not alone. You can help keep her out of here. The angels know they've made a mistake. They'll find the real killer. They were just looking for an easy target."

Sablo huffed before stomping away from the desk.

"My little girl is nobody's easy target," Mom said. "Tempest, you must help your sister. She depends on you, and we're busy with the cemetery."

I looked at Auntie Queenie for support. She simply nodded as she finished what might have been her third pastry. I had no clue where she stored all her pastries, but she was always eating.

Granny Dottie patted my arm. "It's the right thing to do, dear. You'll handle it."

I stared at her and shook my head. "It's better if you help. You're old. You know a thing or two about the law. The only reason I help these angels is because of you." Years ago, Granny Dottie had guilted me into helping these pristine princesses when they couldn't get a handle on a demon who'd escaped their custody. Before she'd married Grandpa Lucius, she'd been involved with the former chief of Angel Force. I still hadn't quite worked out that relationship, but she was loyal to the angels, even if I wasn't.

"I'm grateful for it," Granny Dottie said. "But just because I'm old doesn't mean I'm clever."

She wasn't going to be any help to me. "Grandpa Lucius. Please, you help Aurora."

He grinned at me. "Your mom is right. You're in the best position to help her. You know how Angel Force works. You got her out of here with no problem."

"Because she's innocent. You would have been able to do the same thing." They had no idea how hard I struggled to keep Frank under control. They always assumed I was capable of anything. The role of being a big sister sometimes sucked.

"Tempest, you've always looked out for Aurora. Don't let her down when she needs you the most." Mom's eyes were fixed on me. She had a way of making me feel guilty even though I'd done nothing wrong.

It looked like I was not winning this fight. I had to decide who was a bigger threat here, the incompetence of the angels and their desire for swift justice or my unwelcome demon friend.

The angels were useless but persistent. I had to help Aurora if they had her in their blue-eyed sights. "I'll help but only until we ensure the angels no longer consider Aurora a suspect. Then I'm out of here."

Aurora ran forward to hug me. I stepped away and shook my head. "Then you're on your own again."

Aurora grinned at me. "I knew you wouldn't let me down."

I rubbed my forehead. I might not, but Frank definitely would. I needed to find Deacon's killer and fast.

Chapter 4

Having spent part of the morning calming my family and making sure my not so baby sister was out of immediate danger from the incompetence of the angels, I'd headed back to Cloven Hoof for a long, hot shower and a huge breakfast.

I felt marginally better after stuffing myself with crumpets and tea and deliberately not thinking about what a mess Aurora had gotten herself into.

Wiggles had watched every delicious bite before grudgingly accepting he wasn't getting any and heading to his bowl of dog kibble on the floor.

"It's for your own good." I licked the last of the strawberry preserve from my fingers while sitting in my favorite booth in the bar. "I need a lean, mean fighting machine. Not a dog with a pot belly who inspires laughter. You're my vicious guard dog, not my pet pooch." In truth, Wiggles was a delicious mix of both. When he wanted to, he could be the meanest, most evil-eyed dog you'd ever stumble across. He also had a way of winning you over by rolling onto his back and showing you a cute pink and white dotted belly ready for a tickle.

The door to the bar opened. Merrie strode through. She slowed when she spotted me. "Hey! I heard about Aurora. How's everything going?"

"She's out. It was all a mistake. The angels know nothing. They figured since Deacon had scribbled their date in his calendar, Aurora was the last person to see him alive and therefore she killed him. It wasn't exactly genius detective work."

Merrie walked behind the bar and flicked on the back lights. "Poor Aurora. How's she doing?"

"She's shaken up." I didn't mention that she was hiding something. She'd always been an awful liar. Her nose twitched when she lied. It had twitched three times in that interview.

Merrie shook her head. "Deacon always struck me as the sort of guy who could look after himself. He had decent angel skills."

"Clearly not enough. I have no idea how he died, though. Dazielle wasn't giving much away."

"He was smothered," Merrie said, "at least, that's what I heard. Someone got in his bedroom and smothered him."

"Then it couldn't have been Aurora," I said. "She's not strong enough to hold down Deacon."

"Unless she caught him unawares."

I glared at Merrie. "Not you as well."

Merrie grinned. "Maybe Aurora and Deacon were into kinky stuff. He could have asked her to tie him up and then shove a pillow over his head. Things got out of hand. The next thing you know—"

"Stop! You can't think my sister did this."

"Absolutely not, but it's being talked about. If Deacon was asleep and someone crept up on him and smothered him, he might not have been able to fight back."

"He could have been drugged," I said.

Merrie's eyes widened. "Aurora sells herbal remedies for insomnia at Heaven's Door. Some of that stuff is potent. I've tried it a few times. It can knock out an elephant."

I groaned. "You're not helping by suggesting my sister not only smothered Deacon in a lurid sex game, but she also drugged him."

Merrie laughed. "I'm staying well out of this. But maybe that's what Angel Force is thinking, which is why they questioned her."

"Dazielle muttered something about getting quick results because of Deacon's high standing." I shook my head and snorted. "He wasn't high standing. He was a wannabe mayor. There's nothing special about that."

"There sort of is," Merrie said. "People look up to the mayor. They respect them. Deacon had a good shot at winning."

"So, one of the other candidates killed him."

"Anything is possible."

The snow globe on the bar vibrated.

"Can you answer that?" I asked Merrie.

She shook the globe to activate the message.

"Don't forget lunch at Mom's today." A tiny version of Aurora stood inside the snow globe. "We've got lots to talk about."

I hopped up and shook it to end the message. My whole family around a table, digging up reasons Aurora was innocent. That would be interesting.

The snow globe vibrated again. I groaned and nudged it with a finger. "Don't forget you're bringing dessert."

"Is there some emergency you need me for?" I asked Merrie.

She raised her eyebrows. "Nope. Everything is fine here."

"You're sure there's nothing I need to do that will keep me away from my family?"

Merrie laughed. "Sorry, you can't avoid the family lunch because of me."

I grabbed the tub of stardust from behind the bar and ate a huge teaspoon.

Merrie pulled it out of my hand. "That's not hygienic."

"That's my own personal tub. Label it as so then keep it under the bar," I said. "I'm going to need all the energy I can get."

"You love your family," Merrie said as she placed the lid back on the tub. "You wouldn't have them any other way."

I shrugged. They weren't the problem. I was.

I spent a couple of hours on boring but necessary paperwork. But finding no more excuses to stay at Cloven Hoof, I headed out with Wiggles to find a dessert. There were so many great places to eat. I was contemplating something with lemon or maybe chocolate when Puddles stepped in front of me and held out her hand.

"Your rent." There was no smile on her face.

"I haven't forgotten." I dug the check out of my back pocket and handed it to her.

She stared at it for a few seconds before nodding. "Make sure you're not late next month. I'll have that building back on the market if you're not careful."

I glared at her. "You wouldn't dare."

Wiggles growled and nudged Puddles with his nose.

Puddles took a step back. "Not everyone loves Cloven Hoof."

"I know you do. You buy from us every week."

"I have to. I have nerve issues. It doesn't help when my clients pay late."

I bit my tongue. I didn't mean to be a jerk. Puddles had a job to do just like I did. "It won't happen again."

Puddles nodded. "We'll forget all about it. Give my best to your sister. I hear she's still having a tricky time."

"Not for long," I said. "I'm off to sort this mess right now."

Puddles eyes widened. "You know who killed Deacon?"

"Not yet." I walked away before Puddles questioned me further. The gossip mill was up and running in Willow Tree Falls, and all eyes were focused on Aurora. I needed to grab dessert and head to Mom's quickly before I faced further quizzing.

It was a toss-up between three places for dessert. Brogan Costin's cafe, the Unicorn's Trough, served decent food. I'd never had a bad meal there. If I wanted something fancy, Tilly Machello's restaurant, Bite Me, was always an option. Then Tate Rathmore's Mystic Mushroom take out did a killer chocolate profiterole.

"Choices, choices," I muttered under my breath. I settled on the Unicorn's Trough and headed to the royal blue awning and into the cafe.

Brogan Costin was Romanian and came with a flair for magic and a hint of the undead. He wasn't a full-on vampire but had a liking for prowling around at night and seducing virginal maidens in long floaty dresses. At least, that's what he said he did. Personally, I thought he was more into star gazing than cleavage leering, but we all had reputations to uphold.

He was behind the counter as I entered. He wore a white apron over his black outfit and flashed me a bright smile when he saw me. "What will it be, Chickadee?" His deep voice always sent a pleasant shiver down my spine.

"I'm looking for a killer dessert for lunch. What have you got on offer?"

"For you, anything. I was hoping you might be here for something hot and spicy." His grin widened. His teeth were slightly sharper than the average warlock.

"Just the dessert today." I grinned at him. "Something sweet and moreish."

"You could be describing me."

"I'm sure Auntie Queenie would be happy if I served you up as the dessert."

He chuckled. "She is a sweet lady. I can offer you fudge cake. A warm, sticky, sweet cake that will melt in the mouth. Or I have a caramel jam cake. Sweet, fluffy and a treat in your mouth. Or how about a peanut butter fudge pie? I promise you, when you take a bite, it will make you moan with pleasure."

Every dessert he described sounded a little more delicious than the last. "I could take them all."

"My favorite is the peanut butter fudge pie. It's sweet with a slightly salty aftertaste. It goes perfectly with vanilla ice cream."

I licked my lips. "That sounds ideal. I'll take the biggest one you have."

"I will be with you in one moment." Brogan disappeared into the kitchen and returned with a box in his hand. "I was most sorry to hear about Deacon and your sister's alleged involvement in his demise. I trust everything is being resolved?"

"She's been questioned but released. The angels are figuring things out as am I."

"Aurora is such a charming girl. I knew Deacon was interested in her."

"He spoke to you about her?"

"No, but you can always tell when someone is infatuated with a person." Brogan flashed me a smile. "Deacon used to watch when she walked past here. He had coffee here most mornings. He would hum under his breath as he watched her walk."

I wrinkled my nose. "That's a bit creepy."

"These half-angels, they have issues. Human urges and heavenly urges conflicting. Maybe he was torn between his primal urge to devour your sweet sister and his angelic longings to do the right thing."

I nodded. That was the trouble when angels had children with non-magicals; the resulting offspring were often stunning to look at but came with dubious morals. "Deacon never mentioned he was having trouble with anybody?"

"Not to me," Brogan said. "He spent most of his time discussing the upcoming campaign. He thought he was in with a chance."

"Did you like him for our new mayor?"

"I was undecided. He had his plus points, but he was too ambitious for my taste."

I held out some money, but Brogan shook his head. "A gift from me to your lovely family. I ask you just one thing in return."

I narrowed my eyes. "What's that?"

"You think of me every time you take a bite."

"I'd rather just pay."

He laughed. "I insist. Having a family persecuted for no reason is something I am familiar with. You have a friend here. Every time you need something sweet, just think of me."

I reluctantly put away my money. Brogan was hot, and he knew it. I looked but didn't touch. He was an outrageous flirt but had a good heart.

"Thanks. Aurora will appreciate this."

"As I hope, you do too."

I nodded a quick goodbye and hurried out of the Unicorn's Trough where Wiggles waited for me.

Maybe it wouldn't be such a bad thing to spend some down time with a gorgeous warlock. Brogan was a charmer, but I saw him as more of a friend, someone I could talk to without any fear of being judged.

I turned left at Lula's hairdressers and walked along the lane to Mom's house. She owned a large detached plot, set back from the road and surrounded by large evergreens. The grounds of the house had a wild, untamed feel to them. As a powerful witch, who drew her energy from nature, she loved surrounding herself with it.

My whole family was descended from a particular type of witch. They got their energy from the earth and anything that lived, and died, in it, which was why they enjoyed living away from other houses and the bustle of the village.

The front door opened before I'd reached it, and Mom ushered me in and hugged me. "We've been discussing matters. We've got some ideas you need to hear."

Wiggles bounded through the door, already on the hunt for food.

"I knew you'd figure this out without me being involved."

Mom tutted as she took the dessert box, lifted the lid, and gave an appreciative nod. "We haven't. We still need you. Go on through. Everybody is in the kitchen."

I wandered along the warm, cluttered hallway, full of childhood knickknacks and bookshelves piled high with thumbed paperbacks.

The kitchen was a handmade affair, built when my dad was still around. Some shelves sat at different heights, and a large worn wooden table dominated the center of the kitchen.

Aurora sat at the table, flanked by Auntie Queenie and Granny Dottie.

Aurora looked up and smiled at me, her eyes still looking red. "I'm glad you came."

I looked at the steaming mug of chamomile, cookies, and the box of tissues on the table. "You look like you're doing okay. You don't need my help."

"I do. You know everyone in the village. I don't think there's a single person you don't do business with."

"I take their money. It doesn't mean I know them." I settled in a seat at the table and leaned back, taking a moment to see how Frank felt about being so close to Aurora. So far, so good.

"That gives you a good in," Auntie Queenie said. "If they refuse to talk, you can withhold the goodies."

I shook my head. "It doesn't work like that. It's not like I'm planning to put sanctions in place if people refuse to talk to me about Deacon's death."

Mom placed the dessert on the counter. "Your sister is innocent. We all know that."

"What we need to figure out is who wanted Deacon dead." Grandpa Lucius wandered into the kitchen, sniffing the air as he did so. "Did someone call me down for lunch?"

"No, you old rogue. While you're standing, help me lay out the plates," Mom said.

Grandpa Lucius and Granny Dottie had lived with Mom for five years, ever since she'd gotten worried about their magic becoming unstable. It wasn't; she just loved having them around and needed an excuse to keep them close, especially after I'd moved out and Aurora had moved into the apartment over Heaven's Door.

After Grandpa Lucius had laid out the plates and cutlery, he sat in a seat and rested his hands on the table. "Perhaps Deacon has a jealous ex-girlfriend. Since he set his sights on our Aurora, he could have let someone down. They wouldn't have been happy about that."

"He was seeing Petra for a while," Aurora said. "Deacon said it wasn't anything serious, but maybe it was."

"Petra never takes relationships seriously," I said.

"A jealous, spurned woman is a dangerous thing." Grandpa Lucius helped himself to a large piece of quiche and ignored the salad Mom offered him.

"As if you'd know anything about that," Granny Dottie said. "You've only ever dated me."

He chuckled. "That doesn't mean I didn't leave behind lots of broken hearts when I accepted you."

Granny Dottie caught my eye and shook her head. "Petra is worth talking to. She might have considered their relationship serious. Then she got wind that Deacon was dating Aurora and things turned sour."

"I was wondering about the other candidates running for mayor," I said. "Professional rivalry turned bad could mean someone needed Deacon out of the running."

"He was a handsome beast," Auntie Queenie said. "Lots of women would have voted for him because of that chiseled jaw. And did anyone else dream about his abs?"

Aurora blushed. "He was lovely to look at."

I filled my plate with quiche and salad. "Another candidate might have thought Deacon had an unfair advantage, especially when you compare him to Mannie Winter."

"Some people find chubby dwarves with beards attractive," Mom said as she sat at the table, checking everyone's plates to make sure they had enough food.

"If we're considering other candidates, we should also have Axel Shadowsoul in the mix," Granny Dottie said. "I know you have a soft spot for him, Tempest, but he's a candidate and a half-demon. He'll have evil intentions running through his veins."

I glowered at her. "Axel is as evil as a chocolate frog. He's all talk and no action."

"He'd like some action with you," Aurora said. "He always asks about you when he comes into

Heaven's Door."

"He does not." I shoved a piece of quiche in my mouth. "Even if he is interested, he's wasting his time."

"He is sort of gorgeous," Aurora said, "if you like the smooth and rich type."

"Then you date him." I'd had enough of my sister trying to fix me up. She always chose decent but boring guys. There was no spark when I went out with them.

"There's also Rhett Blackthorn and his gang to add to the list of suspects," Auntie Queenie said.

"What makes you think he's involved?" I asked.

"He's a shady biker. He runs with a bad crowd."

"He's a fallen angel, he sort of has to." If I was going to date anybody, it would be somebody like Rhett. He was hotter than the hell he'd dragged himself out of and made leather pants look so good I sometimes drooled when I saw him in them.

Still, I'd been there and done that and gotten too close to being burned.

"Being part of a bad crowd doesn't automatically make you a killer," Mom said.

"I'm sure I saw his bike parked outside of Deacon's house," Auntie Queenie said. "I remember because I sat on it for a while. That's a sexy beast of a machine. It's a V-twin, four-stroke, with overhead valves and self-adjusting lifters."

I grinned. Auntie Queenie had been in the Dead Tree Witch biker gang. The biker witches were ousted by the fallen angels a long time ago. It was something nobody talked about unless Auntie Queenie had one too many and started trash talking the fallen angels. That was always fun.

"I favor the jilted girlfriend," Grandpa Lucius said. "Women are beautiful, but they can be terrifying."

He should know since he was surrounded by them. As the only man in the household, I felt sorry for Grandpa Lucius. Not that he had anything to be sorry about. He was waited on hand and foot most of the time and even got his laundry done when Granny Dottie was in a good mood. Still, it must be tough when he needed some guy time and had to contend with Mom and her sister discussing the best way to seal a crypt crack and what kind of pot roast to have at the weekend.

"I'll talk to Petra," I said. "See what she knows."

"I can guarantee a strong woman is involved," Grandpa Lucius said.

"I just don't see Petra doing it. Earth witches are usually benign. You need someone with a dark streak in them. Someone who'll hold a grudge."

"A woman scorned," Grandpa Lucius said. "I'm telling you jealousy is a strong motive."

"Petra can hold her own in a fight," I said. "She's got powers, so maybe you're right."

"And I saw Deacon arguing with Petra a few weeks ago," Aurora said. "It was just as I arrived for our first date. I didn't hear what they were fighting about. Maybe she got mad about me dating him."

I scooped up the last of my quiche and hopped up to unbox the dessert. It looked like Petra was my number one suspect. Grandpa Lucius was right; jealousy turned people into monsters.

"I'll head over to talk to Petra after lunch. If I get her to confess, this will be sorted by the end of the day."

Mom reached over and patted my hand as she stood to clear the lunch plates. "You're such a good girl."

I nodded as I sliced up the pie and plated it for everyone. It was a good job I was the only one who could hear Frank at that moment. His laugh echoed inside my head, making my temple throb and my spine tremble. Dark, unhappy thoughts bounced around my head. I tried to stay on the right side, but having a demon living inside you made being good a constant struggle.

I stuffed a spoonful of peanut butter fudge pie into my mouth and urged Frank to stay quiet. He was content, for now, but wouldn't stay that way for long. I had to hope he'd stay under my control for just a couple more days, so I could sort out Aurora and then get out of Willow Tree Falls fast.

Chapter 5

I left Mom's house with a spring in my step as I walked with Wiggles along the lane. Lunch had been delicious, and Frank had behaved himself most of the time, which was not typical of him when I shared air with Aurora.

This mess would easily be sorted. I'd have a quick chat with Petra, maybe twist her arm if she needed it, and she'd be singing to Angel Force in no time. My sister's name would be cleared, and I could get back to being careful about not spending too much time with her and exciting Frank.

I needed to swing by Cloven Hoof before wringing a confession out of Petra. There were packages that needed dropping off. Since I was heading past half of the drop-off sites, it would do no harm to go in and catch up on all the gossip. And I'd be happy to set anyone straight if I caught them badmouthing Aurora.

As I pushed open the main door to Cloven Hoof, I heard laughter.

My eyes widened. Petra sat at the bar with a bowl in front of her and a half-drunk glass of red wine. She was starting early. Maybe she was hiding a guilty conscience and needed a distraction.

I strode over and sat next to Petra. Merrie nodded at me from behind the bar before moving away. Wiggles sniffed around for a bit before laying down at my feet.

"Is there something wrong with the wine at Ancient Imp?" I asked Petra.

She shook her head as she chewed on a piece of dried mushroom. "It always tastes better here, and I'm sampling your new produce. Patti said you had a new supply of Mystic Tail mushrooms. It's good quality stuff."

"It always is."

She nodded, her eyes glazed from the natural power she absorbed from my special variety of mushrooms. Mystic Tail mushrooms were rare, expensive, and exquisite on the tongue.

"I was coming to see you," I said.

"What about?"

"How were things between you and Deacon before he died?"

She slid me a sideways glance as she carried on munching. "I haven't spoken to that loser for a long time."

"You used to date?"

"Sort of. It was casual. He was a good-looking guy. I enjoyed his company."

"Word on the street is that he wasn't all that into you, especially not when he got my sister to agree to go on a date with him."

Petra whistled air through her teeth. "I can't say I noticed who he dated after me. We were never exclusive."

"You cared enough to fight with him a few weeks ago."

She turned in her seat. "What are you talking about? We never fought."

"Are you sure about that? I know from a reliable source that you did. What got you so angry?"

Petra glanced at me before stirring her finger through the bowl of mushrooms. "He was unreliable. It irritated me. It must have been his non-magical side."

"He stopped taking you out, and you didn't like it?"

"I liked the free meals. I loved having a hot guy on my arm. It was nothing. I'd already moved on."

"You're dating somebody else?"

Petra grinned and fluttered her lashes. "Of course. How can somebody who looks this good stay single for long?"

I suppressed a snort of laughter. She was hot in a brassy kind of way. I got the impression most guys were terrified of Petra. "Who are you seeing?"

"Different guys. No one special." She glanced at me. "Are you looking for recommendations? You're dating again?"

"No, and not anyone you want to set me up with."

Petra shifted in her seat. "I'm guessing all these questions have to do with your perfect little sister. You're looking for someone else to blame Deacon's death on?"

I nodded. There was no point in concealing the truth. "She didn't do it. It has to be somebody else. What were you doing the night Deacon died?"

Petra eyed me suspiciously. "Like I have to tell you."

I thought about what Granny Dottie had said about withholding supplies. Petra bought from me at least twice a week. She loved her mushrooms. "You will if you want to keep getting your hands on my products."

Petra huffed out an angry breath. "I'll find another supplier."

"In Willow Tree Falls?"

"You're not the only seller. I can import."

"For double the price and half the quality."

Petra grimaced. "Fine, I have nothing to hide. If you must know, I was home alone eating pizza."

"Where did you get the pizza?"

"Mystic Mushroom, same as always. Tate makes the best double cheese and pineapple pizza in the village. I get the same order once a week. I've been doing so for years. Ask him; he only has to hear my voice, and he knows what I want."

"I might do that." A quick stop at Mystic Mushroom was never a hardship. Petra was right.

Tate did make amazing pizzas. I could check her order and maybe get something for dinner.

"I ate pizza, chilled out, then went to bed. The exciting life of a bar owner. I'm too tired to do anything else." Petra sighed. "I'm thinking it's time I got into a new business and am hoping something established will come up for sale. Something with more regular hours and fewer bar fights."

I could relate to that. Cloven Hoof closed at midnight, and we were never done clearing up much before one in the morning. "You're sure you weren't still interested in Deacon?"

"He was a dumb half-angel. I never loved him. He was fun to hang out with. The fun came to an end, and I moved on."

Petra sounded worryingly plausible. "If you didn't do it, and my sister isn't involved, who do you think wanted rid of Deacon? Did he talk to you about any enemies he had?"

Petra looked around the bar and leaned closer to me. "I reckon it was Mannie Winter."

"Why Mannie?"

"Deacon and Axel were working together. They wanted Mannie out of the running for mayor, so it was the two of them standing against each other."

"Why do that? Mannie doesn't stand a chance of winning this election."

"So you'd think, but he's invested a whole heap of money into new campaign material. He's getting a real buzz going around Willow Tree Falls. Haven't you noticed all the posters and promises he's making to turn the village into a worldwide tourist destination?"

I'd paid no attention to the upcoming mayoral election and had missed all the posters. "That only makes me not want to vote for Mannie. We have enough tourists. We need no more."

"I couldn't agree more. I've watched Deacon and Axel in the Ancient Imp on several occasions. They were as thick as thieves, talking about something secretive and stopping whenever I went over to grab their empty glasses. They were working on something together. My guess is, it had to do with getting Mannie out of the campaign."

"But one of them would still lose. Get rid of Mannie and they'd compete with each other."

Petra shrugged. "Maybe they'd come to some arrangement. They'd keep out of each other's way whoever won. Or they'd do under the table deals between the two of them, so there were no hard feelings. I don't know the details."

"A half-angel and a half-demon working together. I guess I've seen stranger partnerships."

"One thing I do know is that politics is a shady business, and Deacon and Axel both wanted a shot at being mayor. They were worried Mannie's money and experience would go against them. You need to speak to Mannie and see what he knows about Deacon's death. I bet he did it." She pushed back her stool. "I have to get out of here. I'll have the early dinner crowd in soon at the Ancient Imp. I need to make sure the barrels are changed so customers don't go thirsty."

"Hold up. You haven't told me who you're dating." I wasn't letting Petra off that easily. I also wasn't convinced by her not so solid alibi about eating pizza alone on the night Deacon died. What was to say she didn't stuff her face and then kill Deacon?

"That's my business." Petra turned and hurried out of Cloven Hoof.

I dashed after her, Wiggles jumping up and running after me. He loved a good chase. "Tell me who you're dating. All I want to do is double check you're really over Deacon and didn't hold a grudge that he'd moved on."

She ignored me and ran to her sleek black sports car. She was one of the few people in Willow Tree Falls who owned a car. The place was so small it was easy enough to walk to wherever you liked. Wearing the kind of heels she did, Petra needed all the help she could get when it came to walking.

"Give me one name," I said. "It can't be that hard. You can't have that many boyfriends."

"I told you what I was doing that night. That's all you're getting out of me."

"If you're dating that many hot guys, you'd brag about it, not keep it a secret."

Wiggles bounced around my feet as he sensed my growing agitation.

"Keep your nose out of my business." Petra hopped into her car and gunned the engine.

This was my business. Aurora's reputation was at stake, along with a potentially lengthy spell in prison if she was found guilty. I ran toward Petra's car. "Wait! I'm not finished with you."

Petra spun the car around, the tires squealing.

I leaped out of the way, falling backward to avoid being hit by the back of her car as it swerved. I heard Petra crunch the gears and punch the gas.

Wiggles growled, sensing my panic, and leaped in front of the car, his hackles raised as he tried to defend me from a metal beast.

"Get back," I screamed at Wiggles.

It was too late. Petra accelerated and hit him.

Chapter 6

My breath caught in my throat, and my eyes were blinded with tears. For a second, the world froze as I couldn't believe what had happened.

There was a flash of Petra's brake lights as she realized what she'd just done.

"No, you don't." She was not escaping from this. I rolled onto my feet, stretched out a hand, and cast a net spell, trapping the car.

I felt it thump against my magic as Petra put her foot down again.

"No, no, no, no." I ran toward the car. Where was Wiggles? I silently begged all the benevolent witches and warlocks to make sure he was okay. He wasn't a big dog, but he might have survived.

I rounded the car. Wiggles was in front of it. He must have been lifted off the ground from the impact.

My heart stuttered, and I wiped my cheeks with my hands to remove the tears. Anger burned through my grief. I was going to kill Petra.

I dropped to the ground next to Wiggles. He lay on his side, looking like he was simply asleep.

I gently pressed a hand to his furry tan chest. He didn't move.

My tears felt like hot acid as I stood and stalked over to Petra. "What have you done?" I opened the door, grabbed the collar of her dress, and yanked her out of the car.

Petra gasped and looked at Wiggles. "I didn't mean to. It was an accident. He just jumped out in front of me."

"You weren't going to stop." I shook her hard, wanting to hear her teeth rattle. Wanting her to feel the same pain I did. Anger raced through my veins, and I didn't try to stop it. This was one of the few occasions when I was glad I carried a demon inside of me.

I didn't fight as Frank took over. He fed on my rage, and it made him strong. My blood felt like fire as his power raced through my body, making me shake and my vision blur.

Petra gasped and staggered back as she sensed the demon energy sparking through me. She hit her car and scrambled for the door handle.

My hand shot out and wrapped around her neck. "You killed him."

"Please, it was an accident." Petra clawed at my hand.

"Let me take over completely," Frank whispered in my head. "She deserves this. She is a killer."

I nodded. Petra might not have killed Deacon, but she'd definitely killed Wiggles. She deserved to be punished.

I dropped my final barrier and allowed Frank to take control of my body.

He purred in satisfaction. Whenever Frank took control, I felt like I was watching myself have an out-of-body experience. It was my body and my voice, but my actions were controlled by a ruthless demon, who thrived on destruction and death.

At least, this death was deserved. My disembodied self looked back at Wiggles. Through the rage and satisfaction Frank felt at getting a taste of power, my heart clenched with sadness.

I'd had Wiggles for ten years. He'd been with me since he was a pup. I was a surly, uptight teenager when I'd passed by Fur Baby Emporium, run by Abigail Furby. I'd stood and stared at the puppies for at least ten minutes, my attention repeatedly drawn to the little guy in the corner no one else wanted to play with. Abigail had seen me looking and encouraged me into the store.

It had been love at first sight. Wiggles had stumbled over to me on his big paws, hope in his tiny blue eyes that he'd finally found someone who understood him. My heart had melted, especially when I found out how his siblings ignored him because he was the litter runt. We'd been best friends ever since. He was my rock and never judged me, no matter what I did or how badly I behaved.

Now he was gone. Run over by this cold-hearted witch, who couldn't drive because of the ridiculous heels she drove in. She deserved everything Frank gave her. I would sit back and enjoy the show.

I watched as Frank used my hand on Petra's head, my fingers digging into her hair.

"Destroy her," I whispered.

"It will be my pleasure," Frank replied. "A gift to you."

"No, don't do it," Petra said. "I'll do anything. I'll get you a new dog. Whatever you want is yours."

"Tempest, stop!"

I glanced around, not certain where the muffled voice had come from.

Aurora stood at the end of the lane, horror etched across her heart-shaped features.

I shook my head, panic flooding through me. She couldn't be here. If Frank turned his attention on Aurora, I wasn't sure I'd be able to stop him.

I waved her away. "Get lost." She had no idea Frank was in control of me.

Frank laughed. "Two delights in the same day. I feel honored."

I gritted my teeth and forced his energy away. I had to get control of him, or Aurora would be dead. I squashed the anger and rage I felt. That was what had fired Frank up and given him power over me.

"It's time for you to take a rest." Sweat trickled down my back as my internal battle to regain control raged.

"We are not finished." Frank's voice was deep and gravelly inside my mind. "You do not want revenge on the one who killed your best friend?"

My gaze went from Wiggles to Aurora. Revenge for my lost dog or protecting my sister? I loved them both. I wanted them both to be safe.

"Decide what you want," Frank said. "I know what I desire. We both desire it."

Petra sank to the ground, her head bowed as a rush of Frank's energy shot through me and he took control again.

"Tempest, you need to stop." Aurora took a step closer.

I felt Frank's attention drift to her. A lustful hunger burned inside him for my sister. It had always been that way, ever since the night he'd tried to take her. Ever since the night I'd stopped him from devouring her.

My head pounded with the effort of stopping Frank, but I was gaining control and forcing him back.

"Get out of here," I shouted at Aurora. "It's not safe."

She ignored me and drew nearer. "What's going on? What happened to Wiggles?"

Panic engulfed me. Frank was still far from being under my control, and Aurora was ignoring me as she took another step.

I took a deep breath and closed my eyes, forcing Frank down, down, and down, trapping him inside me. I always imagined a big, roomy cage he lived in.

I furnished it nicely, so he had nothing to complain about, but if I were him, I'd not want to spend the rest of my days trapped inside a witch's mind prison. I understood why he fought me.

Slowly, his grip loosened, and his hot, jagged power slid down my spine. I opened my eyes and blew out a long breath.

Petra remained on the ground, my fingers tangled in her hair. She knew better than to mess with a demon like Frank and knew not to provoke me while I got control of him.

"Tempest, what happened?" Aurora repeated.

"When will you ever listen to me?" I gasped. "Frank was out. He could have killed you."

Aurora licked her lips. "I didn't know. Is everything good with Frank now?"

"Just about but keep your distance for a bit longer." I swiped a hand across my sweaty forehead. "Petra hit Wiggles with her car."

Aurora's hand went to her mouth, her gaze on Wiggles. "Is he…"

"Yes. She ran him over." I choked on the sentence and had to swallow a few times to get control of my tears.

"I'm so sorry," Petra whispered. "I promise you I couldn't stop in time. I'd never want to hurt him. I liked Wiggles."

Frank let out an angry howl as he slid back under my control. I felt the same desire to howl. I wanted to scream and cry and smash Petra's car into tiny little pieces.

Aurora's eyes widened. "Are you sure you're in control?"

"For now. Why do you ask?"

"Your eyes are red."

It seemed like Frank wasn't as far away as I thought. "You should leave while you can. Frank was dealing with Petra. He might come back."

Aurora shook her head. "What Petra did was horrible. We all love Wiggles, but you can't kill her."

"I can. She didn't even stop. She doesn't care what she's done."

Petra was still on her knees in front of me. She raised her head. "I got scared. You wouldn't give up on the questioning."

Despite all my warnings to keep her distance, Aurora ignored me and walked over. I staggered out of the way as she caught hold of Petra, helped her up, and eased her back into her car. "You'd better go."

"She is going to pay for this," I said.

"She will. I'm sure of it." Aurora glanced cautiously at me before turning her attention to Petra. "Are you okay to drive?"

"I'll be fine," Petra whispered.

"Then I suggest you leave while Tempest feels calmer."

Petra nodded. "I'm really so sorry. I never meant for this to happen." She glanced at me before steering the car around Wiggles and away from Cloven Hoof.

The anger finally left me, and I dropped beside Wiggles again. He was gone, my best friend had been taken from me. My heart ached, and my lungs burned.

I had no one to talk to. No one to watch terrible movies with. And who would I share lie-ins with, now Wiggles wasn't there to snuggle next to?

Aurora touched my shoulder. "Oh, Tempest, it's so sad. Poor Wiggles."

"He didn't deserve this. He was looking out for me. I was chasing Petra, trying to get answers out of her about Deacon's death. I spooked her, and she wouldn't stop."

"Wiggles was helping you. He was such a loyal dog." Aurora's words wobbled as she spoke.

Frank stirred inside me, restless at how close Aurora was to him. Or maybe he was also sorry Wiggles had gone. He'd known him as long as I had.

"You need to get out of here," I said to Aurora. "I still don't have things under control here. Frank loves to feed on my moods. Right now, I want to punch something hard until my hands bleed. He's only encouraging those feelings."

Her grip tightened on my shoulder. "Before I do, I have an idea."

I glanced up and saw a determined look in Aurora's eyes, mingled with a little fear. "Which is?"

"We're powerful Crypt witches. Although some of our power comes from siphoning nature, we also feed on undead energy, you in particular."

"Sure, I just love to drain all the creepy undead power from our cemetery." That was certainly a quirk in my abilities. I loved being around dead, creepy things, which was why hunting soul sucking demons never fazed me.

"I don't mind it either." Aurora's smile was soft. Her magic had always been gentler than mine. She could draw power from the cemetery but thrived when it came to helping others. She grew strong from positivity. I sometimes wondered if we really were sisters. We couldn't be more different.

"What's your point?"

"We both know a certain spell to reanimate dead things."

I sucked in a breath. "Flowers and birds, we can manage those. We can't bring Wiggles back from the dead. He's a dog."

"The magic works on animals. The birds wake up and fly away. Obviously, Wiggles is much bigger, but between the two of us, we can do it. What do you reckon? Shall we get Wiggles back?"

I jumped up, my knees feeling shaky and my heart racing with uncertain hope, and I hugged her. "Anything! I'll try anything to get him back."

Her eyes glistened, and she bit her bottom lip. "Let's do it."

We sat either side of Wiggles and both placed a hand on his warm chest.

"There's no guarantee this will work," Aurora said quietly. "He'll need lots of energy."

"How about some mushrooms?"

Aurora tilted her head. "I thought they only chill people out."

"I have all sorts in Cloven Hoof." I scrambled to my feet, raced into the bar, and grabbed a bag of dried Regal Bolete mushrooms.

I was already eating a handful as I thrust the bag at Aurora.

She pulled one brown, flat mushroom from the bag. "How many?"

"At least a dozen. We need to feel so buzzed we think we're flying. That's the kind of spark Wiggles needs to come back to me." I swallowed the lump of citrus-infused mushrooms. Sometimes, these little buggers did not taste great if you didn't give them a helping hand with something sweet or tangy.

Aurora gobbled down a big handful of mushrooms, and I ate a few more just in case.

Eating these was like downing a dozen energy drinks but without the caffeine side effects. The colors brightened around me, and I felt like bursting into song and dancing on the spot as the mushrooms worked their magic.

"We can do it. I'm sure we can." Hope fluttered in my chest. I was getting Wiggles back. I settled on the ground opposite Aurora.

With our free hands, we linked fingers. This spell aired on the wrong side of light. It wasn't a full on black magic spell but definitely had shades of gray. Bringing anything back to life was a big deal.

Magic pulsed through my body, my energy mingling with Aurora's and flooding down our fingers as we willed Wiggles back to life.

We sat like that for half an hour, focused on Wiggles. Nothing else mattered. We didn't speak; we barely breathed; we just pulsed magic into him.

I felt my energy ebbing but refused to give up. Wiggles would live. He had to. I sucked in a breath and blocked out everything else.

"Did he move?" Aurora whispered. Her skin was gray from the toll the spell had on her, but she looked as determined as me that this magic would work.

I pressed against Wiggle's chest and gasped as a tiny shiver of movement ran along his spine. "It's working."

Aurora smiled at me as a trickle of blood slid from her nose. "I knew we could do this."

"Can you keep going? You don't look so hot."

She nodded. "We're almost there. The hard part is over."

As my own energy wilted, Frank shifted inside me. If I got too weak, he would break through again. With Aurora sitting so close, she wouldn't stand a chance, and I'd be powerless to protect her.

Only when Wiggles' chest was rising and falling regularly, did I pull back my magic. Aurora did the same. She slumped forward and took several deep breaths.

I hugged her. "You're amazing. Now please, get out of here. Frank could come through at any moment. When he does, your butt is his. I have nothing left to fight him with."

Aurora stood wearily, nodding as she did so. "Give Wiggles a kiss from me when he wakes up properly." She dragged herself away, turning back as she got to the end of the lane and giving me a thumbs-up.

I lay beside Wiggles on the ground and wrapped an arm around him. "For a too perfect to be true sister, she isn't so bad."

Wiggles kept his eyes closed, but his ears twitched, suggesting he was listening.

"She took a huge risk by helping us." I rested my forehead against Wiggles'. I needed to get better control of Frank. I hated not being around Aurora, not able to do all the things we used to do when we were kids.

"Maybe I should let her go to prison for Deacon's murder," I said to Wiggles. "She'd be safer behind bars, and she'd have the guards to protect her. I could decide when I went and saw her. If I was having a bad Frank day, I could leave her alone. It will be much harder to hunt my sister if she's locked away."

Wiggles shifted beside me and grunted. "That's a terrible idea."

Chapter 7

I shook my head and stared at Wiggles. It sounded like he'd just spoken, but that wasn't possible. I ran a hand down his side. That spell must have taken more out of me than I realized if I could hear voices.

Wiggles opened his eyes, and my breath caught in my throat. They were glowing red.

I sat up and inched away from him. "How are you doing? Has that magic made you feel weird?"

"You bet your fuzzy butt it has. And being hit by that witch's car wasn't a fun tea dance full of sprightly grannies." Wiggles staggered to his feet and shook out his fur. "Man alive, that spell had a kick and a half to it."

Holy cow! Wiggles could talk. My mouth hung open as I stared at him.

"Stop catching flies. Anyone would think I'm your first talking dog." Wiggles tilted his head to the side, before settling down to scratch an ear with his hind leg.

I scratched my head in response. "You are my first talking dog. Wiggles, this is amazing. You're talking!"

"It's about time. You've had so many one-sided conversations with me over the years. I've never been able to tell you what I was thinking. Whenever you were about to do something dumb, I always wanted to step in and help but could never say anything other than *woof*. The number of times I've tried to tell you how many bones I wanted, and it never worked."

I choked out a laugh. "Your eyes have changed color."

Wiggles blinked a few times. "They feel the same."

"They're red. Like fire pits of hell red. You look scary cool."

"Huh! No kidding. I guess that's what comes of doing a spell when you've got a demon inside you."

I gasped. "No way. Frank helped with this spell?"

"I felt the fiery dude's energy curl around me. It was like wearing a thermal coat in the desert. Sweaty, gritty, and sulfurous. I don't know how you deal with him sitting inside you like a giant tapeworm all the time."

"Gross!" When I thought about it, that was a decent description of Frank. Nothing I did shifted the son of a demon. "So, if a demon got involved in bringing you back, what does that make you?"

"Well, glowing red eyes, brought back from the dead, and an ability to talk. You got yourself a drop-dead gorgeous hellhound as a best friend." Wiggles raised a paw and examined it. "Which is pretty darn cool if you ask me."

I laughed again and wrapped my arms around his neck. "It is pretty amazing."

"Enough with the cuddles. That's something we need to discuss. I'm not much into the spooning at night. I don't mind a couple of minutes, but you sometimes have me wrapped in your embrace the whole night. I have fur and that gets hot. This hellhound needs his space. He needs room to scratch and break wind and do some serious grooming at night. That's not possible when you're hugging me so tight I can barely breathe."

"I don't cuddle all night." I untangled my arms from around him.

"You have a cuddle addiction."

I rubbed the top of his head. "We've got a lot of talking to do."

"No kidding. First things first, my name. Wiggles sucks. We're changing it."

I stood up, unable to take my eyes off my new hellhound, and resisted the urge to dance around with delight at having him back. "Your name is adorable. I can't think of anything else to call you. You'll always be Wiggles."

"Why am I called Wiggles?"

"Well, when you walk, you have that cute little sway to your butt, like a doggie super model."

He growled and his eyes glowed brighter. "Wiggles is off the table."

"We'll discuss it later." I couldn't help myself and hugged Wiggles again.

He endured it for a few seconds before shaking me off. "And another thing, your sister. Don't go giving up on her so quickly. She might be sweeter than a jar of molasses, but she doesn't deserve jail time."

My eyebrows rose. "How much do you know?"

"I hear everything when you let me hang out with you."

"Okay. That's good; you haven't missed much. The angels don't know how Deacon was killed, although Merrie heard he'd been smothered. His body was found at his house."

"Why do the angels think Aurora's involved?"

"Deacon had their date penciled in his calendar. That's when the trouble begins. I think Aurora lied about seeing Deacon the night he died."

"Your adorable little sister told a lie to Angel Force?" Wiggles shook his head. "That's impossible."

"She's not as innocent as I first thought, and Aurora is a terrible liar. She got herself in a muddle and was almost caught when questioned. She has denied her involvement, but I need to know why she's lying."

"Who else have you got in the frame?"

"Petra pointed the finger at the other mayoral candidates. It's possible they're involved. In particular, she fingered Mannie."

"Axel deserves a visit. I do not trust that guy. He's too smooth talking for my liking. He's always sliming around you and trying to get into your pants."

"Wiggles! That's not true. He slimes a bit, but he knows never to make a pass at me."

"It's true. He sniffs around you like I do when I sniff out a box of Patti's brownies."

I grinned at him and shook my head. It was going to take a while to get used to having a talking hellhound as a sidekick.

"How about a visit to see Axel since you're so fond of him?"

"Why not? If he is in cahoots with the victim, he could be the killer and not Mannie. He might have had a disagreement with Deacon and decided to get rid of him."

"Okay but let me do the talking when we see him."

Wiggles cocked an ear. "I've not been able to talk for ten years. I should do the talking."

"Not everyone is calm about hellhounds. Axel might think you're going to belch brimstone at him."

Wiggles grumbled. "I thought there was something stuck in my throat. I can do that?"

"Isn't it standard practice for hellhounds?"

"Hmmm. I'm new to this game. Let's see if I've got anything to cough up." He sucked in a deep breath.

"Let's stick to fur balls for now. We can try the brimstone belch when we've got more time. But we need to do something with your eyes."

"What are you suggesting, sunglasses?"

"That's not a bad idea. Wait here a moment."

"I was joking," Wiggles yelled after me as I ran to my apartment, grabbed the darkest pair of shades I had, and ran back down the stairs.

"Try these." I settled the glasses on Wiggles' nose.

"How do I look?"

"Odd, but not as scary. I don't suppose you can do anything about the scary red eyes?"

"Not a chance. I didn't even know I had them. The hellhound eyes are here to stay."

"Are you up to questioning some suspects now?"

"Of course, I feel great."

"You have just come back from the dead. You might like to take it easy."

"I've never felt more alive."

"Come on then. We might as well go tackle Axel."

As I walked alongside Wiggles, I realized I was still in shock. I'd seen him run over and then had my sister help bring him back to life. My sister and my demon.

"I was thinking Rocky," Wiggles said.

"For what?"

"My new name. Something solid and dependable."

"It doesn't suit you."

"I'm not solid or dependable?"

"You're both of those things. I just don't see you as a Rocky."

"How about Tiberius? Or Zeus?"

"I like Wiggles."

"It makes me sound like a sap. I should be a hairdresser, not a hellhound, with a name like that."

"People will think it's strange if I change your name all of a sudden. You've always been Wiggles. No one is going to remember a new name."

"They will if I bite them every time they get my name wrong."

"No! No biting."

"You're always telling me to bite people."

"I only mean it half the time."

"Am I allowed to bite Axel if he's too much of a jerk?"

"No. Not even then."

"What if he slimes up on you in his usual way and makes suggestive comments?"

"Maybe a gentle nip." We headed away from Cloven Hoof and walked along the main street. Axel owned a flash bachelor pad on the opposite side of Willow Tree Falls to my family. I'd never been inside, despite his many offers to show me around, but imagined what it would be like. Lots of chrome and minimalistic lines. The total opposite of my home.

As we approached the stark white building, I glanced down at Wiggles. "Best behavior now. You don't want to go scaring the half-demon and making him run if he is involved in this murder."

"I'll do my best. I'm getting used to my new hellhound abilities. I might be unpredictable for a while."

"No talking," I cautioned him.

"I make no promises."

"I should have left you back at Cloven Hoof."

"I've been breaking out of that place ever since we moved in."

"Exactly how have you been able to do that? I lock the door every time I leave."

"We all have our secrets."

"Now you have no reason not to tell me yours."

Wiggles barked a laugh. "That's never going to happen. I like being a mysterious hellhound."

I knocked at Axel's front door. He didn't work. He was a trust fund baby and had been given vast amounts of money by his demon father, Kroni.

As far as I knew, Axel spent most of his time gambling, flirting with anyone he thought was available, and racing around in his fancy soft top.

Axel opened the door. He smiled brightly when he saw me. "This is a pleasant surprise."

"It's not a social call," I said.

"That is a shame." With his slicked back dark hair and perma-tan, Axel looked like someone out of an old episode of Dynasty. The look strangely suited him. Give him a cravat and loafers and I'd be convinced he was an oil baron's son, not demon offspring.

"Did you hear about Aurora?"

His smile faded. "I did. What a shock. Why don't you come in? I can fix us some drinks."

I gave Wiggles a warning stare, which he completely ignored as we stepped inside the house.

It was not as I expected. There was no chrome or glass. A rusty motorbike sat by the stairs, parts littered on the ground, and a huge bookcase full of paperbacks dominated one wall. Everything on the shelves looked well-read.

"I didn't know you liked to read." I stood in front of the shelves. He had everything from the classics to pulp fiction noir.

"I love a good book. This way." He led us past the bike and into the kitchen.

Wiggles headed straight for the trash can in the corner and started sniffing around it.

The kitchen was all white. It felt lived in and well-used, just like Axel's book collection. Maybe I had this half-demon all wrong.

"Anyone would think you were a half-angel, rather than a demon, given your liking for all the white in here," I said.

Axel chuckled. "Blame my interior designer. I told her what I wanted, gave her the money, and she spent it all. Maybe the place could do with a bit of color. What do you suggest?"

I looked around the kitchen. "You've got plenty of room for a sacrificial altar at that end. Maybe you could host parties and invite the neighbors for some gentle bloodletting."

He grinned as he pulled a bottle of white wine from the fridge. "That's tempting. Would you come to the party if I did?"

"Unlikely." I shook my head as he held up the wine bottle. "Not for me. I'll have a soda if you've got any."

He pulled out a can of soda and handed it to me along with a glass.

I opened the soda and drank straight from it. "What do you know about Deacon Feathers' death?"

Axel raised his groomed eyebrows. "It was a surprise. Deacon was a decent guy for a half-angel.

He could be sickeningly good, but that's not a reason to get rid of him."

"Did you consider him a friend?"

"We weren't friends. We also weren't enemies. We had a healthy competition between us. Did you know we were both running for mayor?"

"I did. Did you consider him strong competition?"

Axel's grin widened. "Ah, I see what you're doing. You're looking for someone else to put in the frame instead of your sister."

"What if I am? You could be a good fit."

"Sorry to disappoint you. I was busy that night."

"What were you doing?"

"The same as always. I went to the gym, had dinner, and then headed out to a movie."

"What movie did you watch?"

"They're showing the Witches of Eastwick. It's an oldie but a goodie. Not too true to life but enjoyable."

That would be easy enough to check out. "Where did you eat dinner?"

"The same place I always do, over at Bite Me."

"Have you got any evidence?" I watched him carefully as I sipped my soda.

Axel lowered his wine glass. "I could probably dig out some receipts. Tilly will definitely remember me. I tip well."

"I'd like to see those receipts."

His smile faded. "You really think I'd kill Deacon?"

"Why not? He's an angel; you're a demon. You're old school sworn enemies."

"We're not the only ones around here who have their demon issues." Axel's gaze swept over me. "How's yours doing?"

"I've no problems. I also had no issues with Deacon."

"Deacon was dating your baby sister. Maybe you got all protective of her and decided to get rid of him before he broke her heart."

"Nope. They weren't serious."

Axel shrugged. "Well, I've nothing to hide. Give me a moment and I'll find the receipts. I can't have you thinking I'm a killer." He left me in the kitchen with Wiggles.

"What do you think?" I quietly asked him.

"He's still too smarmy for his own good but check out this trash can. It has four different compartments." He pressed the levers on the bottom, and the lids opened one after the other.

"Stop messing with the trash. You're only looking for food."

"Axel could have hidden evidence in here. I'm sniffing it out and being a good hellhound."

"Has your sniffing helped at all? Is there a murder weapon hiding in there?"

"Woah, something so much better. Axel has dumped half a cake. Come over and take a look."

I shook my head. "I'm not looking at a discarded cake."

"It's cherry and chocolate. It smells great. Barely any mold on it."

"That's nasty, and it's not evidence."

"My stomach disagrees."

"Here we go." Axel returned and handed me a movie stub and a receipt for his dinner. "I can't help with my gym routine, but I'm there every evening at the same time. You can check with the staff if you need corroboration."

The dates were correct, and the movie ticket had been torn. "Did you have dinner with anyone?"

"I'm a sad, lonely bachelor. I always dine alone."

"Don't tell me you go to the movies alone, as well?"

"I prefer to see movies with nobody else. I can't stand anybody talking and spoiling the mood. As soon as the ads start, that's it. I'm focused. I don't need distractions or anyone asking me if I want popcorn or what that person said and guessing the twists at the end of the movies. No interruptions, that's how I like things."

"There were other people there? If I asked around, they'd remember seeing you?"

"Of course. I always like the back row though." Axel winked at me.

"I bet you do," I muttered.

"I am sorry to hear about Aurora getting pulled up for this murder. If you're looking for somebody to blame, you should speak to Petra. Until recently, she was hot and heavy with Deacon."

I sat up straight. That was not what she'd told me. "What changed?"

"Deacon got sick of her hounding him. He told me she never gave him any space. She was always checking up on him. Petra would even accidentally show up at places he went to and pretend it was a coincidence. He was convinced she'd been snooping in his diary, so she could keep bumping into him. One day, he had enough and told her it was over. Petra didn't get the hint. She kept asking him for a second chance."

"Deacon wasn't interested in getting back together?" Petra had acted like she hadn't cared one way or the other about Deacon. Somebody was lying.

"He was looking for a trophy girlfriend, somebody who would look good on his arm during the election. Deacon needed somebody reliable by his side, someone potential voters would find appealing."

I frowned. "And he decided to pick my sister as that replacement?"

"I meant no offense. Aurora is adorable. She'd make a perfect trophy girlfriend."

I reached across the counter and smacked the side of his head.

"Ouch! Okay, she'd make a perfect girlfriend."

"Don't even think about looking at her."

Axel's grin turned sharp. "I like my women on the spiky side. Your sister is sweet, but she's not for me."

"What did you do first?"

His brows lowered. "You've lost me."

"Do you work out first and then stuff your face afterwards?"

"Oh, I see. It's always the gym, then food, and then a movie. I hit the gym around five, head to dinner at about six-thirty, and catch the eight o'clock movie.

It's the same every Thursday. I like my routine. Everybody knows it. You're not going to catch me out."

I wrinkled my nose. He did have evidence to show he was nowhere near Deacon's the night he died. "What time did the movie end?"

"We're always out by eleven," Axel said. "The neighbors don't like the noise. I watched the movie and then wandered back here. I must have been in bed by midnight at the latest. I had a nightcap and then turned in. It's not always high glamor here. I'm an average guy."

It sounded like a pretty good night if you discounted the gym workout. He had a solid alibi. Axel no longer seemed like a likely candidate for Deacon's murder. But what he'd said about Petra interested me. She'd been clear she wasn't interested in Deacon. She'd been almost flippant about it and claimed to be seeing somebody else. Then she'd run off and squashed Wiggles in her panic to get away. Maybe she wasn't being as upfront as she should be.

"How close are you to Petra?"

"Not very. I occasionally go to the Ancient Imp for a glass of wine but prefer my own cellar to what she offers."

"You definitely think she was hassling Deacon?"

"Absolutely. I was there a couple of times when she accidentally stumbled across him. She made some excuse about fate bringing them back together. He seemed embarrassed by the whole thing. You know Deacon. He was never rude, but he politely brushed her off without hurting her feelings. He's too much of a sucker. He should have told her she didn't stand a chance and was wasting her time. She might have left him alone after that."

"Is that how you talk to your conquests after you get what you want?"

Axel smiled at me and raised his wine glass. "Maybe one day you'll get to find out."

I glanced at Wiggles, who shook his head as he ate moldy cake out of the trash.

"I'm going to have to chat to Petra again." Which was a good thing. We had some unfinished dog hitting business to deal with.

"You've already talked to her?"

I finished my soda. "We met earlier today. We've got an issue to clear up."

"From that glint in your eye, it looks like it's not a good issue." Axel glanced at Wiggles. "What's with the dog shades?"

"He's had an eye operation. He's going to have to wear those shades most of the time."

Axel patted his leg. "Here boy. He's always such a decent dog, although I get the impression he's not too keen on me."

Wiggles growled and bared his teeth, displaying all the cake stuck between them.

Axel frowned. "And definitely not today."

I stood. "Thanks for the drink and the alibi."

"My pleasure." Axel walked Wiggles and me back to the front door. "If I can be of any help in clearing your sister's name, let me know." His hand moved to my lower back.

"I'll keep that in mind."

He leaned forward as if he was going to kiss me.

"Take a hike, buddy. She's not into toads."

Axel jumped back. He looked at me and then Wiggles. "Who said that?"

I looked around, trying to keep the smile from my face. "Maybe you have a ghost. Have you had this place checked recently for unwanted spooks? The magic sometimes draws them in."

Axel stared at Wiggles. "I could have sworn that came from Wiggles."

I glared at Wiggles, silently willing him not to say another word. "He's just a dog."

Axel looked around the hallway. "How bizarre. Well, as I said, anything I can do, just ask."

I pulled open the door and left Axel staring around the inside of his house.

I waited until we were out of earshot before speaking. "That was close."

"The guy was being a sleaze. He was going in for some open mouth action with you."

"Don't be nasty. He was going to kiss my cheek."

"No way, that guy is as slippery as an eel. He'd have accidentally planted one on your lips and then gone in for a full-on face sucking session."

"I wouldn't have let him," I said. "And you need to keep your mouth shut until we work out how many people to tell about your transformation."

"What's wrong with me being a hellhound?" Wiggles asked. "It adds an edge. It will get you more respect now you have me by your side. Your amazing talking hellhound, Thunderbolt."

"Thunderbolt?"

"I'm trying it out."

"More like Thunder Fart. Let me tell people about your change slowly. I'll only get questions about what kind of magic I used to bring you back. It will make people jumpy, knowing my pesky demon had a hand in your resurrection."

"You've always been known for your shady magic practices. This is not so different."

I stopped walking and stared at Wiggles. "I am not. My magic is legit."

"As are those mushrooms you sell in Cloven Hoof."

"Everyone needs a little natural buzz now and again. Those mushrooms are Magic Council approved. Hell, some Council members come to Willow Tree Falls to get their own mushrooms. I'm doing nothing dodgy."

"And neither am I," Wiggles said. "All you did was use some powerful magic to bring back your beloved dog. I came back with a few improvements; that's all. I cannot go around wearing sunglasses and keeping my jaw shut the whole time. That would be torture."

"You need to when we investigate Deacon's death," I said. "We don't want to spook any more suspects."

"I'll keep my muzzle shut, so long as the sleazebags keep their hands off you."

I patted his head as we continued walking. "You're a good boy. Anyone would think you were jealous."

"Of course I'm jealous. I'm your reluctant snuggle buddy."

I laughed as we headed back into the village. Wiggles might be a hellhound, but I'd trust him over any of the guys I'd dated.

"Let's go see Petra while she's still racked with guilt over squashing you. Her guilt might force her to open up," I said. "She didn't tell us the truth about her feelings for Deacon, and I need to know why."

"Grandpa Lucius is right. It's always the ex-girlfriend or the wife," Wiggles said. "They get obsessed with a guy, and that's it. It could be lights out at any time."

"How many ex-girlfriends have you got that want to do that to you?"

"A hellhound can dream. Let's go scare this witch and see what she has to tell us."

Chapter 8

Before heading to the Ancient Imp to grill Petra, I made a quick detour to Cloven Hoof. Merrie was behind the bar as usual when I walked in. She raised her hand when she saw me.

"I'm glad you're here. We've got a problem."

"No problems, not today. I'm on a mission to prove my sister's innocence."

Merrie nodded. "Two things. Angel Force has been in touch. They left information about a new job for you."

I slumped onto a stool by the bar. I had said I'd take another job to get me out of Willow Tree Falls. Right now, all I could think about was helping Aurora clear her name, not jumping an escaped demon and teaching him a few lessons.

"What else?"

Merrie pursed her lips. "Two staff called in sick."

"You're kidding. Who?"

"Paula and Mickey."

"They've only been here a couple of months. They're both sick at the same time?"

"It looks like it. Paula is decent, but I was always a little concerned about Mickey. He enjoys sampling the produce too much. He says you need to experience everything, so you can give recommendations to customers. Most of the time, he's as high as a kite and keeps walking into things."

"Get rid of him."

"Isn't that your job as our boss?" Merrie winked at me. "You get all the fun jobs."

I groaned. "Fine, when he's well enough to make an appearance, let me know. I'll happily fire his bewildered backside."

"Will do."

"We've got two parties this evening, haven't we?"

"A stag and a hen party from out of town."

I snitched my nose. "I'll stick around and lend a hand." Merrie was great at her job, but pre-wedding parties were hectic affairs.

"Thanks, that will be great. Most of the prep is done, but it's going to be crazy when the drinks orders come flying my way."

My mission to quiz Petra would have to wait. I knew where she was. She wasn't going to leave Willow Tree Falls, even though she thought she'd run over Wiggles and must be wondering what hideous revenge I had planned for her. I couldn't wait to see the look on her face when we strolled into the Ancient Imp later that night.

I hurried upstairs to change into my usual work outfit, flat black boots, fitted black pants, a red shirt and my hair tied back in a low ponytail.

"I'm starving," Wiggles said.

"Is the moldy cake not sitting well in your stomach?"

"That barely touched the sides."

"What's your favorite food? I'm guessing you're not going to say the dog kibble I feed you since there's half a bowl still in the kitchen."

"It's not great."

"It's a nutritionally complete dog food."

"It's not hellhound food. I'd love a rare steak with a side order of fries, half a bottle of Chianti, followed by a mountain of ice cream."

"No way are you getting any of that. I'm not having you turning into an obese hellhound."

"I'll burn it all off. I run extra hot now I'm fired by demon power."

"Even so, no Chianti."

"How about a smooth Merlot?"

"How about a fresh bowl of water?"

"I'll settle for toilet water."

"No! No more drinking from the toilet bowl. It's nasty and you leave puddles all over the floor."

"There's just something about that heady mix of fresh water, cleaning fluid, and human waste that I can't resist."

I wrinkled my nose. "Stop talking."

"That's not happening. I'm never giving up on this voice."

I sighed. "No wine, no toilet water."

"You are no fun."

"I'm lots of fun. But I don't want my new hellhound felled by a heart attack."

"That's impossible, I think. I can't die from anything so basic, not anymore." Wiggles turned in a circle, checking out his fur as if that would give him a clue as to just how indestructible he was.

"We'll negotiate this later. You stay up here while I get to work."

"I'll get bored on my own."

"Take a nap on your favorite beanbag." I pointed to the squishy tartan bag Wiggles loved.

"I hate that thing. Every time I move, it wakes me up with all the crunchy ball sounds. It's like sleeping in a bowl of rice crackles. Hard rice crackles."

"I had no idea. Where do you like to sleep?"

"Your bed is comfortable."

"You can sleep there only when I'm in it."

"You've got all those pillows. I like to lay between them and roll about. Sometimes, I grab one and put it between my legs—"

"Please tell me you don't hump my pillows when I'm out of the apartment."

"Only now and again. Once a day at the most."

I walked over and closed my bedroom door. "I'm going to have to get new pillows." I grabbed the dog kibble and topped up his bowl.

"I'm not touching that. It tastes like meaty sawdust."

I rummaged in the fridge and pulled out half a pack of chicken sausages. "How about these?"

"Not a fan."

I sighed. Who knew hellhounds could be so fussy. "What do you want?"

"Steak."

"I don't have any steak. I'm not into red meat."

"I bet you've got some down in the kitchen freezer."

"You're not having the bar food. That's for paying customers who get the munchies."

"Just a small steak. I'll forego the wine and the ice cream."

I groaned. I had to get downstairs and help Merrie. "I'll get a steak sent up to you so long as you promise not to hump my pillows."

"You're a diamond." He turned in a circle a couple of times and settled on the carpet.

"I'm a mug." I tucked in my shirt and ran down the stairs. I placed the order for Wiggle's steak with Niall, my amazing chef, and got to work on setting up the tables and drinks orders for tonight's parties.

We often had out-of-towners coming to Willow Tree Falls to visit Cloven Hoof. As the only licensed purveyor of magical herbal enhancements, I had a popular business. Magic users from all over the country came to enjoy themselves.

We were particularly popular with the hen and stag parties. They often got a little out of control with all the naughty behavior as people celebrated a last night of freedom with the soon to be newlyweds.

There were two parties tonight. Fifteen hens and twenty-five stags would be descending on us. They always spent well and partied hard, and they always left behind one hell of a mess.

As I did a final check of the tables, Merrie hurried over. "The hens are here."

"Let's give them a night to remember." I turned and watched as fifteen overexcited witches dressed in sparkly pink outfits pushed through the doors. The bride wore an enormous white veil and already looked unsteady on her high heels.

"Welcome ladies," I said as they entered the bar. "Let me show you to your table."

The bride-to-be, Tennessee Brown, nodded and smiled. "We're here for your mushrooms."

"They'll be on tap, as requested." I gestured to her table, set up as instructed with trays of canapes infused with some of my most potent mushrooms.

"Come on, ladies." Tennessee gestured to her friends as she hurried to the table. Her drunken hens followed behind her.

Merrie lined up shot glasses on the bar and filled them with a shimmering blue liquid as I settled the party.

I walked to the bar and snitched my nose at the shots. "Don't tell me they want star bombs all night?"

Merrie grinned. "Mushrooms and star bombs are our specialities."

"Keep an eye on how much they're drinking. Too many star bombs and our bride-to-be will be floating on the ceiling."

"You're the boss."

I sensed the next party arriving just before they entered the bar. I'd had second thoughts about letting this party in. They were elves. Not your fantasy style elf you see in all the video games. They were more like the ones portrayed in blockbuster movies, lithe with shimmering skin and pointed ears. They always had the ladies drooling. I excluded myself from that. I liked my guys with a bit more muscle and a bit less mouth.

But they'd paid upfront and had been nothing but gracious when they'd made their booking. Plus, they booked the deluxe package. These elves were wealthy and liked to spend money.

I pulled open the door to find twenty-five immaculately dressed elves. They looked too good to be true and mostly were. Elves could be deceitful. There was often some sneaky scheme up their perfectly outfitted sleeves. You had to watch what you said and be sure you agreed to nothing you weren't sure of, or you'd end up in one of their underground caverns dancing until your feet bled. All in the name of their entertainment.

"Welcome to Cloven Hoof." I looked around the group. "Which one of you is Darius Oathfinder?"

The tallest elf in the group with silver eyes stepped forward and bowed. "That would be me. Are you Tempest Crypt?"

"I am. It's nice to meet you. I hope you're having an enjoyable bachelor party so far."

"We're about to," he said. "We've heard nothing but good things about the produce you supply."

"I'm sure you won't be disappointed."

"And if I am?" His silver eyes glinted with the challenge.

I smiled sweetly. I was not going to be tricked by this elf. "Then we can talk in private."

"I look forward to it. I'm sure we can reach a satisfactory deal."

I was not doing a deal with an elf. "Everything will meet your approval. Please, follow me." I led the elves to their table on the opposite side of the room from the witches. I was sure the two parties would be mingling in no time. That was their prerogative. I wasn't a dating agency. I'd serve the drinks and let them find their way to each other.

Once the elves were settled and mushrooms gently melted on their tongues, I headed back to the bar where Merrie was returning with two empty trays.

"How are the witches?"

"Having fun." Merrie removed a pair of devil horns that had been stuck on her head. "Someone has bought a variety of amusing willy-shaped items."

"They've also asked for the same shape of cake," I said. "It's in the kitchen when they request it."

"I'll pass on that if I get offered a slice," Merrie said.

"It's bright pink with sparkles," I said. "You'd be wise to pass."

"You'll be warning me next there's a stripper booked."

"It is a hen party," I said. "What do you expect? And I think it's two strippers for our ladies."

Merrie shook her head. "Please tell me I'm getting a bonus for working this."

"You'll get something." Merrie worked hard and never let me down. I always rewarded her for that.

Once I was sure the witches and elves were happily drinking and eating, I headed back to the bar. "Can you handle them on your own for half an hour?"

"It shouldn't be a problem. If anyone gets too rowdy, I'll be in touch," Merrie said.

"Thanks." I dashed upstairs to find Wiggles standing in the middle of the apartment, a guilty look on his face and couch cushions scattered around.

"What are you up to?"

He ran behind the couch. "There's nothing to see here."

"We'll discuss this another time. Come on. We have a witch to question."

Wiggles bounded down the stairs, and we hurried out of Cloven Hoof.

"What's the plan?" he asked as we headed to the main street.

"We're quizzing Petra." It was getting late, and the Ancient Imp would be closing soon. That should mean it wasn't too busy, and she'd make time to see me. Even if she didn't, I'd convince her she had to.

"Do you think she was lying about her feelings for Deacon?"

"It's possible. If she did, and she still loved him, it must have stung to see him getting together with

Aurora."

"She could have been jealous enough to put a stop to his dabblings with Aurora."

"Dabblings? I don't think they dabbled. They went on a couple of dates."

"That's all you need. Dinner and a drink and a dabble."

"Please don't tell me what you think a dabble is." My talking hellhound had a dirty mind.

He chuckled. "You know what a dabble is. I bet you dabble when the mood takes you."

"Nope, no dabbling allowed. So, if Petra couldn't bear the thought of Deacon being with anyone else, maybe she snapped, killed him, and is trying to frame Aurora?"

Wiggles growled. "First, she frames your sister, and then she squashes me. This lady needs me to take her for a long walk off a short pier."

I shook my head. "That makes no sense. If you were walking with her, you'd fall in as well."

"You know what I mean. We need to teach her a lesson."

We did. Petra would benefit from a scare. It might convince her to give up driving or at least stop wearing such impractical shoes. I pushed open the door to the Ancient Imp, magic flaring on the tips of my fingers.

As soon as Petra saw me, she raised a hand and shook her head. "Not in here. I value my bar." Her gaze shifted to Wiggles, and her eyes widened. "Wait! I thought he was…"

"You thought you'd killed him?" I pointed a finger at her, magic dripping from it and sizzling on the ground.

The drinkers in the Ancient Imp turned to stare at Wiggles and me, all conversations stopping.

"Keep your voice down," Petra hissed as she gestured me to the bar. Her gaze didn't leave Wiggles. "I was so sure I'd hit him."

"You did." I approached the bar and rested my hands on the top, crackling my magical energy across it.

Petra's gaze turned concerned, but she let out a relieved sigh. "I'm glad he wasn't hurt. It wasn't my fault. I didn't see him until it was too late."

"You shouldn't be driving. You're dangerous behind the wheel. I've seen you knock over dozens of trash cans."

"I'm short. I have trouble seeing over the hood of the car. That's why I wear such high heels."

"Wearing heels doesn't make you taller when you're sitting down. And it's lazy. Everything is within walking distance here."

"I love my car as much as you love Wiggles." Petra leaned against the bar. "Listen, no hard feelings about hitting your dog. I promise you it was an accident. Don't destroy my bar."

"You might need to buy him some expensive dog treats to make up for it," I said as I pulled back my magic and felt it absorb into my skin. "He's not going to forgive you easily. Neither will I."

"I will. I am sorry, Wiggles."

Wiggles pretended not to have heard her as he snuffled chips off the ground and ducked behind the bar out of sight, no doubt on the hunt for more food.

I dropped my hands and shook the residual tingles of magic from them. "Why did you run off?"

Petra shrugged and ducked her head. "You spooked me."

"You were spooked because you have something to hide. No one runs like that unless they have a guilty conscience. What's on your mind? Feeling bad about Deacon?"

Petra gestured for me to stop talking. "I told you I'm not interested in him."

"I've been told that you were basically stalking him. He lost interest, and you hadn't. You kept pestering him long after he'd moved on."

Petra's cheeks flushed. "Rubbish. Who told you that?"

"I have my sources."

She huffed and polished a glass with a cloth. "Your sources don't know what they're talking about."

"You didn't follow him around in the hope of bumping into him and making Deacon realize he still loved you?"

"Our paths crossed now and again. This is a small place; it was going to happen. I'm not a stalker."

"You didn't mind the fact Deacon was seeing my sister?"

Petra frowned. "I wasn't thrilled about it. I always assumed he saw me as the perfect match in the lead up to his campaign to become mayor."

I gestured around the room. "The owner of a bar might not have been the quality of girlfriend he was looking for."

"Hey! The Ancient Imp is respected. Everyone comes here."

"Sure, you serve great beer. But the attractive owner of a white magic store is more acceptable on the arm of a future mayor."

Petra shrugged. "Deacon made his decision, even if it was a bad one. I'd moved on."

"You still liked him. Admit it."

She sighed. "Okay, I did care about him, but I had nothing to do with what happened. I'm sorry Deacon is dead, but if he goes around treating people like they're objects and upgrading to help himself, something like this was bound to happen."

"You felt like he used you?"

"Not right away. It was only when he got serious about running for mayor that he changed. I got the impression someone was telling him how he should behave to win over voters. I guess they told him I wasn't the right sort of woman to have in his life if he wanted to be a winner." Petra polished the same spot on the bar so hard it squeaked.

"And you're sure you were home eating pizza the night Deacon died?"

"Go check the trash if you like. The pizza box is probably still there with the receipt in it. That's what I did."

"Someone killed Deacon, and it wasn't Aurora," I said, feeling a spark of magic fire in me as I grew frustrated. "Angel Force will have to look into everybody who had a motive for wanting him dead, and that includes you. They will find out if you went after Deacon."

"It wasn't me! I already told you, if you're looking for the killer, you should talk to Mannie. He has to be involved. He's such a sleazebag."

Mannie Winter was known for his underhanded dealings. He wouldn't be above pulling a few tricks to get what he wanted in order to become the new mayor of Willow Tree Falls. Would he go as far as murder?

"Please, Tempest. I don't know anything about this." Petra placed her hand over her heart. "I miss Deacon, even though he was a jerk to me. How about a beer on the house? My treat. A tiny way to say sorry for what happened to Wiggles."

I looked around. Wiggles was nowhere to be seen. "No beer. I'll take a lemon water but a small one. I need to get back to Cloven Hoof. We've got the place full of overexcited punters tonight."

"What would Wiggles like? I owe him one as well."

"A bowl of water will be fine if you can find him." The door behind me slammed against the wall, and I jumped in my seat.

Petra looked up and blinked in surprise. "Oh! What are you doing here?"

As I swiveled in my seat to see who'd come into the pub, I was overwhelmed by a wall of white and feathers and blasted in the chest by a bolt of magic.

Chapter 9

My head pounded, and my throat felt raw as my eyes flickered open. "What the..." I blinked slowly. The last thing I remembered was being in the Ancient Imp and Petra groveling and offering me free drinks.

This was definitely not the Ancient Imp, and I wasn't about to enjoy a sparkling lemon water while I guilt-tripped Petra.

Feathers! I remember lots of fluffy, pristine angel wing feathers and a thump of halo magic slam into me.

I twisted my head and frowned. From the shocking amounts of white surrounding me, I was at the Angel Force headquarters.

Anger rolled through me, and it stirred Frank into action. His hot unstable energy flooded my veins.

I sat up slowly. My chest ached from where I'd been slammed with magic. What in all of hell's fire breathing demons did Angel Force want with me?

"I can take them down if you let me out," Frank whispered.

"It's tempting," I muttered. I had two choices. I could wait it out and see what the angels wanted, or I could let Frank out and blast my way free and wring some angel necks as I did so.

"Those angels can't keep you here. They've locked you in a cell for no good reason. You have every right to break out," Frank said.

"I do have questions that need answering." I rolled off the bench and onto my feet. I made sure to keep Frank in his shackles as I tried a spell on the door. The magic wavered and then faded before it had any impact.

"A null shield," I said with a grimace. It was hardly a surprise. Angels had the ability to create voids that prevented anyone's magic from working. They'd need it on the cells since everyone they arrested had some kind of magic.

My frustration grew and, along with it, Frank's power and control over me.

"Let me out. I can get us out of here. No angel shield can stop me."

It was so tempting to let Frank take over. He was a pain to carry around, but he was a powerful demon. But once he was let out, chaos would ensue. He'd stop at nothing to get what he truly wanted, and that was Aurora.

"Stay where you are. These feathery numpties must have me here for a reason."

I heard a door open and close. A moment later, Dazielle arrived holding two coffees and a brown paper bag.

"Are those peace offerings so I don't sue you for wrongful arrest?" I pointed at the bag.

She looked down at the bag and shrugged. "I figured you might be hungry. You've been out all night. It's almost noon."

I groaned and rolled my shoulders. "Perfect. What am I doing here? I wasn't breaking any laws that I know of."

"You're here for two reasons." Dazielle opened the hatch and passed me a coffee. "Do you want a muffin?"

"I'll take two."

She smirked and handed me one blueberry muffin.

"I'm waiting."

"First of all, someone in the Ancient Imp reported the dangerous use of magic. They were worried about the safety of the building and Petra."

"For crying out loud! I didn't actually use magic. I might have suggested the use of magic, but no spells were cast. Petra was never in any real danger." She hadn't been on that occasion, but if an angel had happened upon me choking her after she'd hit Wiggles, it would have been a different story.

Dazielle raised a hand. "They thought your demon had you in his control. They needed to be careful."

"I was in control."

"And how is Frank?" Dazielle blew on her coffee as her brilliant blue gaze traveled over me.

"Hating on you right about now."

She nodded. "So long as he knows his place."

"Sadly, he does." I bit a piece off my muffin. It was good, obviously from Sprinkles. "I was angry when I went to visit Petra. That's what the drinkers at Ancient Imp must have sensed. I had a right to be. Petra ran over Wiggles yesterday."

Dazielle's eyebrows quirked. "She did? He looks fine to me."

"Where is he?"

"In the break room. He spent the night there after following you when you were brought in. That dog snores loudly."

"He does it because he knows it annoys people. What's the second reason I'm in here?"

Dazielle placed her coffee down. "I can't afford to have you distracted. Your job is not to investigate Deacon's murder. Your job is to help your family keep the demon prison safe and bring back any rogues we need capturing."

"That's not totally true. Besides, I can do both."

"Finding out who killed Deacon is our job."

"You don't get to tell me I can't look out for my own sister."

Dazielle sighed. "That's not it. We're the experts, and we're already questioning people. If you're doing the same thing, it confuses the issue. We had Petra on our list to talk to. We know about her involvement with Deacon. We know he wasn't all that happy with her."

"Do you also know she basically stalked him after he dumped her? I've been told she wasn't giving up on him so easily."

"We're also aware of that." Dazielle leaned against the bars of the cell. "I've spoken with Axel. He told me about Petra's continued interest in Deacon. He also told me that Deacon was much more interested in Aurora."

"So why didn't you drag Petra in for questioning like you did Aurora?"

"We don't drag suspects anywhere. If you hadn't interfered, I might have done so. You can't get involved in this investigation."

"It's my sister; therefore, I'm going to be involved." I felt the remains of the muffin squish between my fingers as I clenched my fist.

"We don't need your assistance." Dazielle straightened and glared at me.

"You need me for everything else. I only help you because Gran dated the old Chief at Angel Force. She twisted my arm and made me promise to help."

"Castiel has retired. Maybe you can retire your services as well."

"Maybe I will. I can drop you on your feathered butts in a second. You'll have to go out and deal with those demons on your own."

Dazielle shook her head. "I appreciate you leaving Willow Tree Falls to retrieve the demons. But you can't investigate cases whenever you feel like it."

"I've already found several other suspects. Suspects who are more likely to have killed Deacon than Aurora."

"No! Stay off the case. You're too close to our main suspect. You can't remain impartial."

I tamped down on Frank's urge to come out. "Aurora cannot be your main suspect. She's a white witch. She is not about killing guys she dates."

"She's a white witch who can tap into the energy of the undead. You might not know your sister as well as you think you do."

Dazielle was dumber than I'd realized. "I know Aurora wasn't all that into Deacon. He was pursuing her, and she went along with it, so she didn't hurt his feelings. I also know Petra was obsessed with him and stalked him. What's to say she didn't crack when she saw Deacon out with Aurora and did something about it? Then there's Mannie. He's sly and underhanded, and he wants to be the mayor. He saw Deacon as competition so bumped him off."

"So, is it Petra or Mannie who's the killer?"

"Both. Neither. I don't know. But I will find out."

Dazielle's eyebrows rose slowly. "You have been busy."

"Busier than you. Why don't you pursue Petra and Mannie, rather than chase after my sister?"

"We might well do that. But we don't go into any situation without as much information as possible. And you going around terrorizing people into confessing is not helping. There will be more complaints filed if you're not careful."

"I don't care about complaints." I tilted my head as I heard several angels in the nearby office shriek and something crash to the ground.

Dazielle set her coffee and muffin on the table and walked toward the door. As she reached it, it slammed open and knocked her into the wall.

Wiggles barged in, growling as he ran toward me.

"It looks like someone's woken up." I grinned at him and lowered my voice. "Are you having fun with your angel buddies?"

"The number of angels who have tried to rub my belly is embarrassing. If they knew what I really was, they'd be running the other way."

Dazielle scrambled to her feet and hurried over. "Keep control of your dog, Tempest."

I looked at Wiggles and gestured to the sunglasses that had slipped down his nose. It wasn't the smartest idea to reveal he was a hellhound in the middle of a building full of angels.

Wiggles bared his teeth and shook the glasses off. "Lady, you have no clue what you're doing when it comes to helping Aurora."

Dazielle's mouth fell open, and she flapped her lips, no words coming out.

Wiggles eyes glowed, and he advanced on her, his hackles raised.

Dazielle backed away slowly. "You're not Wiggles."

I pressed my lips together to prevent myself from laughing. "He is. He got an upgrade. I was telling the truth about Petra. She ran over him. I decided to bring him back."

Dazielle stared at me. "Your dog is a hellhound. You own a hellhound. Have you got the proper license for that?"

"It got lost in the post. I wasn't going to lose my best friend because Petra doesn't know how to drive. Oh, and if it's of any interest to your investigation, she was running because I was questioning her about Deacon. She has something to hide. Don't let her fool you."

"Is Tempest free to go?" Wiggles asked. "I'm getting bored, and it's long overdue breakfast." His gaze landed on the muffin Dazielle had abandoned, and he grabbed it.

"Hey!" Dazielle said.

Wiggles growled at her, and she backed away again.

"Fine, have the muffin," she muttered.

"Can I go?" I kept the grin off my face as I watched Wiggles scoff her breakfast. "Have I learned my lesson?"

Dazielle shook her head. "Probably not, but you can go. Petra doesn't want to press charges. But I'm keeping my eye on you." She waved her hand over the null shield, and the door clicked open.

"You can watch me all you like, but I'm not stopping. I'm going to clear my sister's name no matter what it takes."

"Then you'll find yourself back behind bars if you're not careful."

I scowled at Dazielle before pushing past her, Wiggles hot on my heels. There was not a chance in hell of that. I still had suspects to question. Until I'd figured out which one of them killed Deacon, I was not stopping.

Chapter 10

I rolled my shoulders as I walked away from the Angel Force headquarters. "What a night," I said to Wiggles.

"You're telling me. It's not much fun being a hellhound surrounded by angels. They kept sniffing the air whenever they got too close as if they could smell something they didn't like but couldn't trace the source."

"Are you sure that wasn't your gas? You did eat moldy cake from Axel's trash."

"I'm telling you they smelt hellhound. I had to fake being asleep for hours and hope they didn't twig."

"It's too late for that now. You revealed yourself to Dazielle. Everyone will know about you. There's no hiding what you are."

"I never wanted to hide. That was always you. Anyone would think you're ashamed of being owned by a hellhound."

I looked down at him. My smile faded, and worry pricked at my gut. "I never asked; you don't mind being a hellhound? I didn't know that's what you'd be when we brought you back."

Wiggles gave a yip of delight. "Are you kidding me? I didn't mind being a regular dog, but now I get to live forever, talk, and terrorize people. I don't see any downside to my upgrade."

"You don't mind that most people are going to be terrified of you? You won't get as many treats if people are too scared to approach you."

"Fewer treats? Huh, I didn't think about that. Maybe I should look into getting lenses to hide my eyes and practise my cute begging face."

"You'd still have that hellhound smell."

"I'm no longer smelling of buttercups and sunshine?"

I laughed. "You always smelt of grass and dog biscuits to me."

"That's not so bad." He sniffed his front leg. "There is a sulfurous tang to me now. I'll get some cologne. That will sort the problem."

"Or you could embrace it. I like you as you are. Others will get used to you over time."

"Yeah, I'm a badass hellhound." Wiggles strutted in front of me.

"You have a cute ass, not a bad one." I grinned as he lived up to his name by wiggling his tush. "Where did you go last night in the Ancient Imp? One minute you were gobbling chips off the floor, and the next, you'd vanished."

"I was clue hunting."

"What clue?"

"I went through Petra's trash."

"Not again. This has to stop. I—"

"I wasn't looking for food. I was hunting for food containers. More specifically, pizza boxes."

"Oh, right. Petra's alibi. What did you find?"

"A greasy box and a receipt that tallies with her story."

"She did eat pizza that night. But maybe she went out after that?"

"She got the pizza at midnight, so unless she ate and killed at the same time, it's unlikely."

I tilted my head from side to side. I wouldn't want to commit murder with a belly full of pizza. "Let's head to the cemetery, see how Aurora's doing and if there are any updates from her end."

There was always at least one member of my family at Willow Tree Falls Cemetery, no matter the time of day or night. Willow Tree Falls had been built over the entrance of the largest demon prison in the world. The village might be small, but what lay underneath it was enormous. And the Crypt family was in charge of it all, making sure the demons didn't break out.

Weaknesses and cracks in defenses appeared for different reasons. Sometimes, a minor earthquake might cause a tiny crack and a demon would creep out. Sometimes, the demons worked together and used their combined strength to blast a hole in the prison. Getting demons to work together was rare.

They all had such big egos that they rarely accepted help from each other, but now and again, it happened. When it did, it was my job to leave Willow Tree Falls and get them back, along with any other jobs Angel Force couldn't handle. Oh, yes, and running Cloven Hoof. I sometimes surprised myself that I had any time to sleep.

As I headed through the high black iron gates of the cemetery, I spotted a checked cloth on the ground by an off-white stone crypt. The door to the crypt was open.

I poked my head in and discovered Auntie Queenie, Mom, and Granny Dottie inside cutting up sandwiches.

"It looks like I'm just in time," I said.

"Where have you been hiding?" Mom said. "I tried to get in touch with you last night at the club. Merrie said you'd gone missing."

"Not out of choice," I said. "Dazielle arrested me. She's warned me off of investigating Deacon's murder." I walked over and grabbed a cheese sandwich.

"That angel has clouds for brains. I hope you didn't listen to her," Mom said.

"Do I ever listen to anything the Angel Farts say?"

"Good girl." Mom patted my arm and swatted away my hand as I made a grab for another sandwich.

"We were setting up a picnic," Auntie Queenie said. "Join us."

I glanced behind me. Surprisingly, Wiggles had hung back. Whenever there was food around, he always forgot his manners and was front of the queue. It looked like he was feeling a little bashful about being a hellhound.

"Before we do, I've got something to tell you." I gestured Wiggles into the crypt.

He slunk in, keeping his head down.

"It's about Wiggles. He's a bit… different these days."

Granny Dottie glanced at Wiggles. "We know. You and Aurora brought him back from the dead."

"Which is very dangerous," Mom said. "You know how exhausting spells like that are. Your sister's nose bled all night. You also know that anything could hop on board a spell like that. You could have brought all sorts of unpleasant characters back with Wiggles."

"We didn't." At least, I hoped we didn't. It had been a selfish move using such strong magic, but I'd do it again to get Wiggles back by my side. "The thing is, we had some help from Frank."

Mom dropped the butter knife and glared at Wiggles. She hated Frank. He'd tried to kill Aurora and now lived inside me and refused to budge. "What did he do to your lovely dog?"

"Nothing terrible. Well, nothing harmful to him. I think Frank has a soft spot for Wiggles."

Wiggles barely moved the whole time we talked. I could see his nose twitching. It must be torture for him looking so contrite when all he wanted to do was launch himself muzzle first into the pile of sandwiches.

"Anyway, the three of us combined energies, and, well, Wiggles has come back as a hellhound."

This time, they all stopped fussing around the food and stared at Wiggles.

Wiggles raised his head, looking like the saddest, most innocent hellhound in the world.

"He does have very red eyes," Auntie Queenie said.

"If he's a hellhound, he's immortal," Granny Dottie said, "or, at least, ridiculously hard to kill. Demon water, maybe essence of Iris would do it. Your dog is now one tough little guy."

Mom shook her head and continued buttering bread. "If that's all, then there's nothing to worry about. So long as Wiggles is safe to be around, then he's welcome."

"He's safe," I said.

"We'd never turn him away just because he's a hellhound." Granny Dottie patted his head. "Would you like a sandwich, sweetie?"

"I'd love one," Wiggles said.

Mom dropped the knife. Auntie Queenie laughed and clapped her hands together.

"He talks!" Granny Dottie yelped. "Even better." She threw Wiggles a sandwich.

He gobbled it down and licked his lips before giving me a quick wink. The family had accepted him, and I couldn't feel any more relieved.

We spent a few minutes ferrying food out of the crypt and all settled on the blanket outside in the early afternoon sunshine.

"What's our next step in clearing Aurora's name?" Mom asked.

"I still like my theory that the biker gang had something to do with it," Auntie Queenie said as she passed around plates. "They're shady. They're always up to no good."

"That doesn't make them killers." Mom passed around the sandwiches. "They're overexcited boys with too much time on their hands."

"They try to undercut my market," I said. "I've had to have words with them several times to stop them from selling things I have at Cloven Hoof." No one trampled on my business niche. I was the mushroom and magic drinks specialist in Willow Tree Falls, no one else.

"I bet they're always happy to oblige." Granny Dottie's smile was sly. "Don't you have a thing for Rhett?"

I studied the sandwich I held. "No, I'm not into Rhett." His muscles and dark hair did nothing for me. Neither did those eyes that were almost black and so intense, nor that smile that could melt an iceberg.

"You've had a thing about him ever since you and Aurora were kids," Auntie Queenie said.

"My daughter does not date a biker," Mom said sharply.

"A few seconds ago, you described him as an overexcited boy. There's no harm in dating someone like that." Granny Dottie smiled at me, a gleam in her eyes.

"I'm not dating anyone," I said. "It's just that I have to see him to warn him off of encroaching on my business."

"You'd think, with those muscles, he could turn his hand to all sorts of physical labor. The kind that gets him all sweaty, so he needs to take his shirt off all the time," Granny Dottie said. "A few of those bikers have even turned my head, and I'm happily married."

"My head is not turned," I said. "Getting back to the point, other than the fact they're a bit shady, why do you think they could be involved in Deacon's death? It's not as if he hangs out with the biker gang."

"Maybe not, but I spotted that bike outside his house. Why visit Deacon if they weren't doing something nefarious together?"

"Maybe they wanted to offer him support in his campaign?" Granny Dottie said.

"They're not interested in who wins the role of mayor," I said. "They do whatever they like, whoever is in charge."

"You should go talk to Rhett," Auntie Queenie said to me. "He must be missing you since you stopped returning his calls."

"I'm not going to talk to the bikers or Rhett. And I didn't stop returning his calls. He stopped calling me."

"Because you didn't pick up or reply to his messages," Auntie Queenie said. "A fine piece of leather clad behind like that is not going to wait forever."

"I've been busy," I muttered.

"We should invite Rhett to dinner one night," Granny Dottie said. "It's long overdue him meeting the family."

"No to Rhett coming to dinner." I glared at Auntie Queenie. "We don't need that hassle."

"You're putting up too much resistance." She waggled a finger at me. "You still have feelings for that young man."

I stuffed the rest of the sandwich in my mouth and chewed. "If it means that much to you, I'll go talk to Rhett." I'd prove her wrong. I wasn't in love with Rhett Blackthorn. He was just hot and tempting; that was all there was to it.

The ground beneath us trembled. Mom, Auntie Queenie, and Granny Dottie were on their feet so fast they were just a blur of movement. They raced into the crypt.

I hopped up and followed them with Wiggles.

"There's a crack opened at the Cornwallis crypt," Mom said as she stared at the glowing map that had appeared on the stone wall. The map showed the layout of the cemetery and highlighted any breaches.

They grabbed long wooden sticks that leaned against the wall. To the impartial observer, they looked like solid, slightly twisted walking sticks. They were much more than that. They were powerful magic rods, imbued with so much magic no demon stood a chance when whacked around the head with one.

"Do you need a hand?" I asked as they hurried past me.

"No, you stay here with Wiggles and enjoy the food." Mom touched my cheek, and I felt her magic crackle against my skin. "We won't be a moment."

I glanced at Wiggles, and he shook his head and yipped. There was no chance we would miss an opportunity to watch Mom, Auntie, and Granny in action. It was easy to forget what strong witches they were when all they did was cook, gossip, and try to match make me.

I ran along behind them with Wiggles, eating another sandwich as I did so.

"You head around the back," Mom said to Granny Dottie. "We'll check inside the crypt and see how bad the crack is. We should have caught it early enough that nothing has gotten out yet."

"I'm on it." Granny Dottie defied her seventy-two years by sprinting around the back of the crypt and leaping over several headstones as she disappeared round the corner.

"There's some serious girl power going on here," Wiggles said.

"No kidding. I hope I can jump over gravestones like that when I'm her age."

The crypt doors blew open. A blast of hot fetid air slapped my face. Mom stood in the entrance, the wooden sticks clasped in both hands. She spun and twirled like a ballet dancer as she slammed into the shimmering form of a demon as he attempted to slide through the crack in the prison.

"He's inside," I yelled to Granny Dottie.

She raced back around the crypt and threw herself into the fight with Mom and Auntie Queenie.

"Those ladies are something else," Wiggles said.

"I learned everything I know from them. They're the best demon hunters in the world." I felt a rush of pride at being connected to this family. It was times like this when I wished I could stay around more and help monitor the prison.

"Get back, demon," Granny Dottie yelled as she slammed her sticks against the demon's head.

The demon roared and rose up, a mass of gray and purple smoke, as he tried to form a solid shape and raked his claws through the air.

Granny Dottie danced out of the way, laughing as she did so, looking suppler than a twenty-something yoga fanatic than a seventy-plus grandma.

Mom had moved behind the demon, and with a nod to Granny Dottie and Auntie Queenie, they linked their sticks together, surrounding him in a circle of magic.

"No," the demon roared, his rough, deep voice echoing off the stone walls of the crypt. "I must be free."

"You must stay where you are," Mom said. "You need to serve your sentence like a good little demon."

"You witches cannot keep me contained," he roared.

"Of course we can, you butt head," Granny Dottie said. "That's our job." She kicked him in the stomach as Auntie Queenie rushed closer and pounded his head with her sticks.

With a final roar, he slid back into the crack he'd come out of, the air surrounding us filling with a dense, eggy smelling fog in his final act of defiance.

Wiggles coughed and backed out of the crypt.

I wafted my hand in front of my face. You could always sniff out a demon by their rotten egg stench.

After a moment, when they were sure he'd gone, my mom placed her sticks against the crack and traced over it several times until it was sealed.

Granny Dottie grinned at Mom. "Nice work, my girl."

Mom nodded and grinned as she patted Auntie Queenie's arm. She looked over at me. "You should be eating sandwiches, not watching the show."

"I wanted to pick up a few pointers. It's been awhile since I've seen you take down a demon."

"Nothing ever changes." Granny Dottie emerged from the crypt with the others. "They roar about injustice and being set free, and we tell them that's not possible. That fight has made me hungry for something sweet. It's time for cake."

We walked back to the blanket and were sampling a delicious, sugary, homemade carrot cake covered in a thick layer of vanilla frosting when Lula ran into the cemetery. She was waving at us, flailing her arms over her head as she approached.

"Don't tell me she's got a half-price cut and blow dry we just have to have," Granny Dottie muttered.

"Be nice," Mom said. "She does a great job on your hair."

Lula stopped and gasped in air as she reached the blanket. "Have you heard the news?"

"I think we're about to," I said.

Lula's gaze went to the cake, and she licked her lips. "That looks nice."

"You can have a slice if you tell us what's made you run like a toad with a rocket up his butt," Granny Dottie said as she brandished the cake knife.

"Oh, yes, of course. Petra's in the hospital."

Mom glanced at me. "I'm sorry to hear that."

I raised my hands. "She was fine when I saw her last night. I didn't touch her."

"That's not the worst of it," Lula said. "Aurora's been arrested for attempted murder. Angel Force think she tried to kill Petra."

Chapter 11

I jumped up and grabbed Lula by the shoulders. "Tell us everything you know."

"That's it," Lula gasped. "Someone trashed Petra's place, and she was injured when she discovered the burglar."

I shook my head in disbelief. "Angel Force think Aurora did that? How dumb are these angels?"

"They seem certain she's involved," Lula said. "I ran to your house to let you know, but you weren't there. I figured I'd find someone here at the crypt."

Mom looked at me, her expression thunderous. "Tempest, you have to get your sister out of the cells. If she keeps being arrested, people will talk."

"Let them talk," I said. "It's none of their business."

"I'll come with you," Granny Dottie said. "We can sort out this mess."

"No, you need to keep an eye out for that demon coming back. If there's a weakness in the prison, you all need to be here." New cracks were notorious for breaking open again. Once the demons found a weakness, they exploited it.

Lula glanced at the crypt behind us, and her cheeks paled. "You've got demons on the loose?"

"Not anymore," I said. "Maybe you shouldn't stick around, though. They like pretty things to play with."

Lula backed away. Her gaze went back to the carrot cake, and a determined look crossed her face. She was nothing if not persistent. "I can stay a few more minutes."

"I'll go see Petra, find out what she knows about whoever attacked her. She must make the angels realize Aurora isn't involved."

"Take your grandpa with you," Granny Dottie said. "He has a thing about nurses' uniforms."

That was something I didn't want to know about. "Send him a message. I'll meet him at the hospital."

"Here's your reward, Lula." Granny Dottie cut a slice of carrot cake and handed it to Lula.

She grinned. "Lovely. Thanks, so much."

"Where's mine?" I asked.

"I'll save you some for later. You need to get to the hospital."

I sighed and ran out of the cemetery with Wiggles, Lula struggling to keep up as she ate her huge slice of cake.

"I hate to say this, but…"

I glanced back at Lula. "Tell me."

"Your sister seems really involved in what happened to Deacon," Lula said. "First, he dies, and now his girlfriend is attacked."

"His ex-girlfriend. If you listen to all the rumors, you'd know Deacon had finished with Petra before asking Aurora on a date."

"Sure, but people are beginning to talk. They think Aurora might be involved."

"Then they're idiots," I said. "Spread the word; anyone who goes badmouthing Aurora will have to answer to me. Make sure they know that."

"What will you do to them?" Lula asked.

"Make sure they never tell another lie again."

Lula slowed as we reached her hairdressers. She had a smear of cream frosting on her chin, which I decided not to mention. "I'll let everybody know."

I left her to her sticky carrot cake encrusted fingers and gossip and ran the length of Sweet Briar Lane to the hospital.

The hospital in Willow Tree Falls was small. There was never much call for sick beds. If someone was ill, they used magic to get better. Now and again, someone would develop a serious illness or an injury that needed rest. Magic was not the solution to everything. Whatever had happened to Petra must be bad if she had to stay in the hospital to recover.

As I reached the hospital doors, I saw Grandpa Lucius materialize. As usual, he was dapperly dressed and sported a pair of bright blue chinos and matching bow tie.

"I heard you needed a bit of help." He kissed my cheek.

I gave him a brief hug. "You don't need to be here, and you could have walked. The hospital is ten minutes from our house."

"It's good to shake out the old magic now and again. I haven't done a transportation spell for a while. What's the situation?"

"Aurora's been arrested again. Angel Force think she tried to kill Petra."

Grandpa Lucius's bushy eyebrows rose. "Petra is in the hospital?"

I nodded. "I need to talk to her and find out what happened before Aurora's name gets any more mud attached to it."

"Lead the way, dear girl."

I looked down at Wiggles. "Sorry, buddy. No dogs allowed."

"Why don't you tell them I'm your assistance dog?"

Grandpa Lucius chuckled. "Dottie mentioned your pooch had an upgrade."

"Not enough of an upgrade to get inside the hospital. Wait here, Wiggles. We won't be long." We headed through the doors and into the clean corridors of the hospital. I strode to the desk where Virginia Mackenzie sat. She was a round-faced witch with a mess of dark curls and a tiny snub nose.

"I'm here to see Petra," I said.

Virginia's gaze ran over me as she chewed on the end of her pen. "Family only."

"My sister's in prison because of Petra. I need to see her now."

"She's recovering. Petra's had a shock. She doesn't need any more unwelcome shocks."

"How badly injured is she?" Grandpa Lucius said.

Virginia smiled at him. "She's had a knock to the head and is under observation. Petra was unconscious when she was found, so we're keeping a close eye on her to make sure there's no serious damage."

I shook my head and scowled. Why couldn't Virginia have told me that? "What does she know about who attacked her? Has she said anything?"

"Not to me. That's the job of Angel Force to investigate. From what I've heard, Aurora hurt her."

"There's been a mistake," I said. "Aurora wouldn't injure Petra. She has no reason to do so."

Virginia arched an eyebrow. "Didn't she steal Petra's boyfriend?"

I kept my irritation in check. "If you mean Deacon, he dumped Petra ages ago, long before Aurora was on the scene."

"That's not what I heard," Virginia said. "Still, whatever happened, Angel Force think your sister attacked Petra. You're not getting anywhere near her. For all I know, you might be here to finish the job."

I opened my mouth to protest when Grandpa Lucius squeezed my elbow and gently pushed me to the side.

"Has anyone told you the color purple makes your skin shine?" he asked Virginia. "It makes you look positively radiant."

I resisted the urge to roll my eyes as I discreetly stepped back. Grandpa Lucius could sweet talk anybody, and it looked like his skills weren't failing on this frosty receptionist.

I heard her giggling and watched her cheeks redden as he continued to shower her with compliments.

Only when he gave me a discreet wave behind his back did I sneak off and start looking for Petra.

I found her at the end of the corridor in a private room. Her eyes were closed when I sneaked the door shut behind me.

Petra's sleepy gaze didn't seem to register me at first as she blinked her eyes open. Then her gaze widened, and she stiffened in the bed.

"Don't scream." I hurried to her bedside. "I heard what happened to you."

Petra licked her lips. "Don't be mad with me again. I never said it was your sister who did this."

"Even if you didn't, they still arrested Aurora. What happened?"

Petra glanced at the closed door before giving a small shrug. "It's all a blur. It was late last night, and I was having trouble sleeping. I often go down to the bar and make myself a cup of cocoa and read a book until I get tired. I got to the bottom of the stairs and heard somebody creeping about in the bar."

"Who was it?"

"I couldn't see them. I wasn't alarmed to begin with. It wouldn't be the first time I'd missed someone who'd fallen asleep on a bench by the fire. It gets cozy back there, and after a few too many, it's easy to doze off. I figured it was just another drunk who'd woken up and was trying to fumble his way out of the door."

"But it wasn't a happy drunk who'd lost his way?"

She shook her head and winced. "I've never seen a drunk move so fast. I'd just walked into the bar when I was slammed from the side. They shoved me to the ground and landed a good kick on my head." Petra touched the lump on her forehead.

"Did you get a glimpse of who did it?"

"No. The lights were off. I know my way around that place so well I don't need to put a light on at night. It only attracts attention if I do. Then I'll have someone looking to get a late-night drink and banging on the door to be let in."

"You have no clue who was in the bar?"

"All I know is that they messed the place up." She frowned. "It was a neat sort of mess, though."

"A neat mess? That doesn't make sense."

"It was as if they'd done it deliberately. It was too staged to be the work of someone looking for money or to steal booze. I heard no noise, but when I got downstairs, there were chairs turned over and drawers opened. Everything was placed just so, messy neatness. Almost like the scene of a movie set."

"Was whoever broke in looking for something specific?"

"I was pretty out of it when I was found. I was awake for a couple of minutes but didn't see anything missing. I had Angel Force check, and the bar takings were in the safe completely untouched, so they weren't after money."

"Why do they think Aurora is involved?"

"It beats me. The first I knew about it was when Dazielle came in and told me she was back in a cell."

I shook my head. "It couldn't have been her. Aurora has no reason to break into the Ancient Imp. She'd never hurt you. She'd never hurt anybody."

"Whoever it was, they were dressed in black, and they were strong despite not being very tall. If it was your sister, she had to be using some sort of magic to give her extra strength. She slammed into me so hard, I blacked out for a second before landing on the floor. And that kick, it was meant to hurt. It was meant to frighten me. Maybe it was a warning to keep my mouth shut."

The door behind me opened. "What do you think you're doing in here?"

I turned slowly on my heel. Dazielle stood in the doorway, her hands on her white clad hips. I pasted on a smile. "I was passing by and heard Petra had taken a fall."

"You cannot be in here. Your sister is the prime suspect in this investigation. You could be manipulating our only eyewitness." Dazielle stalked into the room.

"No, she's not. I've already told you I saw nothing," Petra said swiftly.

"Not another word," Dazielle said. "You are still in shock."

"I need to know why you've arrested Aurora," I said to Dazielle. "What makes you think she had anything to do with Petra's accident?"

"Being kicked in the head isn't an accident," Dazielle said.

"Have you seen the ridiculous shoes my sister wears? She couldn't hurt anyone with those." Aurora liked peep-toed sandals in summer and sparkly ballet pumps when it got colder. The worst she'd do if she trod on you would be to give you a sore toe.

"We have strong evidence to show she is involved. That's all I'm going to tell you," Dazielle said. "Now, you have two choices: you leave, or I'll arrest you and you can spend time with your sister, discussing how you both ended up behind bars."

I gritted my teeth and glared at Dazielle. I couldn't afford to end up behind bars again, but I had to find out why they thought Aurora was involved in Petra's attack.

"What's it going to be?" Dazielle asked.

I huffed out a sigh. "I'm leaving. But I'm not leaving this alone. You're not going to keep Aurora in a cell. She didn't do this."

"She will stay there for as long as I need," Dazielle said. "This time, it's more than circumstantial evidence I have against her."

I raised my eyebrows, but she refused to say any more, simply glaring at me and pursing her pouty lips.

I stomped out of the room and headed back to reception. Grandpa Lucius was now behind the reception, perched on the desk with a mug of what looked like coffee in his hand.

He winked at me as I passed. He seemed more than happy to carry on his flirting with Virginia, so I left him to it. He never meant anything when he flirted; it was just his way. Granny Dottie was the same when it came to any hot guy showing off his toned stomach. They both liked a good flirt but always ended up back in each other's arms.

As I headed out of the hospital, Wiggles met me by the door. "Any luck?"

"Petra has been hurt, but she's not sure it was Aurora who kicked her. She saw nothing. The angels have something on Aurora, though. Dazielle looked smugly confident that she hadn't made a mistake." I stopped as I spotted an Angel Force bike parked. Sitting astride it was my favorite gorgeous but dumb angel, Dominic.

I sauntered over and gave him a smile.

He returned the smile. "What's up, Tempest?"

"I was visiting a patient."

His smile faded. "Of course. Yes, that makes sense. You don't come to the hospital for fun."

I gave him my most flirtatious grin. "What case are you working on?"

"I've got all sorts of things open. Too many open cases and not enough shut; that's what the boss always tells me."

"A smart angel like you should be able to figure everything out easily."

He scratched his fingers through his mess of thick blond hair. "Some of us aren't born detectives."

Dominic had followed his father into Angel Force. It was well-known he hated his job but felt obliged to stick with it to keep the family reputation intact. The trouble was, Dominic was hopeless at his job. He was also terrible at keeping secrets, and that played in my favor.

"Are you working on Petra's case?"

"Yes, that's a nasty business. I love the Ancient Imp. I can't believe someone broke in and hurt Petra."

"My sister seems involved," I said. "I can't figure out why you'd think that."

"Me neither," Dominic said. "Aurora is lovely. She always gives me free candy when I go to Heaven's Door."

I stifled a smile. "She is nice like that."

"She is. Sadly, the evidence doesn't lie. We found one of her shoes and some blonde hair. We're running analysis now. Dazielle is certain it's going to be Aurora's hair."

"Hair and a shoe! That seems suspiciously convenient," I said. "That would mean Aurora left the scene of the crime with only one shoe on."

"Unless she brought a spare pair to change into," Dominic said.

"She changed her shoes and then accidentally left one behind? Aurora loves her shoes. She'd never abandon one."

"She might have had to if she was disturbed," Dominic said.

"What robber carries a spare pair of shoes?"

"Maybe she was breaking in a pair and had a backup option in case the new ones pinched," Dominic said.

I pressed my lips together. It was a good job he was so beautiful to look at. "It's an interesting theory. What about the hair?"

"There was a big mass of it on the floor."

"My sister is not a werewolf. She doesn't go around shedding fur everywhere."

"Yes, that was a bit odd," Dominic said. "It was a big ball of the stuff. It was impossible to miss."

"It wasn't a couple of strands that might have accidentally fallen out when she was fighting with Petra?"

"Nothing like that. It looked more like a bird's nest sitting on top of the bar. Still, it's great evidence. It looks like this is a case of girl on girl rivalry."

"Rivalry over what? Or whom?"

Dominic scratched his chin. "Dazielle thinks they fought over Deacon. This is an open and shut case."

"Perhaps you should look at other possibilities."

"No, it's an easy one. I tell you what, how about we meet up and talk about it?" Dominic asked. "It sounds like you might have some ideas I haven't thought of."

Frank twitched at the prospect of spending an evening with an angel. "That's lovely of you, but I'm going to be busy trying to get Aurora out of your prison cell."

"Oh, yes, you must focus on family. I'm sure it will get sorted out. Perhaps if she apologizes and pays a fine, she'll be in less trouble. Of course, Petra will need to agree not to press charges."

"That might work, so long as you don't keep pursuing her for Deacon's murder. I don't think killers get let off if they say sorry and here's some money to make up for being dead."

"Oh, no, that is tricky. And Aurora seems like such a lovely girl."

"That's because she is lovely."

"What can I say? The evidence is the evidence," Dominic said.

"The evidence is horse poop," I muttered.

"So, perhaps a date another night?" Dominic asked. "I mean, not a date, but a chance to talk all things criminal."

I nodded as I turned away from his bike. "Maybe. I'll see how it goes." I hurried away with Wiggles before Dominic could start suggesting places to go for our never going to happen date. He was cute but not smart, but he'd given me what I needed. The evidence they had on Aurora couldn't be real. It made no sense for her to drop a shoe and a handful of hair. It all sounded too convenient. It sounded like faked evidence.

I had to see Aurora. It was time to find out what she was really up to last night.

Chapter 12

Before I could get Aurora out of Angel Force, I needed to go to Cloven Hoof and drop a big, heartfelt apology on Merrie.

It wasn't my fault I'd been stunned by an angel then shoved in a cell. But she wouldn't know what was going on, and I'd abandoned her to deal with two parties of overexcited revelers.

I headed inside the cool, dark interior and found Merrie stacking glasses on the shelves behind the bar.

She arched an eyebrow and cocked her hip. "I know stag and hen parties are no fun, but you totally abandoned me last night. You said you'd be gone half an hour."

I squeezed my eyes shut for a second. "Forgive me."

She chuckled. "What happened?"

"I ran into an angel, and she blasted me with magic and shoved me into a cell."

Merrie's jaw dropped open. "It sounds like you need a coffee."

"With a big dollop of stardust." I hopped onto a stool. "Long story short, I went to question Petra, and one of her customers freaked out when my magic sparked. They called Angel Force, thinking I was threatening Petra. The next thing I know, I wake up behind bars and get hassled by Dazielle."

Merrie poured out two coffees and handed me a mug. "She hates you."

I shrugged. "I try not to take it personally. I think she senses Frank. Angels and demons never get on."

"Talking of demons," Merrie said as she cocked her head to the right, "Axel has been in here for the last two hours. He was waiting to come in before I opened the doors."

I shifted in my seat and turned around. Axel was a regular, but I'd never seen him here so early. "What's he into?"

"The usual mushrooms."

"How many times has he been in this week?"

"Every night," Merrie said. "And he's having home deliveries too."

My mushrooms weren't addictive. That was the beauty of them. You got a lovely natural buzz, and all your cares washed away, and there were no nasty after-effects. Well, in ninety-nine percent of cases. There was always that one infuriating percent that liked to mess it up for everybody else. Maybe Axel was going to be that annoying one.

I took a big gulp of coffee. "Did you say every night?"

"Always. That's his favorite booth."

"Does that include the night Deacon was murdered?"

"I'd almost guarantee it," Merrie said. "Axel is a regular. When he's not here, I think it's strange."

"Yes, it is strange." Strange that he'd lied to me about where he was the night Deacon had been murdered. Axel had told me he'd gone to the gym, ate dinner, and then watched a movie. He never mentioned coming to Cloven Hoof. If he was lying about that, he could also be lying about having nothing to do with Deacon's death.

Coffee just wasn't doing it for me. I dumped in more stardust and swirled it in the mug.

"Is everything okay with you?" Merrie asked.

I patted my stomach as it gurgled. "The usual demon issues."

"How about a lemon drop? They always calm Frank."

"That would be perfect. Super-size me."

"Are you sure?" Merrie grinned at me. "My lemon drops are strong."

"I'll be fine. I need a big hit of energy. I'm off to tackle Angel Force and get Aurora out. I can't have Frank getting loose in the middle of a room full of angels."

Merrie chuckled again as she mixed her speciality drink. The recipe was a secret she kept closely guarded. It was a customer favorite and left everyone with a warm glow and a shot of energy.

She placed a small shot glass that glowed bright yellow in front of me.

I raised it and downed it in one. The sharpness of the lemon was cut through by a sweet aftertaste. I smacked my lips together. "Just what I needed." I placed the glass down as a loud burp shot from my lips.

"Excuse you," Merrie said. "I told you to be careful."

I covered my mouth with my hand. "It's not me; it's Frank. He hates this. The last time I had a lemon drop, he told me it made him sleepy."

"Which is what you want. No demon is coming out to play today."

I held in another burp as I nodded goodbye to Merrie and headed out with Wiggles to face the angels.

Cassiel was on the desk as I walked into Angel Force. She raised her blonde eyebrows. "You're here to see Aurora?"

"Unless you've already let her go."

"She's still here. I don't think she's going anywhere soon." Cassiel gave me a sign-in pad on which I pressed my thumbprint.

"We'll see about that." I followed Cassiel into a quiet room with a table and chairs and waited a few minutes until Aurora was brought in.

"Tempest! I'm so glad you're here." She hugged me before sitting down.

"What's going on?" I asked.

"I don't know what happened," Aurora said, her bottom lip jutting out. "I was in the store, when all of a sudden, the angels turned up. It was so official. They arrested me and brought me here."

"You do know why you've been arrested?"

"They said Petra was attacked. They're sure I did it."

"The evidence is conveniently convincing," I said. "You left a shoe behind and some hair."

Aurora's hands traced over her blonde curls. "Hair?"

"A big ball of the stuff. Where were you last night?"

"In the store."

My eyes narrowed as I saw Aurora's nose twitch. I glanced at Cassiel, who'd remained by the door. "You didn't go anywhere near the Ancient Imp?"

"No, I was at the store all night."

"Doing what?"

"Tidying up. Making sure it looked lovely for the next day."

"That wouldn't take you all night."

"No, of course not. After that, I had dinner and went to bed."

"Alone?"

"Tempest! Of course, alone. You know I'm not in a serious relationship."

Aurora was seeing someone, though. She'd admitted that to me when I'd come back to Willow Tree Falls. Maybe he was the reason she was keeping quiet. I glanced at Cassiel again. If Aurora wasn't going to reveal to me who she was with last night, she wasn't going to tell Angel Force.

I leaned across the table. "You've got to come clean. There's no point in hiding anything. You'll only get in trouble if you do."

She waved a hand in the air dismissively. "I won't get in trouble. I know nothing about the evidence at Petra's, but she'll stick up for me. She couldn't have seen me there because it wasn't me."

"Petra's no good to you. She didn't see her attacker. It was dark, and she was shoved over and kicked. It could have been you on a magic high."

Aurora bit her bottom lip. "I promise you it wasn't me. I'll see Petra when I get out and explain everything."

Cassiel shifted her feet and shook her head. "Best if you stay away from Petra for a while, at least until we get this matter sorted out."

Aurora's eyes widened, and she looked at me. "They think I did it."

I sighed and sat back in my seat. Maybe Aurora had done it. She was hiding something, and whatever it was didn't want to shift anytime soon. Perhaps a few nights in a cell would get her to start talking and stop being so stubborn. She needed to tell somebody before it was too late.

"You look guilty. Angel Force has evidence, and they're clinging to it. They will charge you if you don't watch yourself."

"Tempest, you have to get me out of here." Aurora's eyes flooded with unshed tears.

"No crying." I rubbed my forehead. "It's not going to be so easy this time. I can't help you if you're hiding things from me."

"You have to. I can't stay here." She grabbed my hand.

I glanced at Cassiel. "Are they mistreating you?"

"No, of course not. The angels are all being lovely. But I'm in a cell and being accused of something I haven't done."

I nodded as I stood. "It sucks, but I'm not sure how to help you. You need to come up with solid proof that you were at Heaven's Door on the night of Petra's attack."

"Isn't my word enough?" Aurora looked from me to Cassiel.

Cassiel shook her head. "Not with the evidence we have."

"Are you sure there's nobody who can vouch for you? You didn't see anybody else that night?" I asked her.

She looked away. "No one."

I sighed. There was that nose twitch again. I was done. My sister was lying to me and making a whole mess of this situation. Since she wouldn't come clean, there was nothing I could do to help her.

Mom would complain that I'd abandoned her, but this wasn't my fault. Aurora was hiding something. Whatever it was, it was a big enough secret to hide it from her family and risk jail.

I moved toward the door. "I'll make sure to come to see you during your weekly visiting privileges."

"Tempest, wait!"

I turned and looked at Aurora. "Is there something you want to tell me?"

Aurora bit her lip again and shook her head. "No, nothing."

"Enjoy your life behind bars." I stomped out behind Cassiel and back to the main doors where Wiggles waited for me.

"No Aurora?" he asked, looking over my shoulder.

"Nope, and she deserves to be in here." I ushered him out the door and away from Angel Force. "I don't know what she's gotten herself into, but Aurora is hiding something, and it's something big. Something she's prepared to stay behind bars for."

"Maybe Heaven's Door is in trouble," Wiggles said. "She's always giving stuff away when a magic user pleads poverty, and she hands out free candy to her customers."

"Which is why people love Heaven's Door," I said. "The locals buy most of their magic supplies there, and the non-magicals get all their tourist stuff from there. My sister is rolling in money. It's not that."

"She's got a secret addiction to dark magic," Wiggles said. "Behind that fluffy blonde exterior lies the dark heart of an evil witch intent on bringing Willow Tree Falls to its knees."

I laughed. "Aurora is about as dark as a bright summer's day. The darkest magic she's been involved in is helping me bring you back to life."

"That's gray enough. It could have tipped her over the edge. Aurora might have been waiting for an opportunity to sink into dark magic."

"It's not that. It could be something to do with this secret guy she's dating. Maybe he's someone she thinks I won't approve of."

"He could be married."

I grimaced. "Then she'd never go near him, no matter how hot he was."

"He could be ugly."

"As if I'd care about that, so long as he made her happy."

"He could be an angel."

"That would be hard to forgive, but I'd get over it, so long as the angel wasn't too bright and sunny."

Wiggles glanced at me. "Or Aurora really did do it. Maybe she fell in love with Deacon, and it all went wrong. Deacon could have rejected her, gone back to Petra, and your sister snapped."

"Aurora has her naïve moments, but she's not the kind of woman to snap over a guy. There's no way that evidence in the Ancient Imp is legit. Somebody else is involved. Someone who wants to take Aurora down."

I slowed as I saw a squat figure hurrying into the Romer's telegram store.

"What's on your mind?" Wiggles asked. "Have you got a snow globe message to send?"

"No, but that was Mannie Winter, one of the mayoral candidates. Petra pointed the finger at him for Deacon's murder." I changed direction and headed toward the telegram store. "It's time we put the thumbscrews on our friendly neighborhood second-hand merchant and see what he knows."

Chapter 13

The telegram store smelt of vanilla and mothballs. It had been run by the Romer family for generations. Giovanni now ran the store. His mom, Mila Romer, was semi-retired but kept a stronghold on the business from her perch in the apartment above the store. She was forever pestering Giovanni to work harder and raise the prices of the snow globe telegrams.

These weren't your average telegrams. We all used the system in Willow Tree Falls. They were like the freaky mobiles used by non-magicals. We sent messages via the Snow Globe communication route that ran across the world. It was easy enough to use snow globes if you had to send a local message. Anything going out of Willow Tree Falls made things complicated because of the magic barrier keeping non-magicals from seeing what was really going on.

That was where Giovanni and his skills with the globes came in handy. If you needed a message sent, no matter where in the world it had to go, Giovanni was the warlock to do it.

I edged closer to the counter where Mannie stood. I couldn't catch everything he was saying, but the message he wanted to send was confidential and urgent.

Mannie Winter was a slick salesman, who ran the Magic Second Time Around second-hand store. Whatever you needed, Mannie could get it for you so long as you didn't mind paying through the nose.

It looked like he ate most of his profits and was a rotund dwarf, who took great pride in the long luxurious beard that sat over his stomach.

I waited until he'd finished his transaction with Giovanni, stepped into the walkway, and bumped into Mannie.

"Oh, Tempest. How are you?" He smiled up at me and smoothed down his oiled beard.

"I've been better," I said.

His expression grew sympathetic. "Of course, your poor family is going through so much. And your sister has been arrested for the second time in as many days. It's hard to believe; she's such a lovely girl."

"She has her moments," I said. "You must be feeling conflicted by everything that's going on."

"Conflicted how?" His smile remained friendly.

"Deacon was a thorn in your side. Everyone thought he would be the new mayor. It must have been a relief to get him out of the way."

Mannie cleared his throat. "I was happy to fight fair, so long as he did. Besides, I never considered Deacon real competition. He was a bright young man but lacked experience. I have years on him. I know everyone in Willow Tree Falls. When people come to vote, they'll realize they need someone experienced and knowledgeable, someone with strong roots and a long foundation."

"The Feathers family has been here for five-hundred years. I'd say that's pretty deep roots."

"Not Deacon. He's only been here a decade. He spent years traveling around the world and seeing what magical delights he could enjoy. We can't afford to have a play boy in a position of authority. It wouldn't do Willow Tree Falls any good. As tragic as it is, Deacon would never have made mayor." Mannie stepped closer to me. "I heard he was thinking about withdrawing because he knew he didn't stand a chance and couldn't face being humiliated when the results came in."

"Is that so?"

"Indeed. And he was thinking about leaving Willow Tree Falls."

"No kidding. Where was he going?"

"I've no idea." Mannie smiled and stroked his beard. "My customers are never wrong, though. That's what they were telling me just before Deacon died."

I arched an eyebrow. "Were you information gathering on the night of Deacon's murder?"

Mannie's fingers twisted into his beard. "I'm not sure I understand."

"Who were you with? Where were you?"

His expression shifted from friendly to cautious. "I don't see how it's any of your business."

"Given that my only sister is in a cell, I made it my business." I smiled brightly. "I'm sure you'd do the same for your own family if they were wrongly accused."

Giovanni hurried out from behind the counter. "May I be of service, Tempest?"

I kept my attention fixed on Mannie. "No, thanks."

"Do you have a telegram to send? I'm doing a twenty percent discount on all long-distance messages this week."

"I came in here to have a chat with Mannie."

Giovanni swallowed noisily. "Excellent, excellent. As lovely as it is to have you in here, perhaps you could take your chat to the cafe? I don't want to distract the other customers."

I looked around. Other than the three of us, the telegram store was empty. "I'm sure they won't mind."

"Of course. You're right. Even so, I don't want any trouble."

"Tempest won't cause any trouble. She knows it's not wise to get on the wrong side of the future mayor," Mannie said.

"A potential mayor who doesn't have an alibi for the night someone was murdered," I said. "Maybe you won't be mayor for long when the rumors get out."

Mannie pulled himself up to his inconsiderable height. "Very well. I was at a campaign meeting that went on until midnight. Actually, it might be of interest to you. We discussed the problem of a number of venues in Willow Tree Falls that have late night licenses. Residents have concerns that people have been leaving late and causing too much noise. We cannot afford the peace and tranquillity of Willow Tree Falls to be disturbed. There was mention of adjusting the license, so you must close by ten o'clock."

"You are kidding me." I took a step toward Mannie.

"Now, now. Nobody needs to get angry. I'm sure it was a healthy discussion with people suggesting different options, nothing more." Giovanni worried around us as I continued to give Mannie a death stare.

"There doesn't sound anything healthy about that discussion," I said. "I extended my license after a public petition. People want Cloven Hoof open late. They're the ones who demanded it, not me. I'd be happy to curl up in bed at ten o'clock and put my feet up for the rest of the night."

"I'm sure you would. What a charming image that is," Mannie said. "Still, I must consider the needs of my new supporters. If they're not happy, I'm not happy."

I glowered at him. My growing anger made Frank shift inside me. I almost wished I hadn't had that lemon drop. It would be fun to watch Frank come out and terrify Mannie with a splash of fire and brimstone.

"I will check your alibi. And I want the names of everyone who doesn't think Cloven Hoof should open late." Even if Frank wasn't in command, I'd be happy to shake down a few suckers for not liking my business. They needed to tell me to my face that they weren't happy and not hide behind this smug-faced dwarf and let him do their dirty work.

"I always protect confidences," Mannie said. "And, might I say, you're being overzealous in your pursuit of somebody else for Deacon's murder. My understanding is that your sister was very fond of Deacon. She spent a number of nights in his company."

I jabbed a finger into his gut. "That's not true. They went on a few dates. Aurora was undecided about Deacon."

"That's not what I heard." Mannie's smile was self-satisfied. "He told me she put on quite a performance in the bedroom one night."

I grabbed hold of his beard and yanked it. "Aurora is not that kind of girl."

Mannie tried to pull his beard out of my grasp, but I held on. "I'm only telling you what I heard."

"Tempest, please, not here." Giovanni touched my arm. "We don't want to upset Mother."

As if summoned by the sound of Giovanni's voice, footsteps stamped down the stairs. Mrs. Romer peered around the door, her black beady eyes staring straight at me. "What's going on down here? All I can hear is you simpering, Giovanni."

"Nothing, Mother. Go back to your puzzles."

"I can't think with all this noise." She stamped out from behind the counter. "Tempest Crypt, what are you doing with that dwarf's beard?"

"Stroking it while he gives me information about Deacon Feathers' murder," I said.

Mrs. Romer's eyes widened. She sniffed and nodded. "I heard all about that. Bad news indeed."

"You need to stop protecting Aurora." Mannie succeeded in untangling my fingers from his beard and brushed it flat against his stomach. "I understand why you're doing it. She's your sister, and you care for her. But if she is guilty, she must pay."

"She's innocent," I snarled.

Frank's interest perked up again. His voice was just a whisper in my head. "It's up to me to decide how guilty your sister is. No one else. Remember, she's all mine."

I slammed the door on Frank and his mutterings. He could keep his demon claws off my sister, as could everybody else.

Mannie grunted and ran his fingers through his beard. "You need to go back and talk to Aurora. Perhaps she isn't as pure as you think."

"You Crypt witches are all the same," Mrs. Romer said.

I turned slowly and glared at her. "Meaning what?"

"Meaning you have too much power. You expect everyone in Willow Tree Falls to be grateful for what you do."

"Shouldn't you be a tiny bit grateful that we keep those badly-behaved demons in prison? I'd like to see you handle a fifteen-foot horned demon who breathes fire and has metal claws."

Mrs. Romer sniffed again. "I'd give it a good go."

"Good luck with that," I said. The Romer women were strong. She probably could give a demon a good butt kicking. I glanced at the panic-eyed Giovanni. The Romer men clearly didn't have the fierce backbone trait of the women, or maybe it had skipped a generation.

"You tell me where and when," Mrs. Romer said. "I'll show you a thing or two about fighting a demon."

"That sounds good. I'll suggest my family go on an extended holiday and forget all about our guardian role at the cemetery. When we get back, there might be a Willow Tree Falls left. I doubt it, though."

Mrs. Romer scowled at me. "Do you want to send a telegram? Or did you come into my store to cause trouble for my paying clients?"

I shook my head. "Don't worry. I'm leaving."

"Don't come back any time soon," Mrs. Romer said as I turned away. "And we don't want your murdering sister in here either."

"Mom, maybe you shouldn't," Giovanni whispered.

"Aurora wouldn't come in here if you paid her." I slammed the door as I left the telegram store, fury seeping through my veins and exciting Frank to the point I had to stop walking, close my eyes, and take several long, deep breaths to get him back under my control.

"You really showed them," Wiggles said.

"That was too close. Frank is kicking up a storm." I looked back at the telegram store. Giovanni and his mother were staring at me through the window.

I resisted the urge to gesture rudely and stalked away. I had to double-check Mannie's alibi, but from what he'd said, it sounded like he was telling the truth and had witnesses to prove it. But I wouldn't accept what he'd said about Aurora. She wasn't into Deacon, and she certainly wouldn't spend the night with him.

My options seemed to be narrowing when it came to finding Deacon's killer. Maybe I should head back to Angel Force and see about raising Deacon from the dead. I could ask him face-to-face what happened and solve this whole thing.

I snorted a laugh. Like they'd let me get anywhere near his body. I looked down at Wiggles. Raising the dead was not easy magic and came with unexpected consequences.

I looked along the street and studied the faint shimmer of the magic barrier surrounding Willow Tree Falls. I should get out of here while I had a chance. Frank was getting strong, and my patience was running out. It was a toxic combination and one that meant trouble for everybody.

Wiggles nudged me with his nose. "Any time you want to share those thoughts whizzing around in your head, you let me know."

I petted his tummy. "As frustrating as it is that Aurora's hiding something, we can't give up on her. We need to talk to other people about Mannie's alibi and find out what was discussed at that meeting."

"That cute little dancing pixie is always at his meetings," Wiggles said.

"Star? How do you know that?"

"She's always going on about it. Before I could talk, I had no choice but to listen. I understood everything."

I glanced down at Wiggles. "Which means you know all my secrets."

"Every dirty one. What do you reckon, shall we go have a dance with a pixie?"

I nodded. "Let's see what Star Fairfax has to say about Mannie's alibi and find out if she knows who wants to mess with Cloven Hoof."

Chapter 14

My nose wrinkled as I pushed open the door to the dance studio. It smelt of rubber-soled shoes and lady sweat.

Star was surrounded by a group of eager-faced teenage girls all wearing lycra, tutus, and ballet pumps.

"The same time next week, girls." Star's blonde hair was pulled off her face in a tight bun, and her cheeks glowed from the exercise. She had the figure of an established dancer, all long limbs and tight muscles.

She smiled as she saw me and Wiggles. "Are you here for the next dance class?"

Wiggles' bark sounded remarkably like a laugh.

"No, it's not my thing," I said, shooting Wiggles a warning look.

"I'm sure you'd enjoy it. I'm teaching beginners Cuban lessons in half an hour."

"I'll leave the dance lessons to the tourists."

Star's smile faded. "It's not just tourists who come here. Several of our local ladies enjoy a good boogie. I've even got a few men on the books."

"I don't suppose you've had any complaints about the studio?"

Her eyes widened. "Never. Everyone loves coming here."

"I meant the noise you make. All that Cuban music must annoy people."

"I'm always considerate of my neighbors," Star said. "Why, do you have a complaint?"

"No, but I've had a few issues at Cloven Hoof. I've been talking to one of our potential mayors. It seems he's had supporters on his back about my late license and the noise that occurs when people roll out at the end of the night."

Star brushed her hands down the front of her sparkly lycra vest. "Oh, that must be tricky."

"You volunteer to help Mannie with his campaign, don't you?"

"Now and again. Only when my dance classes don't occupy my time. Despite what you think, it gets busy here. And then there's the planning, marketing, and choreography to sort out."

"Do you know who was talking about trying to have my license altered?"

Star shrugged and looked away. "I've got to get the studio ready for the next class."

I caught hold of her elbow before she could walk away. "Who's been talking about Cloven Hoof? Who doesn't like the late license?"

Star clasped her hands in front of her. "Don't take it personally, Tempest. It's just that I get woken up with people stumbling back from Cloven Hoof late at night. I'm a light sleeper, you see, and I like to have the window open at night to get fresh air. I often get woken several times a night."

My eyes narrowed. "It was you? You're the one trying to mess with my business?"

Star let out a sigh. "Yes, it was me."

"You don't know for sure that these people are leaving Cloven Hoof. They could be coming from the Ancient Imp."

"I have spoken to Mannie about that place, as well."

"You hate all the local businesses that have late licenses because it disturbs your beauty sleep?"

"No, don't get me wrong. I don't hate Cloven Hoof," Star said quickly.

"I should imagine you don't since you have a monthly standing order with me for Moon Burst mushrooms."

"Your produce is great, and I love your service. It's first class."

"If you think it's so great, you shouldn't make complaints about me."

"I promise you it isn't personal."

"It feels personal. If I have to close early, I'll make less money. I might have to cut staff, which will impact on my produce dispatches. That could include canceling monthly deliveries, especially to people who have tried to put me out of business. I have to look after my loyal customers first."

Star's mouth fell open. "No, I'd never want that. Maybe you can ask your customers to be a little quieter when they leave late?"

"My clientele is always quiet and considerate. They're not hyped-up and energetic. They come to relax and chill out. They don't leave wanting to cause trouble. I'm sure you aren't talking about Cloven Hoof customers."

Star stepped back and looked at the door. "You could be right. I just get so tetchy when I haven't had my sleep. I even snap at my dancers, and they're all so sweet."

"You could always try closing the window."

"No, I need my fresh air."

"How about wearing earplugs?"

"They make my ears too hot, and I don't want to risk getting an infection. If a dancer loses her inner ear balance, it can ruin her."

"How about moving your bedroom into another room?"

Star's nose crinkled. "I don't think that will work."

She was not making this easier or me any happier. "How about you get your own late license? You could run evening dances."

Star pursed her lips. "Actually, that's not a bad idea. People are always asking me about holding evening events. I'm more interested in teaching dance, but I have the space to hold something less formal."

"Then we both have a late license, and you have nothing to complain about," I said.

Her eyes sparkled at the possibility. "Would you come to my dance evenings if I held them?"

"Not likely, but I know Aurora would drag me to one. She loves to dance."

Star's smile faded. "Oh, of course, your sister. How's it going? I heard about her arrest."

"That's something I want to talk to you about," I said. "Mannie was telling me he had a meeting with some of his supporters on the night of Deacon's death."

"That's right," Star said. "We held it at his house."

"What did you discuss?"

"Other than the late license issue," Star tweaked her hair bun, "we discussed new campaign materials and what to do with the empty land over on Mystic Street."

"What time did the meeting take place?"

"I got there just after dinner. I ate upstairs, had a quick shower, and was at Mannie's by seven. We talked for about two-and-a-half hours. I was home by ten at the latest."

"Which means you left Mannie's about nine forty-five?"

"That's right. I was the last to leave."

With those timings, it gave Mannie plenty of opportunity to head to Deacon's and kill him. It also meant he hadn't been truthful as to how late the meeting had gone on. He didn't have an alibi for the whole night. "Do you know what Mannie did after the meeting ended?"

"He didn't say he was doing anything," Star said. "I left him drinking brandy. I assumed he finished that and went to bed."

"Did he have any problems with Deacon that you're aware of?"

Star's cheeks paled. "Oh, no. Do you think Mannie is involved with his murder?"

"They were rivals in the upcoming election."

"I don't think it was Mannie," Star said.

"Deacon was a strong candidate. A rival to Mannie's ambitions."

"Yes, but Mannie had so much support. It wasn't really a fair fight."

"Not everyone was planning to vote for Mannie." I was definitely in the undecided camp.

"You were on Deacon's side?"

"I've given the election no thought. All I know for sure is that my sister is being quizzed by Angel Force for something she didn't do. I'm trying to figure out who had it in for Deacon."

Star frowned. "Mannie had a few drinks that evening and seemed jolly. Surely, someone who was planning a murder wouldn't be happy just before they did it."

"Maybe he went to Deacon's in a good mood, and they fought," I said. "If Mannie had been drinking, he could have gotten angry and lost control."

"But Mannie is so… compact. He's no match for a half-angel. If they'd gotten into a fight, Deacon would have floored him."

"Not if Deacon was asleep and Mannie caught him unawares. He could have overpowered him using the element of surprise."

The shake of Star's head was so fierce her bun came loose. "I can't believe it."

"And I can't believe my sister did it."

Star's eyebrows shot up. "No, of course, you're right to think that. Maybe you should look elsewhere, though. Mannie is a decent guy."

I didn't agree. As far as I was concerned, he was still on the hook. "I'd better get going," I said. "Before you get Cloven Hoof shut down, I need to get some work done."

Star hurried after me as I headed to the door. "I never meant for it to go that far. Please don't cancel my monthly order. In fact, double it. I want to show my appreciation for your business."

I glanced at her. "No more trying to get my license revoked. And maybe look into getting your own late license. It could be fun." And it would give Star something to think about other than messing with Cloven Hoof.

Star let out a relieved sigh. "Thanks, I will."

I left Star to her next dance class and headed out the door with Wiggles.

"Star likes Mannie," Wiggles said.

"She does seem like a super fan. People get crazy over anyone with a little authority. She's convinced he's not involved."

"He needs looking into. I don't trust Mannie. Anyone who spends so much time on beard maintenance is not okay in my books."

"Neither do I. We need to do more digging into Mannie and his alibi." I checked the time. "First, we need to check in with Cloven Hoof before Merrie resigns."

"Then we get something to eat," Wiggles said.

"Good thinking. Work, eat, and sleep."

"You do the working," Wiggles said. "I'll do the eating and sleeping."

Chapter 15

"It's time to get up." My duvet was yanked off me, wafting me with an unwelcome blast of cool air.

I rolled over and blinked sleepily at my mom. "How are you even here?"

She pulled open the curtains and smiled at me. "Wiggles let me in."

I groaned. "I'm going to kill that dog."

"Killing a hellhound is a tricky business. Come on. You need to get up. There's work to be done."

"I worked all night, which is why I'm having a lie-in." I rubbed my eyes, grabbed my pillow, and stuffed it over my head.

"I mean with your sister." Mom's voice sounded quieter, but I could still hear her. "You have to get her out of that awful cell. What progress are you making in finding out who killed Deacon?"

I groaned into the pillow. "No progress."

"I'll make breakfast, and you can tell me everything."

I raised the pillow an inch. "Will you make waffles?"

"Only if you hurry."

The pillow was yanked out of my hands. Wiggles stared at me, the pillow gripped between his teeth. He spat it out. "This one's my favorite."

"Don't remind me about your weird interest in my pillows." I eased myself upright. "We need to have a conversation about who you let into this apartment."

"She's your mom. Of course I'm letting her in."

"Not when I'm asleep."

"Of course I will. Any time. She often brings treats."

"You're such a suck-up."

"She is making us waffles," Wiggles said as he hopped off the bed.

"She's making me waffles." I grabbed another pillow and threw it at his retreating butt.

Fifteen minutes later, I was showered, dressed, and sitting at the table as Mom served up coffee and waffles. She'd even made a waffle for Wiggles.

I gave her a quick update about my talks with Mannie and Star.

Her expression grew increasingly worried as she watched me over the rim of her mug.

"What's wrong?" I asked.

"I know I told you to help your sister, but I don't want you overstretching yourself."

"I haven't got a choice. I can't stop working at Cloven Hoof, and I need to keep questioning people who could be involved in Deacon's murder. Something will soon shake free. Someone must know what happened to Deacon."

"If only Angel Force would set Aurora free, I'd be less worried."

I took another waffle and shuffled the fresh strawberries around on the top into a frowning face. "I can't believe they still have her."

"It's that wretched evidence," Mom said, "the hair and the shoe."

"It was obviously planted," I said. "You know Aurora; she's so fastidious. If she was intent on killing someone, she'd know how to leave no clues behind. She'd probably go to her victim's home wrapped in polythene after having shaved her head. She'd know how to avoid leaving evidence."

Mom's eyebrow arched. "You make her sound calculating."

"I make her sound clean."

Mom sighed. "Which means somebody wants Aurora to go down for this murder."

"It's not happening," I said as I helped myself to another waffle and ignored Wiggles cold nose nudging my calf for a piece. "I'm dealing with it."

"Which is good, but..."

"Go on, what's on your mind? You don't think I can do this?"

"I'm sure you can. But I know stress makes Frank tetchy. Maybe take a day or two off from your interrogations. I had Mrs. Romer send me a rude message yesterday about your visit to the telegram store."

"Mrs. Romer can bite me. My conversation with Mannie was none of her business. She said neither me nor Aurora is welcome in the telegram store."

"She decided to make it her business. We don't want to get on the wrong side of Mrs. Romer. She might cut off our communication link out of Willow Tree Falls."

"She can try," I said. "We won't be cut off. I leave Willow Tree Falls at least once a month to do Angel Force business. We can still get messages in and out."

"It will make things more difficult for you." Mom placed her mug down. "I worry about you."

"There's nothing to worry about." I kept my expression neutral as I focused on my waffle. "I'm certain this will be solved by the end of today. Mannie lied to me. He told me that meeting went on late. Star says otherwise. Mannie had plenty of time to get out of his house, over to Deacon's, and kill him. He's got a perfect motive. Deacon was competition and could have ruined Mannie's chances of being mayor."

"You're ruling out everybody else?" Mom asked. "What about Axel? Granny Dottie is convinced he had something to do with this."

"She only fingered Axel because she doesn't want me to date him. Not that I would, but there is something off about him. He lied about his alibi. Merrie spotted him in Cloven Hoof when he said he was at a movie." I sighed as I finished the last waffle.

"I don't know, maybe they're in this together? Axel and Mannie both want to be mayor, so they teamed up to get their biggest rival out of the way."

"Keep your enemies closer than your spell book," Mom said. "What about Rhett?"

"I should go talk to him too, just to clear his name. Otherwise, Auntie Queenie will keep prodding me to hassle him."

Mom regarded me steadily. "Will you find it tricky speaking to Rhett?"

I spent a long time drinking my coffee. "No."

Mom smiled at me. "It's okay to like a bad boy. Your father was considered a little rough around the edges when we first got together."

I blinked at her. Mom rarely talked about Dad. He'd disappeared ten years ago, simply up and left one day. No one knew what happened. Everyone assumed he was dead.

"Don't look like a startled owl. We were young when we met. I was just out of my teens and looking for an adventure. Your father roared past on this enormous sleek motorbike. He had hair to his shoulders and was dressed in leather. It was lust at first sight."

I coughed down my mouthful of coffee. "Too much information, Mom."

She smiled. "When I got to know him, I realized what a sweetheart he was. Behind the leather and moody looks, he was a giant teddy bear. So protective of me. And you girls."

I nodded. I remembered him quizzing Aurora and me when we first got interested in boys. He warned us not to date anyone with long hair who wore leathers. I smiled at the memory. One day, I'd find out what happened to him and why he had to leave us.

"You've been on a few dates with Rhett."

"It was nothing. I'm not into him."

"If you are, then you have good taste. I know I said not to date a biker, but I don't mind. Make sure you take plenty of time to get to know him. You need to ensure there's more to him than that bad boy image."

"I'll ask him for his resume when I see him."

"I'm serious. Some men have a shady side but a good heart. Others are bad to the marrow. They chew you up and spit you out like a werewolf does hairballs."

"I do not want that kind of guy."

Mom patted my hand. "Rhett is always welcome at our dinner table. If you do bring him, Queenie will be thrilled. She's also got a thing for men in leathers."

I grimaced as an image of Auntie Queenie dragging a leather clad gimp around on a leash came into my mind. "She'd eat Rhett alive."

Mom chuckled. "Quite possibly. Seriously, if he is involved, take care. Rhett runs with a dark crowd. Be discreet with your questioning."

"I'm always discreet."

"That's not what Mrs. Romer said. She claimed she had to throw you out of the telegram store because you were being, let me get the phrase right, too much of a disruptive influence."

"That's not true. I stormed out of there quite happily on my own."

Mom chuckled again. "I just need to make sure you've got Frank under control."

"I always have him under control."

Her expression turned serious. "You do a great job. I know it's not easy. We ask a lot of you to keep Frank away from Aurora." Mom's eyes glistened. "It should have been me. I should have gotten to Aurora in time and stopped him."

A part of me wished that was true. I'd acted on instinct, launching myself at Frank as he'd wrapped his talons around Aurora. It had happened in the blink of an eye, and now, I lived with a demon inside me. "He's never going to get her. Frank tried once, and he failed. I'm never letting him get close to Aurora again."

"Of course not." Mom dabbed at her eyes and finished her coffee. "You always have been protective of her."

I nodded. It was the main reason I was knee-deep in this mess and had no idea how to get out, but I wasn't letting Mom know I felt like I was fumbling in the dark for answers to this mystery.

We left the apartment together. I said goodbye to Mom and headed in the opposite direction with Wiggles over to Rhett's studio on the other side of town.

He lived on Firefly Lane in a converted barn. From the outside, it looked abandoned, but from what I knew of his place, he'd been working on it for a long time, fixing it up himself.

Aside from running with a biker gang, Rhett had a creative side and made enormous metal sculptures from scrap metal. His home doubled as his work studio, and as I got nearer, I noticed several of his sculptures placed along the driveway.

Wiggles stopped and inspected one. "This thing is a beast." A twisted metal image of a two-headed dragon stared down at him.

"It's unique." I was impressed. To create something so striking out of junk needed a good eye and plenty of hard work.

"If we took that home, it would give me nightmares." Wiggles dabbed the claw of the dragon with a paw.

"You're a hellhound. How can you get frightened by that?"

"I might fart brimstones, but even I have phobias."

I laughed. "I promise I won't buy you this as a birthday gift."

"Yeah, stick to giant bones and steaks, and I'll be happy."

We headed to the large metal double doors of the studio. I knocked and waited. No one arrived.

"Maybe he's out doing nefarious things with his biker gang," Wiggles said as he inspected a small metal sculpture of a lizard.

"He's most likely still asleep." Which was exactly what I wanted to do.

"Keep knocking."

Five minutes of knocking later, and I was about to admit defeat. I'd just turned to walk away when I heard a bolt slide across the other side of the door. The door slid back to reveal Rhett. An almost naked, sleepy-looking Rhett.

I tried hard not to stare at his abs. His hair was a tangled dark mess around his stubbled jaw line. He wore a pair of black boxers that looked incredibly snug, and his feet were bare.

"Tempest! What brings you here?" He ran his hands through his hair as he stared at me.

I dragged my gaze from his abs. "I thought no one was in."

"As you can see, I'm in. I was in bed."

"Alone?" I grimaced. Why on earth had I asked that? Who Rhett dated was none of my business. We'd had a very brief fling a long time ago, and it meant nothing. It was ancient history, all brushed under the carpet; no one remembered it. Definitely not me.

He grinned. "I don't usually allow sleepovers. I'm all alone. It's tragic." He looked down at Wiggles. "That's a new look for you."

I glanced over to see Wiggles had shaken off his sunglasses and placed them on the lizard, revealing his glowing red eyes.

I shrugged. Everyone would eventually know what had happened to him. Rhett might as well be one of the first. "He's a hellhound these days."

Rhett's eyebrows rose. "Nice one."

I looked at Wiggles and nodded.

"I think so," Wiggles said.

Rhett glanced at me. "And a talking one. Do you two want to come inside?"

"Sure." I waited until Rhett had stepped aside before walking in to avoid brushing past those toned abs.

"I'll put on some coffee."

"And maybe some clothes?"

He laughed again. "If it bothers you."

I tried not to stare at the lovely view of his butt as he walked away and ran up the stairs. It shouldn't bother me. I'd been the one to cool things off. Rhett had been keen on us dating and had asked me out several times before giving up when I'd repeatedly refused him. He was gorgeous but dangerous. I had enough danger in my life. I didn't need some shady biker guy messing things up even more.

His studio was a huge, open plan space with a giant lounge diner and a mezzanine floor above where a bedroom sat.

Several of Rhett's sculptures sat around the main room. There was a giant cat, some sort of warrior knight with a blade in his hand, and a long-haired woman with a flowing robe staring off into the distance.

"You were my inspiration for that." Rhett appeared, thankfully dressed in dark jeans and a white T-shirt.

I stared at the sculpture. "That's supposed to be me?"

"Not you exactly, but I wanted to capture your emotion."

I stepped closer to the sculpture. "What emotion was I conveying?"

"Repressed love. The desire to do the right thing and protect those you care about, while denying your own happiness."

I tilted my head. "Huh! That's what you think of my emotional state?"

"Sometimes. You're a complicated woman."

The sculpture was starkly beautiful. Rhett had captured a quiet despair on the features of the woman. It wasn't me, though. I had nothing to despair about.

"Coffee?" Rhett asked.

"Thanks, that would be good." I followed him into the kitchen.

"Do you still take it the same way?"

I nodded. "Same as always."

I watched as he expertly worked his way around the kitchen, filtering coffee and pouring cereal into a bowl.

He grinned at me. "As great as it is to have you here, I'm guessing this isn't a social call."

"That's true. I'm here about Aurora."

Rhett blew out a breath as he handed me a mug of coffee. "Jeez, that sucks. Angel Force should never have arrested her. What were they thinking?"

"I often wonder that about their decisions." I leaned against the kitchen counter. "The first time was a knee-jerk reaction. They figured she was the last one to see Deacon alive, so she had to be involved in his death. The second time they arrested her, they had evidence to connect her to an attack on Petra. They're convinced she tried to kill Petra."

Rhett shook his head. "That makes no sense. Aurora wouldn't do anything like that. She isn't into Deacon."

"And you know that how?"

"Oh, you know, you hear rumors." Rhett stuffed a huge spoonful of cereal into his mouth.

I wasn't letting him off that easily. "What do the rumors say?"

He spent an inordinate amount of time chewing. "Well, Deacon was seriously into your sister. He was looking to set himself up as the perfect mayor."

I pursed my lips. "To do that, he needed the perfect trophy girlfriend to parade around at fancy events."

"Something like that. Not that Aurora wouldn't be a great girlfriend. She'd make any guy proud to have her on his arm."

I ignored the faint stab of jealousy I felt. "I wondered the same thing. So did Aurora, which was why she doubted his interest in her."

"I also heard your sister was into somebody else and only dated Deacon because she felt sorry for him."

"That's my sister all over. She never likes to hurt anybody's feelings, even if it means doing something she doesn't enjoy."

"Aurora told Deacon she couldn't date him anymore. From what I heard, he wasn't willing to give up without a fight."

"Who told you that? Was Deacon hassling my sister?"

Rhett shrugged. "It's just local gossip."

"You knew Deacon, though. Is it right that he still wanted to be with Aurora?"

"I can't say for certain. We were friends when we were kids. We've drifted apart over the years. I haven't spoken to him for ages. We didn't have a connection anymore."

I took a sip of coffee. Rhett did something magic to coffee, making it strong and rich without any bitter taste. "What made you drift apart?"

"This and that. Deacon picked the life of an upstanding half-angel. I decided to run with a shady biker gang." He winked at me as he finished his breakfast.

"You won't mind telling me where you were the night Deacon died?"

He chuckled as he refilled my mug with coffee. "No problem. My gang can back me up. We were out late that night."

"Doing what?"

"What gangs always do, causing trouble and mayhem."

"Really?"

Rhett laughed again. "No, not really. We were out on Deadman's Lane, running the bikes. Josh has a new one, and we went to test it."

"You were out playing with your toys all night?"

"Sad but true. I'd rather have had someone fun in my bed to play with, but we're just a bunch of emotionally repressed guys who push our feelings into our giant engines and pretend we want for nothing."

I had to smile. It was probably closer to the truth than he realized. "How about Mannie Winter? How well do you know him?"

Rhett's laugh was startled. "Not at all. I have nothing to do with Mannie."

"You don't like dwarves?"

"I like dwarves just fine."

"You never go to Mannie's store? There's never anything you need him to get you?"

"No way. If I want something, I get it myself." Rhett traced his tongue across his bottom lip.

I was annoyed when I felt my cheeks grow warm. "What about Mannie being involved with Deacon? Does your secret rumor mill suggest the two of them had a falling out?"

Rhett shook his head. "Not that I know of."

"How about the two of you working together?"

"Why do I need to work with Mannie?"

"Maybe he was paying you to get rid of a problem?"

Rhett's dark eyes narrowed. "You're talking about a Deacon kind of problem? Are you suggesting Mannie hired me to get rid of Deacon?" He lowered his mug to the counter.

"You're not close to Deacon anymore. It would only be business if Mannie needed your help to get him out of the picture."

"The business of murder," Rhett said. "Something I'm not into."

The surrounding air crackled with tension as Rhett glared at me. "Could Mannie have done it alone?"

"Not a chance. Mannie is not man enough to do anything like that." Rhett scraped his hands through his hair and let out a sigh. "You're on the right lines if Mannie is involved, though. He'd hire someone to do the dirty work for him."

I looked down into my coffee. "I've been thinking the same thing. I don't suppose anyone in your gang has been talking to Mannie? Anyone who's in need of some cash and would help Mannie?"

"Tempest, we're not cold-blooded killers. We might run on the wrong side of the law now and again, but we wouldn't stoop to something like that. You need to look elsewhere if you're hunting for a killer."

"Then who do you think did it? Who killed Deacon? I have to find out. I have to get Aurora back home where she belongs." The desperation in my tone surprised me.

When Rhett didn't speak, I tipped my head back and stared at him. "What?"

"I hate to be the one to tell you this, but everyone thinks it was Aurora. Anyone I've talked to comes to the same conclusion. She was the last one to see Deacon alive, they were having relationship problems, and she was caught trying to get rid of his old girlfriend."

"You don't believe that," I said. "You just told me you know Aurora couldn't have done it."

"I'm not the one who needs convincing. Angel Force has the evidence. They're being pushed for a quick result. Your sister is their quick result."

"How do you know all of this?" I said. "And why are you so interested in this case?"

"Because a friend of mine is involved." Rhett gave me a meaningful look. "I don't like to think of your sister in trouble. I know what stress does to you and your demon companion. If he's stressed, then so are you, and that's good for no one."

"I'm fine. As is my companion." I let out another sigh. This felt like a failure, and none of it made sense. Mannie still wasn't in the clear, but just like Rhett, I couldn't believe he'd snuck off into the night and killed Deacon.

I was at a dead end. It felt like I was being lied to by just about everybody. What was so wrong with telling the truth? It would be so much easier if the killer wandered in with his hands up and told Angel Force he'd done it and was really sorry.

I glanced up at Rhett. He smiled at me, not pushing, just giving me the time I needed. A tiny part of me relaxed. I was glad Rhett was so convincing. He ran with a shady gang, but there was a decent side to him, the side that had drawn me to him.

"If you need any help, you only have to ask," Rhett said.

"No, I'll figure it out."

"I've no doubt you will. Sometimes, having someone to watch your back isn't such a bad thing."

"I have Wiggles. He does a decent enough job."

Wiggles raised his head from his investigation of Rhett's trash can. A banana skin was draped over his head, and he had a paper cake case stuck to his snout. "Did someone say my name?"

I shook my head. "When he's not scarfing down your leftovers."

Wiggles snorted and continued his trash can diving.

Rhett nodded. "I want to help. I'll ask around and see if anyone's heard anything that will clear Aurora's name."

I finished my coffee. "You can if you like, but I didn't ask for your help." It felt nice to have someone looking out for me, but I couldn't start to rely on Rhett. "I need to get out of here and ask more questions."

"Are you going back to question Mannie? You still think he had something to do with this?"

I nodded. "His chain needs yanking. He lied to me, and I need to know why."

Rhett walked Wiggles and me to the door. "Stay safe, Tempest."

"I always do."

"Just ask if you need a hand." He leaned down and brushed a kiss across my cheek.

I ignored the tingle on my cheek as I hurried away from his house. I wished Rhett hadn't been so obliging. Even when I'd accused him of murder, he'd barely flinched. If I thought he was guilty, I wouldn't get that annoying warm glow inside me when we spent any time together.

"Can we quit with the power walking?" Wiggles trotted alongside me.

"Oh! Sure." I forced myself to slow down. I hadn't even noticed I was almost jogging.

"You have such a thing for that guy."

Maybe I had, but it wasn't important. "I don't."

"Sure you do. Even with my nose stuck in the trash, I could smell the lust."

"It's not like that. We're… friends." We couldn't be anything more, not now, not ever.

"You keep telling yourself that. Neither of you believes it."

"Keep your nose out of my love life."

"I've had to endure watching your sad little lack of love life for years. It's time I got involved and sorted things out. You're young, you're cute, and you need someone."

"Nope, the only thing I need to sort out is who killed Deacon." That was all I could deal with.

Rhett and his abs and his perfect coffee were not getting involved in this.

Chapter 16

Before seeking out Mannie, I felt guilty enough for snapping at Aurora yesterday to stop at Angel Force to see how she was doing. Maybe she'd had a chance to rethink her options. Even if she was still keeping her secret, I could update her on my fruitless search for the real killer. This situation was getting desperate, and she needed to know what little success I'd had.

I left Wiggles in reception and signed in.

Once we were alone in the visitor's room, I updated Aurora as to who I'd been talking to.

"The bottom line is, your name keeps cropping up when it comes to Deacon's demise."

"Everyone in Willow Tree Falls thinks I killed him?" Aurora's cheeks paled, and she clasped her hands together.

"Not everyone. I'm still on your side. Mom's on my back about me figuring this out for you."

"Of course, I know you'll stick by me."

"Even if you did it?"

"Most likely, which I didn't." Aurora pursed her lips. "Look at me, how could I overpower some hulking great half-angel? Deacon was enormous."

"He did have too many muscles for my liking. But you do have magic. Magic trumps muscles."

"White magic only. Magic that helps and heals, not fells gorgeous angels when they get a bit handsy."

I nodded. "I believe you. But we have a job to do to make sure everyone else feels the same."

Aurora slumped back in her seat. A smile played on her lips. "Did you get to see any of Rhett's muscles when you were talking to him?"

I shook my head and ignored the memory of the perfect abs that had welcomed me when Rhett opened the door. "There was nothing to see."

"It was nice of him to offer to help." Her tone was deliberately coy.

"Sure." We were not heading down that road. "So, when are you going to be honest with me?"

Aurora lifted her head. "About what?"

"Where you really were the night Deacon died. I can guarantee you weren't stock taking. You hate stock taking."

"Hate is a strong word. Stock taking is a necessary evil."

"Which you definitely don't do every week."

"I did it that night." Aurora ducked her head. "That's my alibi."

"An alibi where no one witnessed what you were doing is not a real alibi."

Aurora's nose twitched, and she looked around the room. "Maybe you'll find out something useful when you speak to Mannie again. It does sound like he's been up to no good."

"He's not the only one," I muttered. Aurora was still hiding something. That something must be big. She rarely kept anything from me. Was it big enough to involve murder?

The door to the visitor's room opened. Dazielle scowled at me as she entered. "I heard you were here."

"Visiting the prisoner," I said. "I got permission. I even signed in like I'm supposed to."

"That's not the problem," Dazielle said. "You're still investigating this case."

I tilted my chin up. "And if I am?"

"I've told you to stay off the investigation."

"And I told you that's not happening while my sister's in a cell. You're going to have to let her go. You either charge her or release her."

"We have strong evidence to hold Aurora until further notice," Dazielle said. "Evidence collected by my squad."

"Which makes it no less wonky."

We glared at each other, neither one backing down.

"It's not so bad here," Aurora said after the awkward silence stretched out for too long. "The food is okay, and they're nice to me."

I looked away from Dazielle. "You're happy with this being the rest of your life? You want to sit in the same room and stare at smug angels' faces because you won't be honest about what you did the night Deacon died."

"What do you mean by that?" Dazielle asked.

I stared at Aurora, willing her to tell the truth.

She shook her head and bit her lip.

"If you're concealing information, you need to let us know," Dazielle said. "This case could be concluded if you simply confess to your involvement."

I stood from my seat and shoved my chair back. "Aurora is not a killer. You're looking in the wrong place. Are you even bothering to follow up any other leads now you've got her here?"

"The other leads have gone cold," Dazielle said. "We questioned everyone we considered relevant. They either have alibis or we've discounted them from the investigation. Your sister is the only suspect we're looking at."

Aurora's quiet sob was hidden behind her hand.

"Then you're putting away an innocent person." I turned to Aurora and slapped my hands on the table. "Tell her the truth. What did you do that night?"

I glared at Aurora until she looked away. "I've been dating someone."

"Yes, Deacon Feathers. We know that," Dazielle said.

"Not Deacon. He was nice, but there was no spark between us. I accepted his dates because I didn't want to hurt his feelings. I figured he'd work out we weren't compatible and move on to somebody else."

"Were you seeing this mystery guy you've alluded to the night Deacon died?" I asked.

Aurora nodded. "I felt terrible. I was supposed to go out with Deacon that night. I did drop by his place to cancel our date. There was no way I could stand him up. I told him I was busy at Heaven's Door and couldn't get away. He was so sweet and understanding. I almost changed my mind."

"What happened after that?" I asked.

Dazielle cleared her throat. "I ask the questions."

I gestured at Aurora. "Then ask."

Dazielle glared at me and then looked at Aurora. "What happened next?"

Aurora dipped her chin. "I went out with the other guy."

"Who is he?" I asked, ignoring the annoyed sounding tut from Dazielle.

"He's an older guy. He's a divorced warlock."

I scratched my head. "Okay, that doesn't sound so bad. Does he have a name?"

Aurora licked her lips. "Toby Matlock."

My mouth fell open. "Wow! He's really old."

"He's only twenty years older than me," Aurora said. "He's charming and sophisticated."

"And old," Dazielle muttered.

I nodded. Toby Matlock was a wealthy warlock, skilled in the mental magical arts. In particular, he could bend a person's thoughts. He also had a liking for cravats and silly looking hats. I couldn't picture him with my sister.

"Listen, I don't care who you date, so long as you've got a solid alibi for the night Deacon was murdered," I said. "Why didn't you give Toby's name as your alibi in the first place? You could have been out of here by now."

"Or not here in the first place," Dazielle said.

I nodded, for once agreeing with Dazielle.

Aurora sighed. "The family won't approve of Toby. Granny Dottie called him a second-rate wizard the only time I mentioned him. Mom wants me to marry a doctor or a politician, someone respectable. I can't bring Toby home and show him off."

I wasn't sure if I wanted to smack Aurora around the head or hug her. "You're such an idiot. They don't care, so long as you're happy."

"I'm not so sure. Do you remember when you brought Dillon home and Dad chased him away?"

"I was sixteen and thought it was cool to date a fire breather. He deserved to be chased off, especially after he set fire to the table cloth. Besides, Dad's not here to chase any of our dates anymore."

"I bet Auntie Queenie would scare him off."

She had a point. "Does Toby make you happy?"

"He's different, interesting, and he has loads of fun stories. I like being with someone older. When I compared him to Deacon, he's so much more sophisticated."

I looked at Dazielle. "You need to get out there, find Toby, and make sure my sister is innocent and everyone knows about it."

"I didn't realize I was working for you. Do I have a new boss?" Dazielle said coolly.

"Someone needs to be in charge."

Her eyes glittered. "Someone is."

"Come on! You've got an eyewitness to say where Aurora was on the night Deacon was murdered. Don't stand there staring at us; get to work and find out what went on."

Dazielle crossed her arms over her chest. "Perhaps I don't consider Toby a reliable witness. I suspect Aurora's reticence about revealing her involvement with Toby is not just about what your family thinks of him."

I glared at her. Now she was being annoying. "You're only saying that because you know you'll have to start from scratch with this case. All those other suspects you've discounted are back on the table, and you're going to have to scuttle off to your big boss and tell her you made a mess. You'll be lucky if Aurora doesn't put in a formal complaint for wrongful imprisonment."

Dazielle turned her attention to Aurora. "Is that true? How well do you know Toby?"

Aurora focused on her clasped hands. "Well enough."

"So, you know he's being investigated by the Magic Council for the misuse of magic?"

I sucked in a breath. "He is?"

Aurora glanced at me and nodded. "I'm sure he's done nothing wrong."

"Which is why you kept your involvement with him a secret?" Dazielle arched her perfect eyebrows.

"What's he done?" I asked. The Magic Council never got involved unless it was something serious.

"That's under our investigation," Dazielle said. "The Council has made us lead investigators in this matter."

"So, you'll never solve the case."

Dazielle's eyes narrowed, and she pressed her lips together.

"He's being accused of using his ability to manipulate a wealthy widow into giving him money," Aurora whispered.

I stared at her, my mouth open. "And you're okay with that?"

"It's not true!" Aurora's cheeks flushed. "He was with her when we met. She died, leaving Toby her money. A family member claimed Toby tricked her into giving him everything and left her when he met me. They said she died of a broken heart. They tried to claim Toby killed her, but that isn't true either."

"That doesn't sound at all suspicious." I studied Dazielle's neutral expression. "How far are you from solving these accusations?"

"We've got a lot to do, but we're making progress."

Which meant they didn't have a clue what was going on. I looked at Aurora's miserable expression. I sort of understood now why she was reluctant to reveal her alibi. If any of this was correct, Aurora was in love with a thief and possibly a murderer.

Aurora sighed. "I want this over. I need to get back to Heaven's Door. The place has been closed since I've been away. People have orders that need collecting."

"Do you hear that," I said to Dazielle. "The most popular store in the village is going to go out of business because you've imprisoned the owner. Imagine how popular that's going to make you."

Dazielle raised a hand. "I will talk to Toby and see if he supports Aurora's confession."

"She's confessed to nothing, other than being a bit of an idiot."

"Hey, that's not fair," Aurora said. "You can't help whom you love."

I glared at her again until she ducked her head. "Okay, I might have been a tiny bit stupid."

After giving me one more pointed glare, Dazielle left the room.

I sat back down and stretched my arms over my head. "We need to talk about your taste in guys. Toby Matlock, really?"

Aurora shrugged. "I like him. I know he's innocent."

"Mom is going to pop her cork when she finds out."

"Which is why I've said nothing. Can you imagine the grilling I'm going to get about him?"

"He is old enough to be your father. You're not using him as a sugar daddy?"

"Don't be gross. I don't need a sugar daddy. I just need to find a way to get everyone to accept him. I think I want him in my life for a long time."

I twisted my mouth to the side. "It sounds serious."

"It is, I think. I don't know. I'm so confused. Just don't say anything to Mom, not yet. Let me do it."

I nodded. Aurora was in for a rough ride when she finally came clean, but she could handle it. "At least now we have proof it wasn't you; you can get on with your life with Toby, so long as he doesn't get arrested as well."

Aurora snitched her nose at me. "Sure, but what about the actual killer? We need to find out who killed Deacon. You mentioned Mannie, but I can't imagine a less likely killer. He's not the type."

"I'm thinking the same thing. But he lied to me. He had an opportunity and a good motive if he considered Deacon a threat."

"Mannie's such a... weasel. You're right in thinking he'd hire someone to do it."

"When I spoke to Rhett, he laughed off the idea of being involved with Mannie. He assured me none of the other gang members were involved either."

"If not Mannie, Petra, or Rhett, that leaves Axel," Aurora said. "If it was him, did he work alone?"

"Axel has lied to me as well, but I'm not sure he's a killer. He's been hitting the mushrooms hard. I've seen him staggering home a couple of times after overdoing it. If he was in that state on the night of Deacon's murder, he wouldn't have been able to see straight, let alone kill Deacon."

"He could have hired Rhett to do the job for him," Aurora said.

I nodded. That had crossed my mind. "The problem is, Rhett has plenty of people who will back him up. His gang is loyal to him."

"You should go talk to Rhett again."

"I've heard enough from him. The most important thing is we get you out. Once Dazielle has gotten her team in gear and they've spoken to Toby, you'll be released."

"You've got to keep investigating, though. There's a killer on the loose."

"You're doubting the skills of the angels to find out who really killed Deacon?"

Aurora shrugged. "They do like jumping to conclusions, and they have arrested me twice. What's to say the killer won't strike again before the right arrest is made?"

"Until we know the reason Deacon was killed, I can't answer that. You're my priority, that's the reason I'm doing this."

Aurora jumped up and hugged me. "Thanks. I couldn't wish for a lovelier big sister."

"I'm only doing it because Mom told me to." I returned her hug.

"Sure you are." Aurora stepped back. "But I won't be able to sleep knowing a killer is on the prowl, maybe even hunting for their next victim."

"You have an overactive imagination." I stood from my seat. "If it makes you feel any better, I can ask Dazielle to keep you here another few days. You said yourself, you like life behind bars."

Aurora pouted. "Not that much. I want out of here as soon as possible."

"You'll have to sit tight for a bit longer. As soon as Toby comes good, you can get out."

"Then I can help you search for whoever did it."

"We'll see about that." I walked to the door. I did not want Aurora involved in a hunt for the killer. Once she was safely away from the incompetent clutches of Angel Force, I would lock her in her store and set a guard on her until Deacon's killer was revealed.

For now, my next step in finding out who killed Deacon was a trip to see Mannie and get the truth out of him.

Chapter 17

When I arrived at Mannie's house with Wiggles, the place was quiet. All the windows on the grand white painted building were closed. Despite knocking on the front and back doors, no one came to answer.

"We should come back later," Wiggles said. "You do realize we missed lunch, which should have been five hours ago."

"I hadn't noticed." My stomach grumbled as if it had most definitely noticed.

"I'm starving," Wiggles said. "A growing hellhound needs his food."

"You ate out of Rhett's trash can."

"I was tidying up for the guy. A bachelor needs to maintain his standards."

"You were being disgusting."

"I'd have shared if you'd asked."

I stared up at Mannie's house. "I'm sure he won't object to us waiting inside."

"You're thinking of a little break and enter?"

"There might be a door or window open. That's not really breaking anything."

"That sounds like fun. Maybe Mannie has food we can eat."

"We don't want to add stealing to our breaking and entering." I did a quick check of the front door, which was locked. We headed around the side of Mannie's house. None of the windows budged until I got to a small one by the back door. It was unlatched, and after some gentle shoving, it popped open.

"That looks like a squeeze," Wiggles said. "I'll wait out here until you get the door open."

"You're such a hero, but I can't fit through that." I leaned through the window and fiddled with the latch until it unlocked.

When the door opened, I held my breath for a few seconds, listening for the telltale sounds of anybody inside the house. Silence hit me.

"Take me to the kitchen. I'm in the need for a triple-decker sandwich with mustard and pickles," Wiggles said.

"No sandwiches," I said. "We're having a quick look around to see if there's anything in here we can use against Mannie."

"What sort of thing are we looking for?" Wiggles wandered ahead of me along the wide hallway.

"The murder weapon would be nice." I pushed open a door and walked into the living room.

"We don't know what that is."

"A pillow with Deacon's blood on it? If he was smothered, a pillow would be the perfect weapon."

"I doubt Mannie would have brought the murder weapon home." Wiggles raised his nose and sniffed the air. "I'd be happy to test the firmness of any pillows by humping them."

I turned my head slowly. "You'll do what?"

"Isn't that what pillows are for?"

"Humping? No, they're not." I was regretting Wiggles ever finding his voice. "Let's keep everything as it is. We don't want the place to look turned over." Without warning, a gross tasting sulfurous belch shot out of my lips.

"Manners," Wiggles said.

I clamped a hand over my mouth. "It's not me; it's Frank. There's something about this place he doesn't like."

"He's not the only one. It looks like a memorial to Mannie has been set up in here. Have you seen how many pictures there are of the guy?"

I did a slow turn. There were over a dozen framed photographs of Mannie dotted around. There was also an enormous oil painting hanging over the fireplace of him sitting in a throne-like chair with a glass of wine in one hand.

"We should definitely eat while we're here," Wiggles said. "Whenever you get hungry, it makes it easier for Frank to control you."

He was right. I needed to look after myself; otherwise, Frank took advantage. "We'll take five minutes to eat," I said. "And nothing out of the trash."

"That depends what's in there," Wiggles said. "People throw away all sorts of tasty treats."

"No dumpster diving. We're eating food that hasn't passed its sell by date."

We hunted around until we found the kitchen. The units were a sleek black gloss, and the oven looked new. Perhaps Mannie ate out every night and never used it.

I felt another belch brewing and could sense Frank grow increasingly restless. Maybe it was the amount of time I'd spent with Aurora recently. It was always the same; whenever I spent more than half an hour with my sister, Frank sensed her presence and wanted in on the action.

"She's not here," I muttered to him as I hastily made a cheese and pickle sandwich for me and Wiggles. "Stop pushing."

"We can go back and see her," he whispered in my head.

"That's not an option. We're here to find out more about a suspect. Don't you want to see my sister go free?"

"Having her behind bars makes her easier to get to."

Wiggles cocked his head as he accepted his sandwich. "Demon problems?"

"Frank is being troublesome." I looked around the kitchen. "Maybe it's something Mannie's done to the place."

"Does Frank sense a threat?" Wiggles' hackles rose, but he kept eating.

"He's not said if he has. I don't get it; as soon as we got inside, he started acting up. I put it down to seeing Aurora, but maybe it's more than that."

"You don't think Mannie's got a protection barrier around the house?" Wiggles asked. "I've seen them set Frank off before."

My eyebrows rose. "That might be it, but I didn't feel any magic when I came through the door."

"Do you remember that time you broke into Bite Me to steal a tray of caramel meringues?"

I grimaced. "How could I forget? There were spells on all entrances. Once I got in, Frank was enraged by the magic and came out to play. He gorged on everything in the store."

"And you vomited a dozen meringues all over the floor."

"I worked off my punishment for three months. Mom was so embarrassed."

"You and Frank have a sweet tooth. Nobody can blame you for that."

Another belch shot out of me, and Frank's power curled up my spine. "We should get out of here."

"Let me finish my sandwich," Wiggles said. He eyed my untouched food. "I'll have yours if you're not interested in it."

I pushed the sandwich toward him. "Help yourself. But we need to leave."

My gaze went to the kitchen door, and my eyes widened. Hanging next to the door was a small oval amulet with an eye painted on it. "You have got to be kidding me." I stood and inched toward the amulet.

Wiggles followed me, both sandwiches jammed in his mouth. "If looch rike ma bambi let. My of erection."

The eye glittered as I stared at it. "It's an eye of protection."

"That's what I said." Wiggles swallowed the last of his sandwich. "Those things are powerful."

No wonder Frank was unhappy. I clutched my stomach and groaned. It felt like Frank had just punched me from the inside.

Wiggles grabbed hold of my pants leg with his teeth. "Let's get out of here."

I nodded as I stumbled through the doorway, heading to the back door.

Frank's energy crawled up my spine, making me sweat. I grabbed the wall for support to stop from falling.

"Stay away," I warned Frank. "You're not needed."

"I want to come and play."

I sucked in several deep breaths. "Not now. It's just protection magic triggering you." Every now and again, I had no choice but to let Frank's energy come through. It was exhausting keeping him controlled. But I only let him out when there was no risk to Aurora, and I was far away from Willow Tree Falls. Right now, I was in the danger zone. Letting Frank out would mean trouble.

"Tempest, let's go." Wiggles stood by the back door, nudging it with his nose. "What I wouldn't give for opposable thumbs right about now."

"Go through the window," I said. "Get out of here."

Wiggles tilted his head. "Will you be okay?"

"I'll handle Frank. Get outside and keep a look out for Mannie. I don't want him coming home and finding me here when Frank is in control."

"That would be fun," Frank said.

"Not for Mannie," I said.

Frank's hot demon energy crawled up the back of my neck and covered my head. That was when I knew I'd lost control, and he was taking over.

Usually, I could force Frank back, but his power, combined with the magic Mannie had infused through the house, weakened me. I sank to my knees.

"I should stay with you," Wiggles said.

"You're better off outside," I said. "Use the window to get out." I didn't think Frank would hurt Wiggles, especially not since he'd helped bring him back to life. I didn't want to take that risk, though. I didn't like anybody to be around me when Frank was in command, especially not people I cared about.

Wiggles backed up and jumped at the open window. He made it halfway through before his butt got wedged. He wriggled and kicked but didn't get any farther.

I staggered to the window and gave him a shove from behind. "I told you not to eat out of trash cans."

"It's got nothing to do with my diet. I have wide hips. Keep pushing."

I shoved his butt with my shoulder, but he was well and truly stuck.

"You'll have to drag me back in," Wiggles said.

"You're wedged. I can't move you either way."

"I can't stay like this!"

"I'll get some oil and grease you up."

"Don't you dare grease me up! A hellhound has to have some dignity."

"You've got your fat ass wedged in a window of the house we've broken into. You've got no dignity left."

"I'm warning you. Do not grease me up."

I staggered backwards and landed on my knees. My body shook as Frank took away my final slivers of control.

When he gained power over me, it was as if I saw the world through somebody else's eyes. Everything took on a slightly red glow. I could still sense myself and think, but I had little control over my actions and not a chance of shoving a rational belief into Frank's twisted little demon mind.

I raised my head, and the world gleamed red. "Damn!"

"Damn, indeed," Frank said. "Or should I say damned. It's time for us to have fun. You've kept me caged for too long. Seeing your sister imprisoned and so pitiful only made me determined to get out and break free of my own shackles."

"There are worse shackles you could be in," I said, my voice echoing inside my own head.

"And if you ever figure out how to get me out of your body before I kill your sister, you're welcome to try to get me into them," Frank said.

I found myself pushed back to my feet. Frank propelled me over to Wiggles.

"Stay away from him." We fought for a few seconds, my arms trembling from trying to stop Frank from touching Wiggles.

"I will not harm our hellhound." Frank grabbed hold of Wiggles and pulled him back through the window.

Wiggles landed on the floor and jumped to his feet. He looked up at me. "How are you doing?"

"We are doing very well, my splendid hellhound." Frank held out a hand, and Wiggles tentatively sniffed it. "Let's explore properly. There are all sorts of delights in the fridge that need eating. We deserve a feast."

"No binging on junk food," I said to Frank. It always felt so weird to talk to him while I was trapped inside my own mind. Frank could hear me fine, but Wiggles couldn't.

"I am definitely binging. Cake, ice cream, cookies, wine. And coffee. Lots and lots of strong coffee with sugar in it. I miss those things."

"No to all of that. That's not why we're here."

"What do you desire, my hellhound?" Frank asked Wiggles. "I expect you get bored with all that dried dog kibble she forces on you."

Wiggles cocked his head to the side. "I could do with another sandwich."

"You're such a traitor," I hissed, even though Wiggles couldn't hear me.

Frank chuckled at my comment. "Tempest agrees. More sandwiches all around. Then we move on to the sweet stuff."

Within a few minutes, the kitchen counter was littered with meats, cheeses, peanut butter, jelly, and a big loaf of fresh bread. With the sandwiches made, Frank and Wiggles sat in a contented silence as they stuffed themselves.

I hated to admit it, but Frank had excellent taste in sandwiches. Peanut butter and jelly was always my favorite, closely followed by banana and honey.

"Grab those cookies, my hellhound." Frank stood and brushed crumbs off my chest. "Let's explore upstairs."

"No exploring," I said to Frank. "We have no idea how long it will be until Mannie comes back. You've stuffed your face. Now let's get out of here."

I pushed against his energy in the hope he was now satisfied after eating and would be happy to let me gain control. Frank was having none of it. He was strong, possibly stronger than I'd ever felt him.

It had to be those wall amulets. I needed Wiggles to deal with those, or I'd never get control of my body.

I was forced into action, and Frank propelled me up the stairs.

Wiggles followed along happily enough, a family sized bag of chocolate chip cookies in his mouth.

"Let's see what we've got in here." Frank opened Mannie's closet and rifled through it. "Hideous, garish, too boring, too bright. This dwarf has a terrible dress sense." Frank hauled clothing over his shoulder as he inspected each item and passed a scathing judgment on it.

"Stop that, or Mannie will know we've been here."

"He'll know someone's been here," Frank said. "I have no intention of getting caught, which means you will also be in the clear."

"Nice thinking, genius. My fingerprints will be all over this place," I said. "You try explaining that away."

"Everyone knows you carry an evil demon inside of you. Say it was my fault. I'm your perfect get out of jail free card. The demon took control, and you had to sit back and let him."

"All that will do is get us in an Angel Force sanctioned security unit being monitored all the time because I have no control over you. That's not going to be fun for either of us."

Frank ignored my comment. "Hellhound, what's happened to those cookies?"

Wiggles' head poked out from around the side of the bed, his muzzle was covered in crumbs. "I must have left them downstairs."

"Hand them over," Frank said. "You don't get to eat all the cookies. Tempest is right; you're out of shape."

Wiggles growled as he stamped over with the remains of the cookies. "I'm in the prime of my life."

Frank grabbed the cookies and stuffed several in his mouth. Crumbs scattered across the floor as he continued to pull out Mannie's clothing.

"I've always fancied myself as a tailor." Frank grabbed a pair of scissors from the dressing table and turned toward the heap of clothing.

"No, you don't," I said. "Put the scissors down and step away from the clothes."

He laughed. "You don't like Mannie. This will teach him a lesson. He lied to us both, he's hiding something, and he's not helping your sister. This is his punishment."

I shoved hard against Frank's energy, trying to get his control to loosen. My gaze went to the doorway, and I saw another one of those wretched amulets.

There was nothing I could do but watch in dismay as Frank set to work with the scissors, hacking through the arms of Mannie's shirts and tearing up pants legs. He was behaving like some naughty schoolkid, who'd been let out of class early and gone on a massive sugar bender.

Frank dropped the scissors and chuckled. "That was fun. What's next?"

Since I couldn't beat him, I decided to play along and try to get him to make a mistake. "How about we get out of here? Mannie is not coming back. We could go and get something at Bite Me. You love to play with Tilly, and she makes the best coffee."

"Mmmmm, fresh coffee, cakes, and Tilly Machello's throat clasped between my fingers."

"No, there won't be any throats crushed." Tilly was strong. She could stand her ground with Frank, but only if she was ready for him.

"Just a little choking of the witch."

"What's going on?" Wiggles asked. "Who are we planning to choke?"

"Follow me, my hellhound." Frank stuffed a black fedora on my head, ran down the stairs, pulled open the back door, and walked out.

My stomach flipped over. I never got used to the feeling of Frank being in control of my body. It felt like being on a wonky rollercoaster that was about to fly off its rails.

I had to get Frank back in his cage, but he was having far too much fun even to think about giving up his control over me. We were wasting time, and this was not helping me sort out Aurora's problems.

"Ah yes, your pretty sister. We should pay her another visit," Frank said.

I shoved away all thoughts of Aurora. "Let's concentrate on the food."

A hot wave of power ran down my spine. "You don't tell me what to do, witch."

"I do when it comes to protecting my sister."

Frank chuckled. "I can wait for somebody so succulent. She'll be mine one day."

Wiggles trotted along beside us. "I'm lost. Are we going to choke Tilly or play with Aurora?"

"Both," Frank said. "Oh look, Tempest. A friend of yours."

My chest tightened as I saw Axel strolling toward us. He knew all about my unwelcome passenger but had only seen me once when I was not in control of Frank.

Axel grinned at me. "That's a new look for you." He pointed to the oversized fedora Frank had slapped on my head.

"Hello, handsome," Frank said to Axel.

"No, no, no! Don't you dare mess with Axel." I slammed against Frank's energy.

"Handsome! Someone's in a good mood." Axel tilted his head as he looked at the hat I wore. "If I didn't know better, I'd say that was Mannie's hat."

"Would you be jealous if I told you he gave it to me? He's so sweet like that." Frank practically purred as he spoke.

"Stop encouraging Axel," I said to Frank.

"Erm, well, not really. It's a bit big." Axel ran a hand through his hair. "Is everything okay with you?"

"Everything is just perfect, sugar."

"Frank, stop!"

Axel took a step back. "Are you running a fever, Tempest? You look a bit hot."

"Oh, sweetheart, you don't know the half of it."

I groaned. "Please, just let him go."

"This one's for you," Frank muttered to me as he grabbed hold of Axel and kissed him.

My mouth collided with Axel's so hard I tasted blood as my teeth hit his bottom lip. Frank clamped my hands around Axel's head and held on tight as he forced open Axel's mouth and went to town on him.

This was a nightmare. Axel obviously thought so too as he tried to pry himself out of my grip.

I knew there was no point in trying to struggle, but I still tried.

Frank finally shoved Axel away and wiped a hand over my mouth. "I've had better." He plopped the fedora on Axel's head before stalking away.

"What was that all about?" I gasped. My cheeks felt roasting hot after that kiss and not for the right reason.

"He's a half-demon. You owe the guy a break. He's been flirting with you for months. I've had to endure every sleazy move he made in an attempt to draw you in."

"How is kissing Axel going to make him less sleazy toward me? He's going to redouble his efforts after that." I tasted peppermint and realized I'd transferred Axel's gum into my mouth during our make-out session. Could this get any worse?

"The guy deserved a break. But you could be right. I should go back and punch him instead, just so he's clear where we stand."

"No, but spit out his gum and keep going," I said. "Let's forget all about the kiss."

"I doubt Axel will." Frank turned and looked back along the lane.

Axel stood there, his arms by his side and his mouth open.

Frank gave him a cheery wave. "You've just made his day."

"You mean, you have. You were the one who wanted to kiss him. Maybe you have a crush on Axel?"

"That was all for you. You could do worse than a half-demon. And it's been a while since your sheets have seen any action."

"That's because I shut you down, so you have no clue what goes on under my sheets." At least, that was what I always tried to do. But maybe I'd not been as successful as I thought if Frank knew when my last romantic relationship was.

"You should try a full demon. We're not so bad," Frank said.

"You burned down twelve villages."

"They were in my way," Frank said.

"Of what?"

"My view."

Typical demon. Always putting his own needs first.

We arrived at Bite Me, and I hunted anxiously through my red tinted vision for signs of Tilly. There was a method to my madness in enticing Frank here. Tilly was a fiery witch and had helped me in the past when I'd struggled with Frank.

My heart gave a thud of relief as I saw her behind the counter, handing change to a customer.

Tilly's smile faded as she saw me walk through the door. Her gaze shifted to the occupied tables. She knew trouble when she saw it. "Is there something I can help you with?"

"I'll take a dozen of your desserts, flame witch." I tried to shake my head, but Frank held me in position, so my body froze to the spot.

Tilly looked down at Wiggles. "You know the rules." She pointed at the door.

Wiggles looked up at me and shook his head.

"It is best the hellhound remains outside. His loyalty might be tested," Frank said. "I would not like him harmed."

"Good idea." Tilly opened the door. She petted his head. "Everything will be okay." Wiggles backed out of the door, his eyes full of concern.

I was grateful they both wanted Wiggles out of the way. He would try to protect me. When he did, Frank would hurt him as punishment. I couldn't have that happen. He might be a hellhound, but he was still my fur baby.

"Are you having a party?" Tilly moved cautiously around the counter. She was a tall slim blonde with pale blue eyes that were fixed to me with an unnerving intensity.

"Yes, a party for one."

"You need to be careful with all that sugar." Tilly gestured to the dessert counter.

"I can handle a little sugar. I can even handle your sugar." Frank closed the gap between them.

Tilly raised her eyebrows. "I'd be too sweet for you."

"Frank, stop flirting and eat your damn desserts," I said.

He laughed in response. "What do you say, flame witch? Shall we dance?"

Tilly squared her shoulders, and red sparks of magic flickered across her fingers. "Everybody leave."

The half-dozen diners knew not to question Tilly. They grabbed their purses and food and ran for it.

When the last customer fled, Tilly flexed her fingers. "I've done enough dances with demons to know how this will end for you."

I found myself bowing in front of Tilly as Frank laughed. "Then this should be entertaining for us both."

Tilly raised her fingers, and a fireball appeared in her palm. "Give Tempest control of her body and slither back to whatever prison she keeps you in."

"I am impressed you saw through my disguise," Frank said.

"I don't serve demons. You need to leave."

Frank grunted, and his hot energy spiked inside me. "I haven't had my dessert."

"Let go of Tempest." Tilly raised the fireball to eye level, a flicker of indecision in her eyes.

I wished I could let her know she could do whatever she needed in order to loosen Frank's grip. I could handle being singed with Tilly's fireball if it meant Frank disappeared and I got control of my limbs.

Tilly seemed to understand because she raised the fireball and slammed it directly at my head.

At the last second, Frank lunged out of the way. I hit the floor and stayed there, feeling the heat of Tilly's fireball skim past.

"I don't want you injured," Frank said to me. "This lovely body of yours needs to be able to walk around, so I can visit Aurora whenever I desire."

"I'd break my own legs to stop you reaching her," I hissed at him.

Tilly leaned over me. "I'll try not to mess you up too badly."

"As if you could," Frank said.

"She will. Tilly is a bad ass," I said.

Frank launched my body upward, and he leaped over the dessert counter in a fluid motion.

"You stay away from those cakes," Tilly shouted.

Frank plunged my hands into a strawberry pavlova and stuffed the sweet gooey mess into my mouth.

Tilly launched another fireball.

Frank grabbed a brownie before ducking behind the counter. "Our flame witch has a terrible aim."

"She only has a terrible aim because she's trying not to kill me."

"Then she's a fool." Frank dragged a tray of chocolate tiffin to the ground and gorged himself on them.

"You're paying for those desserts," Tilly said.

"You'll have to catch me first," Frank said.

"My pleasure."

An unnerving silence filled the room, occasionally punctuated by Frank's noisy open-mouthed chewing.

"Quit it, will you? That's enough cake." I focused on stopping Frank grabbing another tray of desserts. Any more cake and I'd be sick for days.

"You are not in control, and neither is that—" Frank shot to his feet, cakes tumbling around us as he bashed into the trays.

Tilly held two large white moonstone crystals. Her eyes gleamed with anger. "Are you sure you want to stay?" She edged the crystals closer.

Frank snarled. "You will harm my carrier if those stones touch."

I wanted to tell her to do it. Those crystals drained a witch's energy. If I was unconscious, so was Frank. He couldn't influence me when I was asleep or unconscious. The easiest way to knock out a witch was to drain her using moonstone crystals charged in the moonlight in our stone circle.

"Get back in your cage, demon," Tilly said.

"You will not do it. You value this witch too much." Frank's heat radiated off me in sulfurous waves.

Tilly shook her head. "I also value my cakes." She slammed the crystals together, and I blacked out.

✦✦✦✦✦✦ ✦✦✦✦✦✦

"Tempest, are you okay?" Tilly caught hold of my shoulder and rolled me out of the face full of lemon cheesecake I'd landed in.

I groaned and licked my lips, feeling like I'd gone several rounds with a heavyweight prize fighter. "He's gone. I've got Frank under control."

Her gaze was full of concern. "He was strong this time."

"The worst for a while." I blinked up at the ceiling. "I've been in Willow Tree Falls too long. It's my own fault. Frank gets like this when I'm around Aurora."

"Then you need to leave," Tilly said. "I don't want you to go, but it's not safe for you or anyone here."

I laid flat out on the ground, my stomach churning from all the food Frank had stuffed into me and the smell of burnt sugar filling my nose. "I know, but until Aurora is in the clear, I can't abandon her. The family is relying on me to clear her name."

"It's a good job my crystals were charged, or I might have no store left and definitely no desserts from the way Frank was stuffing them into you."

I wiped cheesecake off my face. "Sorry. I had to come here. I knew you'd sort out Frank."

"Of course, any time. Let's get you up and clean some of this off you." Tilly looked around at her ruined dessert counter. "It's going to take me all week to get this place back together."

I raised a weak-feeling hand. "I'll help. You won't even know you battled a demon in here by the end of the day."

Tilly caught hold of my hand and pulled me into a sitting position.

The movement made my head spin. "Just give me a second." I slumped down again and passed out next to a destroyed pile of chocolate profiteroles.

Chapter 18

I awoke to the taste of sugar in my mouth and a pounding head.

My gaze shifted around an unfamiliar bedroom as the memory of the fight filtered through my thoughts.

I groaned and gingerly rubbed my forehead.

Wiggles' face appeared over the edge of the bed. "You look terrible."

"I feel worse."

"You passed out."

"I guess I did. Where are we?"

"In Tilly's place. She brought you up here to sleep off the after-effects of Frank."

I pulled on a strand of my hair and discovered sticky, sour smelling cream in it.

Wiggles didn't seem to mind as he tried to lick it clean.

"Enough of that. I'm going to need a long, hot soak to stop smelling like a gone off dairy farm."

"I helped Tilly clean up last night," Wiggles said. "I'm not hungry for once."

I eased myself carefully up on the bed, and my stomach rolled over. "I'm guessing that means you ate a truckload of ruined desserts."

"I might have eaten a few. Tilly didn't mind. She said I was a great help."

"Your waistline will mind." I tried standing, and the room only tilted a little. "How long was I out?"

"All night."

I groaned again. I inched out of the room and made a stop in the washroom. My face was bloated from too much sugar, my eyes were puffy, and my hair stuck up at odd angles from being mashed together with cream and icing.

I washed off the worst before walking down the stairs into the restaurant. My eyes widened. Apart from an empty cabinet of desserts, you wouldn't have known a demon and a fire witch had fought with each other last night.

The smell of strong coffee and sweet muffins drew me toward the kitchen.

As I pushed the door open, I saw Tilly. She wore a white apron wrapped around her middle and was busy mixing something in a large bowl.

She looked up at me and smiled. "Who's in charge this morning?"

"It's me. I promise."

"I'm glad to hear it." Tilly looked down at Wiggles and shook her head. "No dogs in the kitchen. I'll lose my license if your fur is found in my soufflés."

"Some might consider my fur a delicacy."

"Not in this restaurant," Tilly said.

"You'd better wait outside," I said to Wiggles.

He gave a dejected sigh and slumped away.

"He has nothing to complain about," Tilly said. "He ate so much last night I thought he would burst."

"That pooch has a bottomless pit for a stomach."

She filled a mug with coffee and handed it to me. "And he's now a hellhound. When did that happen?"

"That's a story for another time."

"I'll look forward to it. How are you doing?"

"I feel like I drowned in a vat of sugar. I'm never eating cake again."

"I've never met a demon with such a sweet tooth," Tilly said. "The two of you should make good companions, given your love of brownies."

"You'd think so. If he wasn't such a nightmare when it came to Aurora, I might not mind having him around."

Tilly shook her head. "You mentioned last night that you needed to leave because he's getting twitchy with Aurora."

I took several sips of my coffee before answering. "I'm not safe around Aurora. The whole family is also at risk. They pretend not to notice how difficult Frank can be, but they must realize how strong he is."

"Have you told them that? You get an A star for hiding how you feel most of the time."

"We don't talk about our feelings much," I said. "It's how we roll. We get on with what we have to do and protect the world from demons. There's no point crying every time we fight a bad guy."

"That doesn't mean you can't tell your family that it's a struggle at times. Maybe Aurora will be more cautious around you if you do."

I drank more coffee and stared into space. I didn't want that, not really. I wanted the normal relationship everyone had with their sisters. I wanted her bugging me and hassling me and asking me questions. I didn't want her to be scared of me.

Tilly patted my hand. "Families are complicated. How come Frank was in charge last night?"

I grimaced. "That was sort of my fault. I was looking for evidence of Mannie's involvement in Deacon's murder."

"Do you think he has something to do with it?"

"It's a hunch. He's not been totally honest. I went to ask him some questions, but he wasn't home."

Tilly arched an eyebrow. "And? There's more to that story."

"I found an open window and decided to take a look around."

"You broke into Mannie's home and that triggered Frank?"

"Not that." I told her about the amulets, gorging on Mannie's food, and ruining his clothes. "Then Frank got talking about going to see Aurora. I had to distract him. I mentioned you and your desserts, and he thought it was a great idea to come over. Frank's so full of himself. He always thinks he can come in here and take what he wants. He has a selective memory when it comes to the times you've beaten him down."

"And I'll keep on beating him down as long as he keeps threatening you and your family." Tilly jammed her hands on her hips.

"Thanks. I'm eternally grateful for that." Tilly had always had my back. "But it was a waste of time going to Mannie's. I found nothing that connected him to Deacon's death."

"You said he wasn't telling you the truth. About what?"

"He lied about the time his meeting ended," I said. "It was something to do with his campaigning for the mayoral election. He said it ended two hours later than it did. It took place on the night of Deacon's murder, and he used it as his alibi."

Tilly grinned. "You know why that is?"

"Because he killed Deacon and is trying to cover his tracks?"

"No, well, I don't think so. Mannie's got a mistress."

My mouth fell open. "What about his wife?" I was always amazed Mannie was married, but he had a mistress as well. His personality regularly slid to the wrong side of smug to be considered attractive.

"He uses his campaign meetings as a cover story. He ends his meetings early, so he can have a couple of hours of naughty fun. Mrs. Winter knows nothing about it. If it comes out, Mannie will not be happy."

I puffed out a breath. "Which is why he lied to me. Who is he seeing?"

Tilly grinned. "You are never going to guess."

"I'm sure I can't. Mannie is an acquired taste."

"He is also a rich acquired taste. That business of his makes some serious cash."

"Put me out of my misery. Who is he seeing?"

"Star Fairfax."

If my jaw could drop any lower, it would. "But she's young and attractive and full of energy. What does she see in Mannie?"

"His bulging bank balance," Tilly said. "He is one wealthy dwarf. He gives his wife all the gifts she demands, spends a ton of money on Star, and still has plenty to go around when it comes to funding his campaign for mayor."

"Hold on. I thought Star was dating Giovanni Romer."

"You're right there. Mannie is cheating on his wife, and Star is cheating on Giovanni with Mannie."

"Star does not have great taste in men." I grimaced. "Imagine Mrs. Romer as your mother-in-law to be. I bet she grills Star about her intentions toward her precious Giovanni."

"It can't be pleasant. What that means though is that Mannie was most likely with Star when Deacon was killed."

"You know for sure they are a couple?"

"No doubt about it. I saw them late one evening. I'd just finished doing the cooking prep and was taking the trash out to the back alley. I heard voices and laughter and snuck along the alley to take a look.

Mannie was wrapped around Star. They were… enjoying themselves."

I raised a hand. "I don't need to know any more. But I do need to confirm they were together on the night of Deacon's murder." I ran my fingers through my damp, soured cream scented hair. "Since I couldn't find Mannie yesterday, I'll talk to Star again and see what she knows. If she confirms they were together, it means Mannie wasn't involved."

"So, who did it if you rule out Mannie?"

"I've ruled out Petra and most likely Rhett. That only leaves me with Axel." My hand went to my head, and I groaned as a vivid memory of me snogging Axel came to mind.

Tilly looked startled. "Is there something I should know?"

"Just Frank making my life complicated. We ran into Axel yesterday when he was in charge. There was an incident."

"What kind of incident?"

"The kissing kind."

Tilly laughed. "Frank likes Axel?"

"No! Well, I don't think so. He wants me to hook up with Axel because of his half-demon status. He loves to stir things up when he's in control."

"He wouldn't be a good demon if he wasn't. Well, a bad demon." Tilly shrugged. "You know what I mean. How was the kiss?"

"It hurt." I remembered my teeth crashing into Axel's full lips.

"That doesn't sound good."

"I feel sorry for Axel. He got a split lip, and I stole his chewing gum."

Tilly chuckled. "The two of you should talk. He's sweet on you, but you don't want to give him ideas."

"Axel is sweet on a lot of women. I don't consider myself anything special."

"He might."

I shook my head. "I'm not interested in dating."

Tilly nodded, knowing this conversation would go nowhere. "And you're no closer to figuring out how to remove Frank safely, so this won't happen again?"

"Nothing works." I'd lost count of the number of times I'd talked to Tilly about how to remove Frank. Every time I tried, he clung to me like a love-struck limpet. It was as if he liked his home inside me and had no intention of ever leaving. We'd tried different spells and potions to remove him, and some did temporarily weaken him, but they got nowhere close to having him exorcised.

"One day, we'll find out what your demon hates. You're not going to spend the rest of your life living with Frank." Tilly touched my shoulder.

"That's definitely one relationship I can do without." I finished my coffee. "Thanks again for everything last night. I'll pay you back for all the desserts I ate. Well, all the desserts Frank made me eat."

"Don't worry about it. I was happy to help." She passed me a brown paper bag. "Muffins for later. Give yourself a bit of a sugar detox first."

"Will do." I headed out of Bite Me, Wiggles at my heel.

"Where to next?" he asked, his nose pointed at the bag of muffins.

"The dance studio. It's time to confirm an alibi and catch a killer."

Chapter 19

It was still early when we arrived at Star's studio, and classes had yet to begin.

I discovered Star dressed in a pale cream tracksuit, warming up in front of a huge wall of mirrors.

She turned and waved at me when she saw me in the mirror. "I see you're back." She walked over, her gaze going to my disheveled hair. "Did I tempt you with the idea of private lessons?"

I shoved my soured cream scented hair off my face. "No, but I am interested in the private lessons you have with Mannie Winter."

Star's eyes widened. "I don't teach Mannie."

"You don't teach him *dance*."

She blushed and looked away. "He's just a friend."

"What kind of friend?"

"The usual kind." She bent and fussed with a loose tie on her shoe.

"I know you're seeing him," I said.

She stood up swiftly. "Who told you that?"

"That's not important. I need to know if you saw Mannie on the night of Deacon's murder."

Star sighed and nodded. "I did. I knew Mannie couldn't have been involved in what happened, so I kept quiet about it."

"Are you still dating Giovanni?"

Star twisted a loose thread from her top around a finger. "Sometimes."

"You're seeing Mannie behind Giovanni's back?"

Star ducked her head. "Giovanni is a lovely man, but he's not got much get up and go. I have to make the effort in that relationship and feel like I'm nagging him to do anything spontaneous. With Mannie, it's different. He swept me off my feet. He showered me with gifts and compliments until I agreed to go on a date with him. He's such a romantic."

"He's also a married romantic."

"Mannie told me he's leaving his wife after the election. That's the only reason he's waiting. He doesn't want negative publicity attached to his name before such an important event."

I crossed my arms over my chest. "I imagine he doesn't."

"He knows people like to gossip. Mannie wants to make sure his personal life doesn't impact the outcome of the election. After that, he promised me he's going to tell his wife that he's leaving her for me."

I didn't agree with Star seeing Mannie behind his wife's back, but it was their business and their guilty consciences. "You're sure you were together that night? Mannie didn't leave you at any point?"

"No, it was the same as always. His campaign meetings are a great excuse for him to have a night away. He tells his wife he's going to work late and sleep over at his office. She doesn't seem to mind. In truth, I think she's glad to get rid of him. They haven't been friendly for a long time."

They always looked friendly enough to me when I saw them together. "You spent the whole night with Mannie?"

"That's right. He has an apartment on the other side of the village. It's for his exclusive use. I like to call it our little love nest."

I tried as hard as possible not to grimace.

"He's a big sweetie. He'd never be involved in anything as awful as killing Deacon. They had a friendly rivalry with the campaign, but that was it. Mannie was convinced he would win the election."

"Maybe he was only convinced because he'd planned on wiping out all competition until he was the only man standing. That would guarantee him a win."

"I promise you he's not like that."

Although any man who cheated on his wife was a scumbag in my books, Mannie did have a decent alibi.

Star touched my arm. "Does that mean you're back to square one with proving your sister's innocence?"

I sighed. "It looks like it."

"I wish I could give you better news, but I promise Mannie is not involved."

I tipped my head back. There was the vaguest of possibilities Star was lying and covering for Mannie. Or maybe he'd slipped out when she'd fallen asleep and he'd killed Deacon, but it didn't seem likely.

"Where is this secret love nest?"

"It's in the woods on the very edge of the village," Star said. "It takes about twenty minutes to get there on foot. Thirty if you stop for a little canoodle like we do. It's tucked out of the way; no one can see you."

"Is it easy to find?"

"No, you have to trek through the woods. There's not even a proper path. It's super private and very romantic. If Mannie ever left me in the woods on my own, I'm sure I'd be lost forever."

I twisted my mouth to the side. That was doubtful. The woods weren't that big. But it would make it hard for Mannie to creep back to Deacon's house, kill him, and then return. It would probably take someone at least an hour and a half, and that was providing they didn't get lost. It looked increasingly unlikely that Mannie was involved.

But if it wasn't him, it must be Axel. Despite the embarrassment that burned inside me about our unexpected kiss yesterday, I would have to go confront him.

"You will keep quiet about this," Star said. "We only need to keep it a secret until the election. Once that's out of the way, Mannie will come clean to his wife, and I'm going to cool things off with Giovanni. We only need to keep up the pretense for a bit longer."

"It's not my secret to tell, but you know it's a lousy thing to do."

"I didn't mean to fall for him," Star said. "I don't like being a husband stealer."

"What's so wrong with Giovanni? There must have been something about him that appealed to you when you first got together?"

"He's okay. He's actually quite a nice guy when he gets away from work."

"So why stray?"

Star shrugged. "It's his mother. She terrifies me. The last time I was in the store, she stamped down the stairs and accused me of taking her son away from her. Then she started asking when we were going to have babies. First of all, I can't have him, and then I need to have kids with him. Mrs. Romer needs to make up her mind. It's too stressful being around her. I want a mother-in-law I can have fun with, go out for long lunches and have shopping trips with, that sort of thing. Not creep around terrified of her in case she decides to insult me or tell me I'm not fertile enough for her darling boy."

I saw Star's point. My encounters with Mrs. Romer were never pleasant. "I won't say anything. But you need to sort this out. It's not fair to lead anybody on."

"Of course. I wish I could have been more help in getting Aurora's name cleared. Do you have anybody else you think might be involved?"

I pinched the bridge of my nose. "There is someone else. I need to go talk to him before making any decisions about what to do next."

Star smiled. "I'm glad we got that all cleared up. Do let me know if you want a private dance lesson. I teach one-to-one, so no one else has to see until you feel ready to shake your stuff in public."

Wiggles did one of his indiscreet barking laughs from the corner of the room where he was investigating the used dance tights.

"I'll bear that in mind." I hurried out of the dance studio and away from the unappealing invitation of a dance class with Star.

I muttered under my breath as I walked. I had to see Axel and work out what he knew about Deacon's murder. He would understand what happened yesterday. He knew about Frank, but I still didn't want him getting any ideas about us. There was no us.

"If there's anything you feel like sharing," Wiggles said as he trotted along beside me, "I'm happy to listen, especially if you want to break out those muffins Tilly gave you. I'm a better listener when I'm eating."

I opened the bag and passed him one. "I don't want Axel getting the impression that yesterday meant anything."

"You mean after you snogged his face off?"

"Yes, that. I wasn't in control. Frank did it to mess with me."

"Tell Axel that," Wiggles mumbled around a mouthful of muffin.

I knew I had to, but all I wanted to do was hide under my duvet for a week and forget the last day or two had ever happened.

If only Aurora hadn't decided to date a cute half-angel. If only Deacon hadn't gone and gotten himself killed. I'd be happily accepting a new job to hunt a demon and heading out of Willow Tree Falls with my dignity intact. Instead, I still smelt of gone off cream, had an upset stomach from too many cakes, had probably gained five pounds, and had some explaining to do after my unexpected snog-fest with Axel.

Still, I had to do it. I had to put my humiliation to the side and see him. If Axel was the killer, I needed to confront him and save my sister.

Chapter 20

It was late in the afternoon as I stamped along the main street of Willow Tree Falls. I'd tried Axel's home, dropped by Cloven Hoof to see if he was enjoying himself there as seemed to be the norm these days, and even tried the Ancient Imp. He was nowhere to be found.

In my eyes, that made him even guiltier. Only the guilty hid. He had to be involved and must have figured out I was onto him. Axel could have realized what I'd been doing at Mannie's and assumed I'd found information that linked him and Mannie. Could it be that I had the right idea but the wrong people? Could Mannie and Axel have been working together to bump off Deacon? Was it such a big deal to ensure victory in this election? Willow Tree Falls was a special place but special enough to kill for?

There was one place I knew Axel would be. Tonight was the evening the results of today's election would be announced. Axel would have to be there. He wouldn't resist the opportunity to brag about his victory if he was successful. I would get him then when he went to claim his new position. He could be the shortest serving mayor in Willow Tree Falls if I was right about him.

Putting my search for Axel temporarily on hold, I made a detour to Angel Force to check-in with Aurora and see how the angels were treating her.

As we reached the front doors, there was a new sign on the wall: *No hellhounds allowed.*

I grinned. "It looks like you made quite an impression the last time you were here."

Wiggles growled at the sign. "That's discrimination."

"We should put in a complaint."

"You can bet your butt I'm complaining. I did nothing wrong."

I tilted my head. "I do remember you threatening Dazielle and stealing her muffin."

"That wasn't threatening. These angels need to stand up for themselves."

"Wait here. I won't be long."

Wiggles grumbled to himself before cocking his leg up the side of the building, right under the new sign.

Sablo stood at the desk as I entered. She gave me a puzzled look when I asked to see Aurora.

"She's been released. She left an hour ago."

My eyebrows shot up. "Nobody told me."

"I processed her. Your mom, along with the rest of your family, came to collect her. It was quite a celebration."

I shook my head. Thanks for keeping me in the loop, family. "Does that mean you're no longer investigating her?"

"For now." Dazielle appeared in the doorway at the back of the reception.

"What about the evidence you had on Aurora? The rock-solid evidence that she attacked Petra?"

Dazielle shrugged and walked over to the desk. "When I looked into it more closely, it didn't stack up. I interviewed Petra again, and she wasn't convinced it was Aurora in the pub. Also, the evidence we found showing Aurora was the attacker was—"

"Obviously planted? So ridiculously obvious that it couldn't be true? No one loses a massive clump of hair and a shoe at the same time."

Her eyes narrowed. "Yes, well, maybe it was a little too convenient. Plus, there was an unknown fingerprint on the shoe."

"Whose fingerprint?"

"They're not on any database we have. They don't have a criminal record. I have to assume that they took the shoe from your sister, along with her hair, and planted it in the pub."

"To make her seem guilty and involved with Deacon's murder?"

"It would appear so," Dazielle said. "For now, Aurora is in the clear, especially since her alibi checks out too."

"You spoke to Toby?"

She nodded. "He confirmed everything. He needed no prompting and said they were together that evening. There is a small window of opportunity that your sister could have gone to Deacon's and smothered him, but it's not likely."

"If only you'd listen to her in the first place, you wouldn't have wasted all this time trying to pin this crime on her."

Dazielle's expression remained unapologetic. "She looked good for it. I wasn't going to ignore such a compelling motive and evidence."

As tempting as it was to rant at Dazielle for being such an idiot, I bit my tongue and turned to leave.

"While you're here, are you interested in getting the details of a new case?"

I turned back and nodded slowly. I should jump at the chance. Now Aurora was free, there was no reason for me to stick around. In fact, it was better if I didn't. It would be good for Frank to have a break from Willow Tree Falls and reduce the risk of him taking over again.

But I wasn't sure I wanted to go just yet. I loved it here. I loved being around my family when my demon wasn't threatening them.

"It's not a difficult case," Dazielle said, "a quick in and out. A demon absconded from custody and he needs rounding up."

"I'll take a look at the file notes. What are the conditions?"

"Same rates as always," Dazielle said. "Round him up, bring him back here, and we'll do the rest."

"I'll let you know." I grabbed the file Dazielle offered me and headed out of Angel Force. Although Dazielle could be a thorn in my side at times, she gave me a legitimate reason for leaving without upsetting my family. They always supported me when I left to go demon hunting. It was a win-win all around, but sometimes it felt like a hollow win as I left behind the safe bubble of magic and my family and endured the noise and chaos non-magicals thrived in.

"No Aurora?" Wiggles asked as I stepped outside.

"They let her out."

"That's great news."

"It is."

"So why do you have a face like a smacked butt?"

"I do not. It's just that—"

"Now you think you have to go. That you're more trouble than you're worth." Wiggles nudged the file I held with his nose.

"It is safer if I'm not around."

"It's boring. I get bored when you're not here. You should stay and keep me entertained."

"This isn't about you."

"It should be. I'm your hellhound."

I shook my head. I sometimes wondered who owned who in this relationship. Who was I kidding? I always put Wiggles first. Now he was a walking, talking hellhound he was going to keep me on my toes even more.

"Come on, let's go celebrate the prisoner getting out on early release." I headed along the lane to Mom's house. I'd only just started walking up the garden path when I heard laughter inside. I slowed, and instead of going to the front door, I walked around the side and peered in the kitchen window.

Everyone was inside. Aurora was surrounded by Mom, Auntie Queenie, and Granny Dottie. Grandpa Lucius sat off to one side, smiling to himself as he rocked backwards and forwards in his ancient wooden rocking chair. Only Uncle Kenny was absent, most likely left to stand guard in his man cave in the cemetery.

I wanted to be a part of that, but I held back. I could feel Frank stirring, and I wasn't even in the same room as Aurora.

"You keep your demon snout out of my family's business," I whispered to him. "Aurora is not yours."

Frank didn't reply, but I felt a trickle of his hot energy run up my spine. One day, he'd beat me. One day, I'd lose control around Aurora. I could never let that happen. I had to keep my distance.

"Are we going in?" Wiggles asked. "I bet there's a cake."

"No." I turned and walked away. Everything was fine here. Aurora was safe, and everyone else was happy. I'd do a quick check-in with Cloven Hoof and make sure Merrie had everything covered for the next few days then I'd pack a bag and get out of Willow Tree Falls while I could.

"Where do you think you're going?" Auntie Queenie stood on the front porch, her arms folded under her ample bosom.

I looked back at the house. "How did you get out of the kitchen and onto the porch so quickly?"

"I'm a witch." She grinned at me and beckoned me over. "You can't go sneaking off without seeing us. Anyone would think you don't love us."

I walked over and sat on the front porch steps. "That's just it. That's why I have to do it."

Auntie Queenie sat next to me and wrapped an arm around my shoulders. "I know that. We all do."

I leaned against her and breathed in the scent of elderflowers and cinnamon. "It's not easy keeping Frank under control."

"You put on an excellent show of having no problems with him. You let everyone believe you're capable." Auntie Queenie raised a finger and pressed it to my lips. "But I know the truth. I see how you struggle with him. I know how strong he is. Whenever you're around me, I get the chills."

I gently pushed her finger away, so I could speak. "You've never said anything before."

"I didn't want to alarm you and give you another reason to avoid us. I know you like to pretend nothing ruffles your feathers, but that demon you hold is a nasty one." She stroked my hair behind my shoulders. "When you found him in your sister's bedroom all those years ago, he was going to kill her. He would have if you hadn't trapped him. You are an incredibly strong witch. You have powers we've never seen before in this family."

"I don't know about that. You and Mom are amazing at kicking demon butt if one of them dares to creep out of the prison."

"That's because we have decades of experience on you. And that's our speciality. We've honed our skills in demon butt kicking. You have to handle much more than that. You use your body as a demon prison, containing a powerful and dark force. You leave the protective environment of Willow Tree Falls and surround yourself with non-magicals when you go demon hunting. You're never sure what you're going to find out there, but you always come back having trapped the demon. I doubt either your mom or I could achieve that."

"You make me sound like a super-witch."

"You are a super special witch, especially to me." Auntie Queenie kissed my forehead. "Don't be afraid to say when you're having problems. We're all here for you. And Aurora understands."

"She doesn't. She never understands that she needs to stay away from me."

"Aurora does just that. She barely visits you and hardly ever sees you when it's just the two of you. She would like nothing more than to hang out with her big sister every night. Aurora tries as hard as you do to make sure Frank doesn't get the upper hand."

My bottom lip jutted out. Maybe Auntie Queenie was right. I always acted so annoyed whenever Aurora came too close, but she didn't do it often. She passed on lots of messages between family members that reached me, and she used the snow globe system a lot. It would have been so easy for her to walk down the road to Cloven Hoof. Instead, she was keeping a distance. Aurora was doing her best, knowing how difficult the situation was.

"You've done an amazing job helping to keep her safe," Auntie Queenie said. "I'm sure Angel Force would have charged her with Deacon's murder if it weren't for your involvement. You're turning into a regular little sleuth alongside your demon hunting."

I shrugged. "You see? I am a super-witch."

"You're also my super niece, and I want to keep you that way. You let me know if you have any problems. You can always talk to me, whatever the trouble is."

"Thanks, Auntie Queenie. I do struggle sometimes to control Frank. I lost control of him yesterday. There was magic interfering with my abilities, and he beat me."

Auntie Queenie nodded. "I know. I was at Tilly's this morning. She mentioned you were upstairs. I decided to let you rest."

"If Tilly hadn't helped me, I'm not sure I could have stopped Frank." Sadness filtered through me. Hosting a demon was the hardest thing I'd ever done. It kept me apart from the people I loved the most.

"Let me give you a piece of advice that has always worked when it comes to diffusing tension and getting control of the situation."

"Anything. I'll try anything if it means Frank doesn't keep slipping out and taking control."

She patted my hand. "You need to have more sex."

I choked out a laugh. "I do?"

"It works for me. Whenever I'm experiencing tension or am frustrated about something, I go see your Uncle Kenny. He's a man of few words, but he's also a man of action. I only have to say to him, *Kenny, I'm frustrated*. He jumps straight to it. That man has so many moves it makes my head spin. I remember one occasion when—"

"Err, if it's okay, I really don't want to know about your love life."

Auntie Queenie chuckled. "Maybe you don't need to know the details, but you need to know the basics. A lot of sex with the right partner is good for you. You need to get yourself a regular man and make good use of him. Don't be shy in coming forward when you tell him what you need. It's important you keep control of Frank. If that means you have to get busy with your significant other on a frequent basis, then you do that. I've got books I can loan you if you need inspiration. They show all kinds of different positions."

I eased myself out from under her arm. "I appreciate the offer. But before I read the books, I need to find myself a significant other."

She patted my knee. "Of course, you do. I'm happy to share, but I want those books back. I make use of them most evenings."

I blew out a breath to try to cool my hot cheeks. Auntie Queenie needed to check her inappropriate discussion filter was working. "What's making you so tense that you have to get busy so often?"

"I kick demon butts for a living. We look after a demon prison. Not every day is a picnic."

I nodded. Living in Willow Tree Falls, it was easy to forget that protecting a demon prison wasn't an everyday thing, especially when your family did it for a living and you'd been raised talking about crypt cracks, demon powers, and how to fell a demon with a single punch.

"Aurora tells me you're still looking for Deacon's killer," Auntie Queenie said.

"I should let Angel Force do it, but I'm not sure they've got any angles. Aurora told me it's the right thing to do, find the killer."

Auntie Queenie smiled. "How's that going?"

"I have my suspicions about Axel. I've ruled out Petra, and I don't think Mannie was involved or Rhett."

Auntie Queenie snorted. "Axel wouldn't get his hands dirty with a murder. He's too much of a pretty boy."

"He's a half-demon pretty boy."

"Even so, he's a weak half-demon. I still have my suspicions about the biker gang."

"Nope, I've spoken to Rhett. They were out running a new bike on the night of the murder."

"Do you believe the biker gang?"

"I believe Rhett. He wouldn't lie to me."

"Have you spoken to the rest of the gang?"

"Well, no. I took Rhett at his word."

Auntie Queenie tutted. "You get your head turned too easily by him. I'm not saying he isn't gorgeous, but you should double check the information. Just because you went on a few dates with him that doesn't mean he's always going to be honest with you. The biker gang is his family. They'll protect each other. It would be easy enough for them to come up with an alibi like that. What's to say they weren't running that bike just as Rhett said? He didn't need to be there. And remember, I did see his bike at Deacon's house."

"Are you sure it was his bike?"

"I know my bikes. If it's Rhett's bike, I'd know it if I saw it again."

My head sank into my hands. If that was the case, then Rhett had lied to me. "He told me he hadn't been in contact with Deacon for a long time. Why lie? What is he hiding that means he needs to conceal a visit to an old friend?"

"We should go." Auntie Queenie hopped up.

I peered up at her. "Go where?"

"To see the biker gang."

"Now?"

"There's no point in hanging around. There's a killer to be found."

"I can talk to Rhett again. There's no need to see the whole gang." I wasn't scared of the bikers, but I didn't want to drag Auntie Queenie into this search for a killer.

"There's every need. Come on. There's no time to waste. We've got a biker gang to intimidate." Auntie Queenie strode along the path and out the gate.

I jumped up and hurried after her.

"Are you sure this is a good idea?" Wiggles asked as he followed along behind.

"No, it's a lousy idea. But you know what Auntie Queenie is like when she sets her mind to something. Nothing stops her."

"She turns into you on a triple dose of lemon drops."

"That's not fair."

Wiggles barked out a laugh. "Trust me. I've been around this family long enough. You are just like her."

I shook my head and broke into a jog to keep up with Auntie Queenie. Maybe we were similar, but I wondered what I'd gotten myself into by going with her to interrogate Rhett's gang.

Chapter 21

"Are you sure you don't want to slow down?" I was having trouble keeping up with Auntie Queenie's fast pace as she strode away from the house and toward the woods.

"I'm fine. It's all the sex, you see. It's a great aerobic workout," Auntie Queenie said.

"Maybe I should try it more often if it keeps you this fit." My forehead was damp with sweat, and my chest heaved. I was half Auntie Queenie's age, but she wasn't even out of breath.

"I highly recommend it." Auntie Queenie slowed as we turned down an overgrown path.

"Do you know where you're going?"

"This is the place. Most people don't come here on foot. The gang uses an ancient cave system on the edge of the woods. Very few people know about it."

I tripped over a tree root and bashed my knee. "I can see why."

We walked for about five minutes, the trees getting denser and all signs of a path vanishing.

"Hold it right there, ladies." What looked like an enormous moss-covered brick moved in front of us.

Wiggles jumped and ran behind me. So much for being a badass hellhound.

As my eyes adjusted to the gloom, I saw it was a huge, tattooed, bearded guy, his eyes narrowed and his hand holding a large wooden stick.

"Hello, dear. You must be a part of the biker gang," Auntie Queenie said as she peered up at the giant of a man.

His expression remained neutral. "You're on private land."

"We're looking for Rhett." I stood next to Auntie Queenie, sensing the pulse of menace coming off the guy. "Is he here?"

"I don't know anyone by that name."

"Of course you do, dear," Auntie Queenie said. "He's gorgeous and wears tight leather pants and has a lovely bum to fill them. A bit like a ripe peach, all ready for biting."

The bearded guy snorted a laugh, and his gaze flicked to the side. "You could be describing me."

Auntie Queenie chuckled. "You're more meat than muscle."

The guy scowled at her. "He's not here. Leave."

"Maybe you can help us if Rhett's not available," I said. "He told me he was out on Deadman's Lane the night of Deacon's murder."

"What of it?"

"Is it true?"

"Why do you care?"

"Because someone murdered Deacon, and I want to find out who."

"It wasn't Rhett. It wasn't any of us."

"Rhett was there on the night of the murder?"

"If he says he was, then he was."

I shook my head. "That wasn't a real answer."

"Why don't you take us to your leader?" Auntie Queenie said. "We can sit down, have a nice cup of tea, and you can tell us everything."

"We don't have a leader, and we don't serve tea." He stepped forward and went to grab hold of Auntie Queenie's arm.

She sidestepped him and planted her knee in his stomach. "My apologies, but it's not polite to grab a lady."

The bearded guy grunted as he clutched his stomach. "Leave. I won't ask you again."

"You weren't asking. You were trying to manhandle me. Only my Kenny gets to do that."

The guy pulled himself upright and rubbed his stomach. "I'll do more than manhandle you." He lunged at her.

Auntie Queenie grabbed a low-hanging branch over her head and swung her feet forward, connecting with the giant biker's chest. I sensed the magic she pushed into her feet as she kicked him.

The biker was launched through the air and slammed into a tree. He didn't get up.

"I did warn him." Auntie Queenie jumped down from the tree branch.

"Some guys can't take a hint," Wiggles said.

"Where were you when the fighting went down?" I asked him.

Wiggles inspected a spot on the ground. "I have an upset stomach. I needed an emergency comfort break."

I sighed. "It looks like we're going to have to find Rhett ourselves."

The surrounding air shimmered. Three more bikers stepped into view, blades in their hands.

"We've got unwelcome visitors." A tall lean guy with a scar above his right eye stepped forward, a blade glinting in his hand. "And they've not been too friendly to Josh."

"Young men, behave yourselves and put down those knives," Auntie Queenie said. "I raced against your parents, so I know you, Jimmy Blackmouth, and you, Ian Blaine. You should respect your elders."

A guy with bulging biceps and a mess of brown curls squinted at Auntie Queenie before laughing. "You're telling us you used to be in a gang?"

"Not this gang. I ran with the Dead Tree Witches."

Ian hissed. "You were our rivals."

"Until we ran them out of town," Jimmy said.

"Where are your manners?" Auntie Queenie said. "You're not too old for me to bend over my knee."

"He's into kinky stuff," Ian said. "He might like having an older woman discipline him."

The bikers chuckled and bumped fists.

"You can watch your tongue, as well."

I touched her elbow. "We're not here to cause trouble."

"It's too late for that," Ian said. "Josh is out cold. What did you do to him?"

"Schooled him about his appalling manners," Auntie Queenie said. "You will be next if you don't watch yourself."

"Promises, promises."

"We're just here to see Rhett," I said as I moved to stand in front of Auntie Queenie before she challenged the entire gang to an all-out fist fight. "We need to check his alibi for the night of Deacon's murder."

"You're accusing one of our own of being involved in that?" Ian sneered.

"No, but he needs to be scrubbed off the list of suspects, so we can find the killer."

"What list?"

"My list of suspects. I'm not having my sister's name tarnished with this murder."

"He was with us," Ian said.

"Where was that?"

Ian glanced at his friends. "Wherever he was supposed to be. Wherever he told you he was. We've got his back covered."

"You're lying to protect him," I said. "If he had anything to do with this, I need to know."

"Then what are you going to do?" Rhett stepped out from behind a tree, his dark eyes blazing with anger. "Are you planning on arresting me and taking me to Angel Force?"

I sucked in a breath. He was even more gorgeous when angry. "You lied to me. You told me you haven't spoken to Deacon in ages."

"I haven't." Rhett signaled his guys to move back, and they all obeyed.

"How come my Auntie Queenie saw your bike outside Deacon's house?"

"Who says it was my bike?"

"If I saw the bike again, I'd know it," Auntie Queenie said. "That was a one-of-a-kind Harley. There's nothing else like it in Willow Tree Falls."

"You know your bikes, Grandma?" Ian asked.

Auntie Queenie glared at him. "I'm no one's grandma. But of course, I know my bikes."

"She reckons she ran with the Dead Tree Witch gang," Ian said to Rhett.

Rhett's lips quirked. "Is that so? Then you know what we like to do with witches in that gang."

"You had a lucky break running them out of town," Auntie Queenie said. "If I'd been in charge, it wouldn't have happened."

Auntie Queenie opened her mouth to keep arguing, but I shook my head at her. We needed to get the information we came for and get out of these woods before more gang members showed up.

"You still haven't answered the question," I said to Rhett. "What were you doing with Deacon?"

Rhett sighed and turned his attention to me. "Even if I was there, it doesn't mean anything dodgy was going on. What's to say I didn't stop by to chat with an old friend?"

"Because you told me you haven't spoken to him, and you weren't close anymore."

"It could have slipped my mind. Maybe I did drop by one day. It still doesn't mean anything was going on or I had a problem with him."

"It could mean Deacon wanted you involved with his campaign."

Rhett laughed, and his gang members chuckled along with him. "I have no interest in small town politics. I leave that to the suits and the social climbers. That's not for me."

"You don't need to like politics. Maybe Deacon wanted you to help him get rid of the competition."

"Which would mean I'd have killed one of the other candidates, not Deacon."

"If not that, then maybe you were at Deacon's looking for a way to get into his house and smother him without anyone seeing you."

"That's how he died?" Rhett asked, surprise clear on his face. "He was smothered?"

"That's not our style," Ian said.

"Murder is not our style." Rhett shot a sharp glance at Ian. "I'm not involved. This gang isn't involved with Deacon's murder. We weren't close, but I had nothing against the guy. I was sad to learn of his death, but this is not our business."

"I'm making it your business," I said.

"We should teach these ladies a lesson." Ian's blade rose.

Wiggles growled, and his eyes glowed. It looked like his courage had returned just in time.

"They need to show us the proper respect," Ian said. "They're on our turf and accusing you of murder."

I glanced at Auntie Queenie as the tension grew. She appeared perfectly calm and had somehow managed to find a pastry about her person and was eating it. "I want a straight answer. I need to clear my sister's name."

"You won't be able to clear her name when you're in the hospital," Ian said.

Frank kicked inside me, sensing the growing danger.

Auntie Queenie looked at me and shook her head. "We don't need Frank. We can handle this lot on our own."

I pushed against Frank's energy. He needed to stay where he was. Fallen angels and demons battling against each other was never a pretty sight, and I always ended up getting covered in demon goo, which was a look no one could pull off.

Rhett raised a hand, and his gang stilled. "It doesn't need to come to this."

"Agreed. You tell us what you were doing with Deacon, and we'll get out of here. We won't bother you again," I said.

"Rhett had nothing to do with that dude." Ian lifted his blade higher. "He's already told you."

"I don't believe him."

Rhett glanced at Ian, shook his head, and sighed. "Deacon asked me for a favor. He needed to beef up his security. He'd had a couple of weird messages sent to him and was unsettled."

I kept an eye on the blade in Ian's hand. "What did the weird messages say?"

"He didn't show them to me. Deacon said someone had shoved them through his letter-box. He didn't see who it was. They threatened him and told him to stay away."

"Stay away from what?"

"He didn't know. Deacon assumed it had something to do with the mayor's campaign. He asked me if I'd sign on for a few shifts as his unofficial muscle. He didn't want me anywhere near the campaign, and he definitely didn't want anybody to know he was using a gang member to keep him safe."

"So why ask for your help?"

"Deacon knew he could rely on me. We were buddies when we were younger. I guess he figured he could still trust me."

"That's what you were doing at his house?" I asked. "Going through security details?"

"That's about it. Deacon asked me to keep an eye on his house for a few evenings and see if the secret note writer returned. I did as he asked."

"Who did you see?"

"No one. A week later, there was nothing and no new notes. When Deacon had no further contact from whoever wrote them, he assumed it was some overenthusiastic opposition supporter. He paid me what I was owed, and I left him to it. A week later, he was dead."

I let out a sigh. Rhett wasn't involved. He hadn't been working with Mannie or Axel to bump off Deacon. And since I didn't think either of them had the guts to kill Deacon on their own, I was all out of suspects. I must have missed something, but what? Who else could want Deacon dead?

"Are we done here?" Ian asked.

Auntie Queenie nudged me. "We should go. They'll be announcing the new mayor in a couple of hours."

My eyebrows rose. "Of course. If this murder has to do with who becomes mayor, the killer could be there."

"I would be if I'd gone to so much effort to get the job," Auntie Queenie said.

"Do you need a hand?" Rhett asked.

"No, we've got this," I said.

"It doesn't seem like it," Ian said. "A few minutes ago, you thought Rhett was your killer."

I glared at him, and Ian glared right back.

"What's your next move?" Rhett asked.

"I'm going to find the killer," I said. "They won't be able to resist being at the event tonight and seeing who the new mayor of Willow Tree Falls is. If the wrong person has won the vote, they might decide to do something about it."

"You think this is down to some overzealous supporter?" Rhett arched an eyebrow. "How can anyone be that interested in boring politics?"

"You're asking the wrong person," I said.

"But we need to be there," Auntie Queenie said. "If this is about the election, the other candidates' lives are at risk."

"We'll escort you," Rhett said. "We can get you there quicker on the bikes."

"There's no need," I said.

"There's every need," Auntie Queenie said, a big smile on her face. "It's been awhile since I've had a ride. Ever since your Uncle Kenny banned me from riding after that little incident when I hit the magic barrier and broke it, he doesn't think I'm safe."

"We don't need their help," I muttered to her.

"Of course we do. Since they're not the killers, they might as well lend a hand. Hey, big guy with the beard, get on your feet and show me to your bike." Auntie Queenie strode over to the biker she'd knocked unconscious and pulled him upright.

Rhett stifled a smile behind his hand, his gaze on me.

Auntie Queenie dusted down the biker and checked him over. "Oh dear, you're not fit to ride. I'll use your bike, and you can be my pillion."

The guy's jaw dropped, and he stared at her. "You want to ride my bike after you knocked me out?"

"I've shown you I'm strong. I can handle a throbbing beast of an engine between my thighs." She strode off, dragging the bemused-looking biker behind her.

Rhett chuckled as he watched them go. "What do you reckon, Tempest? Can you handle having a biker gang as your escort?"

I kept my expression neutral. It was no big deal accepting a ride. "It looks like I don't have a choice."

We walked along in silence for a moment, Wiggles by my side.

"I'm not going to hide the fact I'm disappointed," Rhett said.

"What have you got to be disappointed about?"

"I told you my alibi for the night of Deacon's murder. I thought you trusted me."

I shrugged. "It isn't that I don't trust you, but I need to get Aurora's name cleared. You could have been involved. I had to be sure. Only an idiot wouldn't check the facts."

"And I never had you pegged as an idiot." Rhett nudged me with his shoulder. "It stung that you think I might have killed Deacon. I liked the guy. He'd gotten a bit uptight as he'd grown older, but he was decent enough."

I tried not to care that Rhett was disappointed in me. I was doing what I needed to protect my family. That had to come first.

I glanced at Rhett. "You must miss him."

"I guess so. I didn't even realize it, but I always looked out for him. Even after we'd grown apart, I kept an eye out to make sure he was doing okay. I never let Deacon know, but I was sort of proud of him. He'd done so well for himself. If he'd won this election, he'd have been the youngest mayor of

Willow Tree Falls. We'll never know how good he could have been."

We reached Rhett's enormous sleek, black Harley. He hopped on and glanced at the seat behind him. "Climb aboard. Let's go see if we can find you a killer for your Auntie Queenie to beat up."

Chapter 22

The sun was sinking below the horizon as we pulled up outside the village hall. Bunting was strung outside, and music drifted from the open doors as we all climbed off the bikes.

I tried very hard not to think about how good it had felt to wrap my arms around Rhett's waist as we'd sped out of the forest and along the streets. Nope, it hadn't made me at all breathless to be so close to him.

True to her word, Auntie Queenie had ridden Josh's bike as he'd clung to her on the back.

"What a ride. I need to get myself a bike again. I'd forgotten how much fun they could be."

"I'm never riding with you again," Josh said. "You corner way too sharply."

"You just have to lean into it," Auntie Queenie said. "Never let the fear take over. That's when you lose control and wipe out."

"Is that what you said to yourself when you broke Willow Tree Falls magic barrier and almost exposed us to the non-magicals?" I asked.

Auntie Queenie sniffed. "That was different."

"You're one crazy rider, lady." Josh patted his bike and rubbed a hand across his sweaty brow.

"Thank you." Auntie Queenie caught hold of my elbow. "Shall we go inside?"

Rhett touched my shoulder before I could answer. "We'll hang around in case you need us."

"You don't have to. I appreciate you bringing us here, but we've got this."

He shook his head. "Even so, in case you need backup. I'll be here. We all will."

My insides flipped over, and this time, it wasn't because Frank was kicking off. Rhett had an honorable streak. He looked out for the people he cared about. I could relate to that. It was the whole reason I was hunting Deacon's killer. Aurora needed me, and I wasn't letting her down. I had to solve this murder. Only then would the rumors disappear about Aurora's involvement.

As I entered the village hall with Auntie Queenie, the sound of talking and laughter filled the air. Voting had been going on all day, and the final votes were being counted before the new mayor would be announced.

There was a stage at the back of the hall with a curtain drawn over it and different stands displaying all the candidates' promises if they became mayor.

We stopped beside a tasteful memorial for Deacon. There was a picture of him smiling. Tea light candles and small bags of herbs covered the memorial.

"He was taken far too young," Auntie Queenie said. "And such a good-looking boy. It's a shame your sister didn't take to him."

"Perhaps he's not to her taste." Aurora had yet to reveal to the family just who she was interested in. A part of me hoped her relationship with Toby would fizzle out after the novelty had died off. But that was Aurora's battle to fight. I was here to clear her name. She'd have to deal with her romantic entanglements herself.

We passed the memorial, and I spotted Mom with Granny Dottie and Grandpa Lucius. Aurora was checking out the refreshment stand.

"Why don't you wait with the others?" I said to Auntie Queenie. "I need to find Axel and have a chat with him. Even though it's a long shot, he's the only one left who might be involved with this."

"I still don't see it being him," Auntie Queenie said.

"There's nobody else," I said. "He wasn't telling the truth about where he was the night Deacon died. Maybe there are other things he's lying about."

"Tempest." Mom engulfed me in a hug. "We were wondering where you were. And what happened to you?" She looked at Auntie Queenie. "One minute you were off getting more drinks and then you vanished."

"I needed to spend quality time with Tempest." Auntie Queenie winked at me. "We had a few things to deal with."

"They're about to announce who's going to be our new mayor," Granny Dottie said as she walked over. "I voted for the best looking one."

"Who do you consider the best looking?" I asked.

"Axel, of course. He's such a charming half-demon." She gave me a knowing wink.

He might be a charming half-demon, but he might also be a killer. "I'll be back in a few minutes." I left Auntie Queenie with the rest of my family. Wiggles had abandoned me in favor of the refreshment table and I started hunting for Axel.

There was no way he'd miss out on tonight. He'd have to know the outcome of the votes and if all his hard work had been worth it, especially if that hard work involved murder.

He wasn't anywhere in the crowds of waiting people, so I snuck behind the curtain in front of the stage to have a snoop around the back.

There were two rooms backstage. I was about to check in one when I heard footsteps behind me. I turned and discovered Axel.

He slowed as he saw me. "This is a surprise. Don't tell me you've come to give me an early congratulatory kiss? Or should I say, another kiss?"

I grimaced. "Not a chance. I'm sorry that happened. I wasn't myself."

His grin faltered. "Oh, well, it was out of the blue."

"Frank thought it would be funny to jump you."

"Frank! Right, it makes sense now. I was taken aback when you lunged. I did wonder if you'd finally given into your desires and stopped pretending not to like me."

"No, sorry. That's not going to happen. I mean, I like you. I just don't..." I waved a hand in the air. This was stomach clenchingly cringy, but I couldn't lead Axel on. "I do need to ask you a question, though."

He shrugged. "Fair enough. You can't blame a guy for trying. Your question will need to be quick. I want to run over my acceptance speech one more time before the curtain goes up."

"You've lost me."

He grinned and pointed at the heavy red fabric. "It's Grenville's grand idea. The plan is that the winner will be told a few seconds before the curtain goes up. We're supposed to stand on the other side of the curtain and be revealed to the waiting audience and welcomed by the old mayor. I guess people will like it. After that, I give my winner's speech."

"I don't think you'll be giving any speech."

Axel's smile faded, as did the color in his cheeks. "You don't like speeches?"

"What I mean is, I think you were involved with Deacon's murder."

Axel's mouth dropped open. "No, that's not true."

"You knew you didn't stand a chance of winning against him, so you got rid of him."

Axel raised a hand. "Wait a second. I'll admit that, with Deacon gone, I was the next best option. I never considered Mannie strong competition."

"I heard otherwise. I heard Mannie has plowed lots of money into this campaign. He wants to win. Did you have him as your next target but run out of time?"

"Mannie can push as much of his money into this as he wants. The people know a trustworthy face when they see one."

"Are you really that trustworthy?"

Axel cocked his head and smiled tentatively. "Of course. Are you questioning my trustworthiness? As the almost new mayor of Willow Tree Falls, I'm offended."

"You lied to me about where you were on the night of Deacon's murder."

"No, I didn't. I had the same routine that evening as I do every week. Gym, dinner, and a movie."

"Maybe you did all of those things, but you were seen at Cloven Hoof. You must think I'm an idiot. Merrie spotted you."

Axel rubbed the back of his neck. "Merrie is mistaken."

"She doesn't make mistakes."

He stared at me for a second and shrugged. "I might have left the movie a little early. I occasionally do that if I figure out the ending. Then there's no point in staying."

"How much of the movie did you see that night?"

"Maybe half. I wasn't ready to go home, so I headed to Cloven Hoof. I thought I was being discreet."

"We are very discreet at Cloven Hoof, but my staff misses nothing." I noticed a tremble in Axel's hands. "Is everything okay with you?"

"Other than the stresses of trying to be the next mayor of Willow Tree Falls and you just accusing me of killing Deacon, everything is fine. Why do you ask?"

"You need a detox from Cloven Hoof." Axel had slipped through my net thanks to my focus on finding Deacon's killer. He was hooked on my mushrooms.

"From what?"

"I'm cutting you off from Cloven Hoof."

Axel grabbed my arm. "You don't need to do that. You're losing good business by turning me away. There's nothing wrong with regular mushroom consumption. It's been proven. You tell everyone that."

"There is a problem if you rely on it. I've seen you staggering away some nights. You shouldn't eat that many."

"They help me relax. I have it under control. It's not a problem."

"It will be my problem if you don't get a handle on things," I said.

"It will be different once the election results are in," Axel said. "I needed a little extra boost. I've been working long hours on this."

"You've never worked at anything in your life."

"Which is why I'm so stressed out. Tempest, I need this, or my dad is turning off the tap. He told me I need to find a passion and said to try politics. Well, he actually said I should work toward world domination, crushing as many skulls as I can along the way. I thought I'd go for something a little less messy. Demon dads, what are you gonna do with them?"

I pressed my lips together. "You're running for mayor to keep your trust fund?"

He nodded. "This is important to me."

"Do you need it enough that you'd kill for it?"

"No, I want to win fairly. And once I got into it, it wasn't so bad. I've spent weeks getting to know what everyone wants. I don't want to turn the place into some cheap tourist destination like Mannie does. Willow Tree Falls is all about magic and protection and keeping people safe. It's not about exploiting our healing stones or thermal spas. The magic we use and the way your family protects the rest of the world from dangers they can't even imagine is incredible. That needs protecting."

"That's quite some speech."

Axel nodded. "Dad wrote it for me. He wants to keep Willow Tree Falls just as it is."

I sighed. "I don't disagree with any of that."

"The balance we have is ideal. We don't need to change things. I love Willow Tree Falls and only want to make it stronger. If we fill the place with overexcited non-magicals, it could tip the balance the wrong way. It could make our jobs harder."

I nodded, surprised by his emotive outpouring. There was more to Axel than I'd realized. Sure, he'd been pushed into this by his dad, but he cared about Willow Tree Falls.

"I promise you, Tempest, I would never kill for this. I had nothing to do with Deacon's murder."

"Where were you the night Deacon was killed? After you left Cloven Hoof, where did you go?"

He ran a hand through his hair. "This is a bit embarrassing, but I was so out of it, I passed out and woke up the next morning on the edge of the forest."

I groaned. "When I opened Cloven Hoof, I made assurances that no one would get themselves in trouble. Everyone would use my produce responsibly."

"It's my fault. Merrie always cuts me off before I get too bad."

"But not the night of Deacon's murder?"

Axel ducked his head. "I might have bought somebody else's mushrooms off them. I paid double the price you sell them for."

I smacked him around the side of his head. "Don't ever do that again."

He rubbed the side of his head. "Jeez, I'm sorry. Even more so because you think badly of me."

I blew hair out of my eyes and tilted my head as I heard people approaching.

"Mom, you need to leave this alone." A harassed sounding Giovanni strode behind the curtains, closely followed by his mother, who fussed at the collar of his shirt.

I grabbed hold of Axel and shoved him into one of the rooms, easing the door almost shut, so I could peek through the gap.

"Why are we hiding from the Romers?" Axel whispered.

"Mrs. Romer hates me, and she looks furious." I did not want another run-in with her anytime soon.

"That's her default face. Even when Mrs. Romer is supposed to be happy, she can make small children cry if they see her."

I pressed a finger to my lips as I waited for them to leave.

"Remember, you need to keep quiet. Keep your head down, and no one needs to know what happened." Mrs. Romer continued to fuss with her son's collar.

He shrugged his shoulders and stepped away. "I'm hardly going to tell anybody what happened."

"Make sure you don't. I know what you're like when you get nervous. We have to keep the family name intact."

"What are they talking about?" Axel whispered.

"I'm not sure."

"This doesn't feel right," Giovanni said. "It had to be done, but—"

"But nothing. Action had to be taken. You worry too much."

"I'm right to be worried."

Mrs. Romer slapped her son's cheek. "Less cowardly talk. Be a man. Be the man your father would have been proud of."

"I try," Giovanni muttered as his chin dropped to his chest.

"Try harder. And stop pouting. What happened was the right thing. You stay quiet and everything will be fine."

"Yes, Mom." Giovanni's shoulders were slumped as he followed Mrs. Romer back out into the main hall.

"What was all that about?" Axel said.

I eased the door open and stepped out, my thoughts racing and my heart thumping. Giovanni was a mommy's boy, but even they snapped if pushed hard enough. "I think… I'm not sure, but I think it had something to do with Deacon's murder."

Axel followed me out and closed the door. "How do you figure that?"

"Mrs. Romer needs Giovanni to stay quiet about something. Something important enough to ruin the family name. Murder would ruin their reputation."

"Why would Giovanni want Deacon dead?"

"I don't think he did. This has nothing to do with Deacon. This has everything to do with Giovanni's relationship with Star."

Axel's eyebrows shot up. "I didn't even know they were dating."

"The problem is, Star is also seeing Mannie Winter behind Giovanni's back."

Axel snorted a laugh. "You can't be serious. If that's true, Star has terrible taste in men."

I stared hard at the curtain that concealed us. Could Giovanni have done this? "Giovanni killed Deacon. He planned to frame Mannie for the murder to ruin his chance to be our new mayor, but something went wrong, and Aurora got dragged into it."

"It's not possible. Giovanni can't be a killer." Axel waved a hand in the air. "He's so... so, apron-whipped. His mom would never let him get away with it. She watches him like a hawk. I bet he even needs permission to go out at night."

I rubbed my forehead. Axel had a point. Giovanni was a sweet guy and his mom ruled his life.

"Their conversation must have been about something else," Axel said.

My pulse quickened. "Maybe I'm looking at the wrong Romer. My mom always says how strong the Romer women are. She's always telling me to be careful around Mrs. Romer and not get on her bad side. You don't think..." I shook my head.

Axel stood up straight. "You're thinking the old lady did it?"

"She might be old, but she comes with a hell of a power. And she's fiercely proud of keeping the family name respectable. What if she found out Star was cheating on her son? Some mothers will stop at nothing to protect their children."

"She killed Deacon because..."

"Mrs. Romer killed Deacon, meaning to frame Mannie." I shook my head again. "But something happened, and she didn't get the chance."

"It definitely did, since your sister was in the frame."

I paced backwards and forwards. I was still missing something. "Why kill Deacon and attack Petra? And why try to frame Aurora?"

"Ladies and gentlemen," Mayor Grenville's voice boomed over the PA system, "I would like to introduce you to your new mayor."

The curtain shielding us was yanked up. Everyone stared at Axel and me.

Chapter 23

"Tempest! Axel!" Mayor Grenville stared at us. "I wasn't expecting either of you to be here. You're not even running for mayor, Tempest."

I stared around at the sea of curious faces. Since everyone was in the hall, now seemed like the best opportunity to reveal what I knew about Deacon's murder.

I stalked over and held out my hand for the microphone. "Can I borrow this?"

"Well, we do have a new mayor to announce." Grenville looked over his shoulder at Axel.

"I'll just be a minute. It's important."

Mayor Grenville scratched his head. "Everybody, I'd like to welcome Tempest Crypt to the stage, who, by the way, is not our new mayor. He will arrive shortly."

The sound of cautious clapping filled my ears. I raised my hand. "I need you all to know that Aurora

Crypt is innocent of Deacon Feathers' murder."

A murmur went around the room.

"I know she's been arrested twice and questioned, but she's innocent." I sought out Aurora in the crowd and nodded at her. She gave me a thumbs-up, a worried look on her face.

Mannie stood to one side of the stage looking uncomfortably sweaty in a lurid pink shirt and plum colored slacks. Star stood near him while keeping a safe distance from the pinch-faced Mrs. Winter. Star's gaze kept moving from Mannie to Giovanni, who stood with his mother. Mrs. Romer had a wicked scowl on her face.

At the back of the room stood Rhett and his biker gang. He nodded at me as I caught his eye.

I took a deep breath. I was either about to reveal a killer or make a complete fool of myself. "I know who killed Deacon Feathers." I saw Dazielle approach the stage, a furious look in her eyes. I was running out of time. "Let me explain. Mannie Winter and Star Fairfax are seeing each other."

Mrs. Winter made a squawking sound and spun on her heel toward Mannie.

Everyone's attention shifted to the two of them.

Mannie adjusted his shirt collar and muttered under his breath to his wife.

I noticed Star discreetly moving toward the exit. Smart girl.

"Star is also dating Giovanni Romer."

Giovanni's head shot up, and he stared at me.

I glanced at Mrs. Romer. If looks could kill, I'd be hung, drawn, and quartered by now. I had no evidence she was involved with Deacon's murder, but if I was right, she'd do anything to protect her son.

"Giovanni killed Deacon in order to discredit Mannie and ruin his chances in this election."

"That's not true," Giovanni said. "I had nothing to do with Deacon's murder. I liked him."

"Be quiet," Mrs. Romer snapped, her hand clamped on his arm.

Star stared at Giovanni. "You love me that much that you'd try to frame Mannie to get me all to yourself?"

I shook my head. And they say romance is dead.

"If that's true, why was my bar broken into?" Petra moved to the front of the stage. "What has Giovanni got to do with that? And why did he plant evidence to frame your sister?"

Everyone's attention returned to me.

I cleared my throat. "Petra, didn't you mention something about wanting to get out of the business of bar ownership? What do you think you'll do next?"

Petra glanced at Giovanni and Mrs. Romer. "Well, I have done some investigation into opening a new telegram service."

"Which would put you in direct competition with Mrs. Romer."

Mrs. Romer glared at Petra. "We don't need another telegram store in Willow Tree Falls. Ours works just fine."

"You overcharge. There's no competition. I figured I could set up my own service and undercut you. People have no choice but to use you."

"No one would use your service," Mrs. Romer snapped. "Everyone comes to us. The Romers have run the business for hundreds of years."

"That doesn't mean you run it well," Petra said.

I tapped the mic to get their attention. "No matter who would run a better service, perhaps Giovanni decided he needed you out of the running. He couldn't risk a rival setting up and making things difficult for him."

Giovanni opened his mouth, but Mrs. Romer glared at him, and he kept quiet.

"What nonsense," Mrs. Romer said. "Giovanni had nothing to do with that. You should ask your sister who killed Deacon and injured Petra."

"It wasn't her. Even Angel Force figured out the evidence implicating Aurora in Petra's attack was planted."

Dazielle glared up at me but then nodded.

"Aurora was an easy target," I said, thinking on my feet as the pieces fell into place. "Giovanni saw the angels were interested in her, so he made their job easy for them."

Mrs. Romer glanced over at Aurora. "My boy did no such thing."

"Aurora, when was the last time you saw either Giovanni or Mrs. Romer in Heaven's Door?" I asked her.

Aurora tapped a finger against her lip. "It was a few days ago, after I was arrested for the first time. I remember because Mrs. Romer needed a particular type of herb, and I didn't have any on the shelves. It was a rare type of marigold. I was sure I had some dried in the back, but it took me ages to find it."

"You left Mrs. Romer in the store with no one watching her?"

"I did. But I trust Mrs. Romer."

"And I bet you left your door unlocked, so she could have gotten into your apartment if she wanted to."

"Oh! Well, yes. I never lock it. There's no one in Willow Tree Falls that I don't trust."

"That means nothing," Mrs. Romer said. "I'm an old lady. I can't climb the stairs."

"You can," I said. "The last time I was in the telegram store, you stamped down your own staircase well enough. It would have been easy for you to sneak up to Aurora's apartment, steal hair from her hairbrush, take one of her shoes, and plant them in Petra's bar. You wanted to divert attention away from your son and onto my sister."

"You cannot prove that," Mrs. Romer said.

Annoyingly, she was right. I looked at Dazielle, who shook her head and shrugged.

"Angel Force will take Giovanni in for questioning. It won't take them long to get him talking."

"They'll do no such thing," Mrs. Romer said. "My son is innocent."

Giovanni nodded, not even bothering to try to defend himself, while his mom did such a good job.

I agreed with Mrs. Romer about Giovanni's innocence. I was sure she wasn't innocent, though.

"Giovanni, what's your alibi for the night Deacon died?"

He glanced at his mother, and she nodded, giving him permission to speak. "Well, I don't recall."

"He was with me," Mrs. Romer said, "all night. We closed the store, I cooked Giovanni dinner, and we stayed in together."

He bowed his head and nodded.

"Wasn't that the night we were supposed to meet?" Star asked from her relatively safe place close to the exit. "We were going to have an early dinner before I went and met..." She stopped and looked over at Mannie. Her cheeks flushed bright pink. "Well, I was going to meet Mannie later that night, so I said we could meet early. You were with me until eight o'clock. You mentioned nothing about your mom cooking you dinner."

"That doesn't mean he wasn't with me," Mrs. Romer said. "I'm an old woman. I simply got my timings muddled."

Giovanni backed away, his hands fluttering against his chest and panic in his eyes. "I had nothing to do with this." His anxious gaze shifted to his mom.

"I told you to keep quiet," she hissed at him. "And stop shaking."

"If that's true, you won't mind talking to Angel Force, so they can clear your name," I said to

Giovanni. "And they also have an unidentified fingerprint on the shoe planted at the Ancient Imp. I reckon it will be a perfect match for Giovanni."

"It will not." Mrs. Romer licked her lips, a hint of panic flaring behind those beady black eyes.

"There's nothing to talk about." Giovanni bumped into several people as he backed away. "I was with my mom."

"And Star," I said. "You forgot that bit. What else have you forgotten?"

"I wouldn't forget killing someone," Giovanni said.

I noticed Rhett and his gang move to block the door to prevent anyone escaping.

"You should confess now, Giovanni," I said. "Angel Force will go easier on you if you do."

I ignored the fact Dazielle shook her head and glared at me.

"I can't," Giovanni said. "Mom, help me."

"Mrs. Romer, is there anything you'd like to add?" I asked.

"My son is innocent." She hurried over and grabbed Giovanni's arm. "Stop bothering him."

"He'll be in for a lot more bother if you're not truthful."

Dazielle approached the Romers and touched Giovanni's elbow. "We should talk at the station, where it's private. It seems you've got a few things you need to get off your chest."

"No!" Mrs. Romer's hand shot out, and a blast of magic slammed into Dazielle, knocking her to the ground. "Keep your hands off my son."

I clutched the microphone as the crowd dispersed away from Mrs. Romer. Magic shimmered around her, threatening anyone who got too close.

"You killed Deacon," I said to Mrs. Romer. "You were so worried about the Romer name being discredited if people found out your son's girlfriend cheated on him that you had to do something about it."

Giovanni glanced from me to his mom. He opened his mouth.

"Not a word," she snapped at him.

I could see Giovanni was weakening, so I pressed on. "Mrs. Romer snuck out that night, killed Deacon, and planned to discredit Mannie and Star. When that didn't go to plan, and Angel Force accused Aurora, you took advantage and used it to get rid of a business rival. You tried to kill Petra and frame my sister."

Giovanni stared at his mom, horror on his face. "I never knew you hurt Petra. I love the Ancient Imp. I can't let anything happen to that place."

"Be quiet," she spat. "That's your problem. You always want the easy life. Sometimes, we have to do things we shouldn't to get what we need."

Dazielle jumped to her feet, a glimmer of white magic on her hands. "Is there something you need to tell me, Mrs. Romer?"

She glared around at the anxious faces in the room. "The Romers are strong. We have traditions to uphold. If anyone joins our family, they must be loyal. We do not allow people who cheat and have low morals be involved with us. And we do not allow rivals to take what is ours. My son deserved so much more than some dancing tart in his life."

Star gasped as her hand went to her mouth.

I sort of agreed with Mrs. Romer. It was never cool to cheat.

"Is that a confession?" Dazielle asked.

Mrs. Romer lifted her chin. "Deacon was a decent enough person, but his death meant the family name would remain intact, a harlot and her lover would be discredited, and our business would remain safe. His sacrifice was a worthy one. I would have found another way to ruin Mannie before long."

"And Aurora?" I asked.

Mrs. Romer shrugged. "As you said, she was easy to implicate. I have nothing against your family other than your superior attitude, but when Angel Force stopped me from framing Mannie, I had to cover my tracks."

I let out a sigh and handed the microphone back to Mayor Grenville, surprised to see my fingers shake a little. My job was done. Aurora was in the clear, and the killer had been found.

I felt a hand go round my waist and discovered Axel standing behind me.

"Nice job," he whispered. "You should consider a job full-time with Angel Force. They'd never have figured that out."

I looked up at him and grinned. "I only just did. When I saw them all standing together, it clicked into place. Mannie, Star, and Giovanni. Add in Giovanni's domineering mother, who'd do anything to protect him, and there was the answer. I didn't have a clue about Petra's idea for a rival snow globe business, but I knew she was thinking of making a change."

Axel surprised me by kissing my forehead. "There's more good in you than you realize, Tempest."

I shrugged and smiled. Maybe there was some good in me, and maybe Frank wasn't always such a bad demon, but I would always need to be careful not to go too dark.

Axel stepped back as Aurora ran onto the stage and flung her arms around me. "I'm innocent. You've cleared my name and in front of everybody."

I gasped as she squeezed me tightly. "You could have done it yourself. You didn't need me."

"I'll always need you," Aurora said. "No matter how mean that demon is inside of you, you're my sister and I'm yours. We're in this together."

I grinned at her and looked around the room again. Mrs. Romer was being escorted away by an angry looking Dazielle, who rubbed her chest where she'd been blasted with magic. Giovanni was right behind her, slumping along like a scolded puppy. My gaze locked onto Rhett's, and I saw him scowling. As I tracked the direction of his scowl, I saw he was glaring at Axel.

Could he be jealous of Axel kissing me? He couldn't seriously imagine I was interested in Axel. I watched as Rhett left the hall with his biker gang behind him.

Grenville tapped a finger on the microphone to get everyone's attention. "I know we've just had something of an exciting time, but we still have our new mayor to announce. I need to pass the baton of power to someone else, so I can get practicing my golf swing."

Everyone laughed politely and looked back at the stage.

"Please don't be me," Axel whispered as I moved out of the way and stood next to him.

"What about your great speech about keeping Willow Tree Falls traditional?"

"Hmmm, it's a nice idea but think about how much hard work it will be. I'm a playboy at heart. I'm not cut out for authority. I'll have to find something else to impress my father with."

"Ladies and gentlemen, I'd like to welcome the new mayor of Willow Tree Falls to the stage, Mannie Winter."

"Three cheers for our new philandering mayor," I whispered.

Axel let out a relieved sigh and nodded.

Mannie managed to look both happy and chastised as he stepped onto the stage. He had the cheek to wink at me as he passed and took the microphone from Grenville. "Well, this has been something of an illuminating evening. First off, I must apologize for my unusual outfit. I had something of a wardrobe malfunction and limited choice as to what to wear on this important evening. I hope it doesn't make you change your mind about voting for me."

I suppressed a smile. Trust Frank to leave only the truly revolting clothes untouched in Mannie's closet.

"Thank you all for your votes. I promise to do my best for Willow Tree Falls. No more murders and no underhanded business dealings. We don't need rivalry here. We can all work together in harmony."

I looked at Mrs. Winter and Star, who both stood awkwardly by the side of the stage. There was no chance they'd ever be harmonious. Mannie would have a lot of apologies to make before this evening was over.

"We're all a part of an incredible community. I have big plans for Willow Tree Falls. We are going to turn this into an even more amazing place. Everybody's business will be booming."

The audience politely applauded, many of them peering intently at Star and Mrs. Winter in the hope they'd start the next round of entertainment for the evening.

I had to hand it to the ladies. They were doing an excellent job of pretending the other didn't exist.

"I sort of wish you had won," I said to Axel as we slipped off the stage. "I do not like change."

"Who does?" Axel scrubbed at his chin. "About cutting me off at Cloven Hoof—"

"It's for your own good."

"I'm not sure I can manage on my own."

I glanced at him. "You'll be fine."

"Maybe you could give me some pointers, you know, how to stay clear of future over indulgences?"

"Are you looking for a sponsor to keep you clean of my produce?"

"No! Well, maybe for a while. Until you think I'm a responsible, solid citizen again." He grinned at me. "It would mean you stopping by my place more often."

My mouth twisted to the side. I did feel a sliver of responsibility. I should have kept more of an eye on all my customers at Cloven Hoof. If I had, Axel wouldn't be in a mess and need babysitting.

"What do you say? We could make it a regular date."

My thoughts went to Rhett, and I shook my head. "It won't be a date."

"Okay, an intervention."

"For a month, that's it, then you're on your own."

Axel grinned. "A month is all I need."

My eyes narrowed as I looked at him. "To do what?"

His grin widened as he strolled away. "You'll see."

Mom appeared before I could chase after Axel and convince him we were never getting romantically involved. She handed me a carrot cake cupcake and tucked an arm around my shoulders.

"Thanks, this looks lovely."

"You deserve it after helping your sister." She squeezed me tighter.

I smiled as I leaned into her hug and tried to remain calm. I could sense Frank shifting inside me, excited by all the action and pushing to get out now Aurora was around.

I stuffed the cupcake in my mouth. Frank would have to wait. I couldn't abandon my family, not right now.

Wiggles bounded over, chocolate frosting on his nose. "This is a great party."

I looked around the room. It felt too closed-in and hot. I eased away from Mom. "I'll be back in a second."

She nodded, a knowing expression on her face. "Take your time. We'll be waiting."

I walked away as Frank became increasingly frustrated at being trapped.

Wiggles bounded along next to me. "Get a grip on your demon. We cannot miss the celebrations. Plus, I want to see when Mrs. Winter is going to explode and slam dunk Star."

"I'm trying." I stopped in a quiet corner and turned my back, so nobody could see me. "Stop fighting me. You're never going to win."

Wiggle nudged my fingers in a show of reassurance. "You can beat him."

"I will," I whispered.

"One day, I'll win," Frank said in my head. "When you least expect it, I'll get out. Then nothing will stop me."

I leaned my head against the wall and focused on everything good in my life. I had my family, I was surrounded by people who cared about their community, I'd just solved a murder, and I had Wiggles. But Frank was right. I could only fight him for so long. It was a struggle to be here, but I wasn't giving up. I loved my home, and I loved my family. It was selfish of me to stay, putting Aurora at risk, but I couldn't help myself.

A chocolate brownie appeared on a plate in front of me.

I took a deep breath and turned. Aurora stood there, her smile pensive. "I thought your blood sugar might need a boost."

I swallowed slowly and looked anywhere but her. "I've just had a cake."

"This is different. It's a brownie." She handed it to me. "Is everything okay?"

"Everything is perfect." I discreetly belched into my hand as Frank made one more failed attempt to come through. I rubbed my stomach until he finally settled. Not today, Frank, today was all about me celebrating with my family. My sister was innocent, her name had been cleared, and we had a new mayor in the village.

I took a risk and slung an arm around Aurora's shoulders. "It looks like there's going to be some changes in Willow Tree Falls."

"So long as you're here to see them happen, I don't mind what they are." Aurora glanced at me. "You aren't going anywhere for a while, are you? I sort of like having my big sister looking out for me."

"I'm staying." We walked back to the rest of our family. "It looks like you're stuck with me, at least for a while."

I couldn't stay forever, but I could stay for now. Being surrounded by my loved ones helped make everything better. I looked around at all the people and smiled. This was Willow Tree Falls, and this was my family. The whole thing was a weird and wonderful mess.

As I watched Wiggles chase a fallen sausage roll across the room, people scattering out of the way to avoid the hellhound, my heart warmed, and I leaned against Aurora. I wouldn't have it any other way.

About Author

K.E. O'Connor (Karen) is a cozy mystery author living in the beautiful British countryside. She loves all things mystery, animals, and cake (these feature in her books.)

When she's not writing about mysteries, murder, and treats, she volunteers at a local animal sanctuary, reads a ton of books, binge watches mystery series on TV, and dreams about living somewhere warmer.

To stay in touch with the fun mysteries, where the killer always gets caught, justice is served magic style, and the familiars talk, join her newsletter.

Newsletter:
www.subscribepage.com/cozymysteries
Website: www.keoconnor.com/writing
Facebook: www.facebook.com/keoconnorauthor

Also By

Luck of the Witch

Hell of a Witch

Revenge of the Witch

Curse of the Witch

Son of a Witch

Framing of the Witch

Trickery of the Witch

Wishes of the Witch

Harmony of the Witch

Remedy of the Witch

Gift of the Witch

Toil of the Witch

Jinxing of the Witch

Craving of the Witch

Union of the Witch

Chaos of the Witch

Sleighing of the Witch

If you enjoyed

Luck of the Witch

turn the page to read an extract from the next Crypt
Witch Mystery

HELL OF A WITCH

ISBN: 978-1-915378-00-2

Chapter 1

It was official; I hated the city. Not this particular city but all cities. And crowds, not a fan of those either. As I shoved my way through the throng of non-magicals turning out from their office jobs, I made sure to keep my breathing shallow. The smell of stale coffee and what might have been desperation wafted off people's clothes as I passed them.

The fumes from the vehicles crawling by almost made me gag. I'd never considered myself a country girl, but every time I came to a city like this, I changed my mind. What I wouldn't do for a lungful of clean, fresh air from Willow Tree Falls and only the occasional buzz of a bike or car dawdling past me. This stress-fueled, horn honking misery did nothing for me.

I stepped to the side to get out of the worst of the commuter foot traffic and reluctantly took a deep breath. I filtered out the stench of the non-magicals around me. I was seeking one smell. The stench of a demon. Every demon came with an unpleasant whiff of sulfur. Some were worse than others, like they'd spent their morning bathing in a bucket of rancid eggs. This one was your average smelly demon. Raksh was a sneaky one, though. He'd eluded me for three long, city stinking days.

I blamed Angel Force for giving him such a good head start. Dazielle hadn't told me he'd eluded their custody until almost a week had passed. His head start caused me more of a headache than I needed. Not that I needed another one.

My nose wrinkled, and I stepped into the alleyway on my left. I was running this gig solo. Before Wiggles had turned into a hellhound, he'd often accompanied me away from the magical bubble of Willow Tree Falls on the demon hunts. He was good at finding demons when he wasn't distracted by food. And it was nice to have company, especially in the world of non-magicals, where everything felt a little off and weird.

Since Wiggles' transformation, he was confined to Willow Tree Falls forever, unless I could figure out a way to maintain his magic away from the sanctity of our home. He didn't seem to mind; he loved Willow Tree Falls, but I did miss hanging out with him.

No matter, I had a demon to hunt in an alleyway, and time was not on my side. I'd already had three urgent messages from Mom on my mobile snow globe, reminding me in an increasingly shrill tone that I needed to get back in time for the mid-summer solstice celebrations that evening. It was a big deal in Willow Tree Falls. Solstice was a time when we recharged our magic batteries and gave thanks to the power at our fingertips, a power that none of the non-magicals around me knew anything about.

That was why I was creeping along a grimy alleyway. I was searching for this demon to keep the non-magicals safe. I sometimes wondered why I bothered to risk my neck to keep their eyes shielded from the magic truth. Every non-magical I met seemed unhappy. When they came to our healing stones or to try our thermal spas, it was in the hope of a restorative cure for their stress aches. If they knew what really lurked around many a dark corner, they'd be even more stressed.

The noise of the busy street faded as I continued along the alleyway.

"Here demon," I whispered. "Come take a nap in my cute little bag." I patted the plain brown bag that hung from a belt loop on my black pants. This wasn't your normal bag; there was no make-up or hair spray in here. This bag was a miniature demon prison, just like the one my family looked after in the cemetery at Willow Tree Falls. The Crypt family was in the business of demon hunting and incarceration and had been for centuries.

My bag had nothing on the prison, but could hold a demon as I transported him to Willow Tree Falls and let the angels determine the fate of the demon I'd captured.

My sister, Aurora, was always trying to make it pretty by attaching pin badges and sticking on sequins. They never lasted. Demons hated the bag. They fought tooth and claw to avoid being shoved into it, and all the pretty stuff fell off.

The sulfurous smell grew. I glanced up at the grimy brick walls surrounding me. Nope, no demon hiding there waiting to pounce on my head. Raksh was a shapeshifter and could fly short distances. All demons had the potential to live forever if they looked after themselves. Raksh was several hundred years old and wanted for three ritualized sacrifices of non-magicals. In his defense, he'd said he needed to conduct the rituals to maintain his strength, given that so few non-magicals worshipped him anymore. But he'd broken magic laws. We never harmed non-magicals, unless they directly threatened us, no matter how annoying they could be with their giant purses and obsession with cell phones.

A door slammed open behind me. I spun on my heel, the bag raised, ready to capture Raksh.

A red-faced man wearing a white apron slung two black bags of trash out the door. He glanced in my direction, and his eyes widened. "What are you doing out here?"

"Enjoying the view." I lowered the bag and acted like it was my right to be lurking around a dark, damp alley.

"You shouldn't be back here."

I shrugged and looked away. I hoped this guy wouldn't give me trouble. There was a demon around here, and the non-magical wouldn't want to be anywhere near us if we fought. Demons liked to use non-magicals as shields.

The guy snorted before pulling the door shut behind him, muttering something about junkies and ending up dead in the gutter.

"As if," I said quietly to myself. The kind of drugs they served in the non-magical world held no appeal. Now, if you placed a bowl of my own home-dried magic mushrooms and a few lemon drops in front of me, I'd be tempted.

I scratched my way through some trash, grimacing as I did so. A hot swell of Frank's energy shifted up my spine as if he sensed danger. Frank, my unwelcome resident demon, was my constant companion, no matter what I tried to get him evicted. Having swallowed him to save my sister when we were kids, he now lived inside me but often tried to get out and finish what he'd started with Aurora. He also didn't react well to stress or danger, something I often found myself in.

"You can stay where you are," I muttered to him. "I'm dealing with this one."

He chuckled quietly but made no further attempt to get out.

I'd given Frank a couple of hours respite as soon as I'd left Willow Tree Falls and was a safe distance from my family. He had to come out now and again; otherwise, my resistance weakened, and he could take control whenever he wanted.

I remembered little about those hours and had woken with a banging headache, the taste of whiskey on my breath, and the remains of two takeout pizza boxes beside me. Who'd have thought demons were junk food addicts? And Frank had the sweetest tooth imaginable.

I glanced down at whatever disgusting thing I stepped on as it squelched beneath my black boot. It might have once been a used diaper.

When I looked up, a long-limbed, green-scaled demon stood in front of me, his pinprick sharp teeth bared. I shook my head. Why couldn't Raksh have shape-shifted into something cute, like a unicorn or a fluffy kitten? Why did it always have to be something gross and scaly, something with teeth and long jagged-looking claws?

I opened my bag. "I hope you're going to come quietly."

Raksh hissed and swiped his claws at me.

"I take that as a no."

Raksh inclined his head. "I am honored that a Crypt witch would come for me."

"Don't be. I was the only one with free time on my hands."

Raksh chuckled. "I know you, Tempest Crypt. You work for the angels."

"I work for myself." It always grated that I freelanced for Angel Force. If they only knew how to do their jobs properly, I wouldn't have to go running around clearing up their mistakes. But my family insisted we help them. It was an old tradition, starting back in the days when my Granny Dottie dated the old Angel Force police chief. Even though he was retired, she still felt we needed to give them a hand and capture all the mad, bad demons who escaped their clutches more regularly than they should.

The demon capturing fell to me if it happened outside of Willow Tree Falls. The rest of my family spent their time guarding the prison and kicking any demon butt that decided to sneak out.

"You're a pretty witch," Raksh said. "I'd like to wrap my claws into your long hair and take a bite of that creamy skin."

"If you're hungry, there's a pizza parlor a block away."

"I prefer my food alive when I eat it." His forked tongue flickered across his teeth.

I shrugged. I'd met worse demons. I lived every day with a worse demon inside of me. Raksh could issue all the threats he wanted, but this demon was going in my bag. There was no way I'd miss the midsummer celebrations because of this rule breaker. The celebrations meant lots of home-baked goodies and partying, and I was always down for some of that.

Plus, my own business, Cloven Hoof, was hosting a stall and selling pick me ups and tonics to give everyone a little extra buzz. My bar manager, Merrie, would cover the stall, but when Willow Tree Falls was full of celebrating locals and non-magicals, she'd need all the help she could get. I promised her I'd be back in time.

Raksh twisted his neck unnaturally. "How about we play a game?"

"I don't have time for games."

"How about I guess the real name of your demon?"

My breath hitched. No one knew Frank's real name. To know a demon's true name was to have power over him. It didn't mean you could completely control the demon, but it gave you leverage and weakened them. I'd deliberately chosen the name Frank for my unwanted guest because it sounded like such a harmless name, and I knew it annoyed him.

"I see I have your attention." Raksh tapped his claws on the brick wall.

"You can't know who he is," I said. "Nobody does."

"Some do. Your demon does."

"He's not going to tell me, and I doubt the two of you ran in the same circles when he was free."

Raksh shrugged. "If you're not interested—"

"I didn't say that. What do you know?"

His sharp-toothed smile grew. "Lower your bag, take me for a pizza, and we'll talk."

This was a con. It had to be. Still, I was tempted. If I knew Frank's real name, it would make my life so much easier. I'd be able to spend more time in Willow Tree Falls with my family. As much as they annoyed me at times, I still loved them. It hurt to have to leave in order to keep them, and Aurora in particular, safe.

"I'll buy you one slice, and you tell me everything you know about Frank."

"I want a family-sized stuffed crust with twelve toppings. And I want dessert."

"Two slices."

"A medium Margherita with a stuffed crust."

"A small Margherita and no dessert."

Raksh scowled at me. "Very well."

The door behind me opened again. Two guys stepped out with cigarettes in their mouths.

The demon lunged at them, screaming in an ear splittingly high range as he did so.

"Oh, balls!" I threw myself in front of the two men. Raksh would try to injure the non-magicals in the hope he could slip away in the chaos.

"What the…" One of the men jumped backward, and his cigarette landed on the ground.

Demons could reveal themselves to non-magicals, but they usually only saw a blur of movement when a demon was around.

"There's nothing to see here," I yelled. "Get back inside." I took the full force of Raksh's charge and stumbled into the non-magicals as his energy slammed into me.

Raksh bounced away, his laugh echoing off the walls.

I felt hands on my shoulders and quickly shrugged them off. "Get inside. It's not safe out here."

"Are you a cop?" one of the non-magicals asked as he scanned the alley with wide eyes. "Is something going down out here? Bruce said there was some junkie hanging around in the alley and to be careful when we came out for a smoke."

"Bruce would be right. I'm much worse than the cops." I blasted a throwback spell into Raksh's chest as he dove at me, giving me a few seconds before he launched himself at the non-magicals again.

"What did you just do?" The taller of the two non-magicals stared at me with his mouth open.

"Nothing. It was a camera flash. I'm collecting evidence of the junkie. Now, get inside." I gestured at the door. Why weren't they getting the hint? They'd be dead if they didn't get their butts out of this alley.

"Are you sure we can't give you a hand? You look kind of small to handle some doped-up loser."

"I can handle plenty more than that. Let me help you find the door." I grabbed hold of them by the collars of their work shirts and threw them through the doorway, slamming it behind them and sealing it with a spell.

As I turned back to face Raksh, he threw himself at me. There was no time to open the bag as his claws flashed in front of my eyes.

I took a breath, steeled myself for what was about to happen, and swallowed him. He struggled and spat curses at me. He also exuded a sour tasting green goo that had me using all my willpower so as not to spit him out.

Tears ran down my cheeks as the hot acid sensation of a demon sliding down my throat tore through me. It was never my preferred method of capturing a demon. The bag was so much kinder on my stomach. This was a rare gift of mine, if you can call it a gift, being able to contain a demon inside me.

A loud belch shot out of my lips. That was another side effect of hosting demons. I almost lost my grip on Raksh. It didn't help that Frank was already inside me and occupying so much space. He did not like to share his living accommodation with anyone.

"Stay down," I muttered as I gripped my stomach and leaned against the wall, feeling the demon's power trickle through my body, the hot energy heating me from head to toe.

After several minutes of deep breathing, I had Raksh under my control and a gross coating of green demon goo all over my favorite black shirt and sliding down my chin.

"There she is," came a shout from the end of the alleyway.

I looked up to see two cops staring at me. The guys I'd shoved through the door stood next to them.

"She's the junkie who attacked us."

"Thanks for nothing, guys. Next time, I'll let the demon play with you." I pushed myself away from the wall. It was time to leave. I'd gotten what I needed, but this had been a messy search and retrieval operation. Whenever possible, we didn't use magic around non-magicals. It left them confused and reporting they'd seen some alien or a ghost to a tabloid paper.

I was out of options and trapped in an alleyway with two cautious looking cops heading my way, their hands too close to their guns for my liking. I also had two restless demons on board. I had about two hours before I lost control of them both. I had to get back to

Willow Tree Falls and release Raksh. I needed to use magic again.

I focused my energy on a transportation spell. This was taxing magic, so I needed to concentrate.

"Miss, what are you doing in this alleyway?"

I ignored the cop and imagined stepping through a door and finding myself on the main street in Willow Tree Falls, seeing the pastel pink sign of Sprinkles bakery and Wiggles racing toward me with his tongue hanging out.

"Miss, place your hands where we can see them and walk toward us."

I shook my head, closed my eyes, took a deep breath, and stepped forward.

Hell of a Witch is available to buy in paperback and e-book.

ISBN: 978-1-915378-00-2